THE BIRTH

OF A NEW AGE

John Reynolds stood with a full-sized scalpel in his gloved hand, drawing a blood-red line on the nine-month-old brown scar coursing down the orange-white flesh. The flesh heaved once and was split asunder with the skill of a master technician. Down went the knife, and down again until the wound ran with blood that spilled onto the white sheets.

Blood washed in waves from the mangled uterus and torn uterine arteries over the beautiful face of a boy named Pan onto the surgeon's green gown and splashed in giant crimson drops into slippery puddles on the floor.

Thus, Pan was born. And his mother was dead.

PAN

Birney Dibble

LEISURE BOOKS ❧ NEW YORK CITY

A LEISURE BOOK

Published by

Dorchester Publishing Co., Inc.
6 East 39th Street
New York, NY 10016

Printed in the United States of America

Chapter 1

He sat hunched at his microscope, thin shoulder blades protruding against the starched white lab coat, sensitive fingers spinning the fine-focus knob impatiently. Color rose in his pale cheeks as he ripped the slide from the stage and sailed it in the general direction of the wastebasket.

"Child's play," he said, and slumped on the backless stool, his fingers clenching and unclenching spasmodically. He turned toward his lab assistant with the creaking care of an old man reaching for his heart pills. "Anybody could do this, Jan. Anybody."

Unobtrusively, Janice Wheeler bent to retrieve the slide and washed it carefully in the sink before she slipped it into the drying rack. Out of the corner of her eye she watched John Reynolds cross the kitchen-sized, apparatus-filled lab and stare out the window at the roofs of the medical school buildings directly below. He leaned foward and rested his hands on the sill.

"How about some coffee, Jan?" he asked.

"Sure, doctor."

She smoothed her blouse over her rounded belly and plodded heavily down the corridor to the automat.

"Hell of a note," she thought angrily, "for a really great scientist like Dr. Reynolds to be doing the scutwork for a bunch of egotists. Should be doing the research *himself.*"

When she returned he was still leaning on the window sill, but his face had lost its flush and he seemed in control again.

As he took the coffee cup from her he smiled and said, "Sorry, Jan. I shouldn't take out my little troubles on you."

"It's o.k., doctor, I know how you feel. And you sure as hell can't talk to anybody else around here."

He sat in the swivel chair and put his feet up on the almost empty desk. Only a year ago his desk had been piled high with papers, notes, books, and magazines. Ten years of research had lain under his elbows as he wrote feverishly to complete a paper, which when published would make his name known not only to other scientists but to millions of people on the street. But just months before he was ready to publish, his dreams were shattered when a previously obscure laboratory in Milan, Italy, duplicated his work and published first. At the outset, he had been incredulous, then indignant, and finally ragingly mad. He had stalked the laboratory corridors, slapping at the magazine with the back of his hand, then wrathfully tearing it into bits which he threw helter-skelter in his wake.

The door from the corridor opened and in stalked a young man of twenty-five or so. "Have you got those slides correlated, John? The old man wants the stuff today."

Reynolds eyed him venomously. "No, not yet."

"How the hell can you just sit there drinking coffee, then? Come on, man, get your ass in gear."

"It'll get done, Jim. It'll get done." Across the room Jan watched the black eyes glitter under hooded lids and she was not at all reminded of soft candlelight and wine. After having worked for him for almost five years she knew better than anyone, perhaps even his wife, Sylvia, that despite this last year of frustration he would not be pushed around by anyone. As Jim left, somewhat mollified but certainly now cowed, Jan watched Reynolds ease his long, lean body up off the back of his spine into a sitting position. He sat tensely now, fingers pulling at the ends of a luxuriant black mustache, then combing back the fringe of black hair alongside his almost bald pate. At thirty-three, he had been losing his hair for almost ten years and looked forty or more. The deep grooves in his cheeks did nothing to dispel the appearance of middle age.

His hands trembled slightly as he stuffed a big church-warden pipe, scraped a kitchen match on the underside of his chair, and lit the pipe with a rolling motion of his head. As the smoke curled around his face he blew it away and rubbed his eyes with his knuckles.

"Damned pup," he said finally. He blew smoke through his nose and tipped the paper cup of coffee to his lips. His eyes stared into the swirling black stuff, then slid slowly across the room toward Jan. She saw again, for the thousandth time, the hurt, the humiliation, the longing, which had dominated those eyes for almost a year.

"Don't worry, Jan," he said, the faintest intimation of a smile crinkling the corners of his eyes. "I won't start in again."

Might as well say it as think it, she thought, for she had heard it all before, many times, and knew what periodically he had to expurgate himself, had to verbalize the demons which gripped him. From time to time he needed a sounding board off which to bounce his frustrations, and she was the usual target. No longer could he risk it with his colleagues for fear of being labeled as the fox who couldn't reach the sour grapes.

Now, back on his high stool at the microscope, black coffee burning the inside of his mouth, and smoke burning his nose, he methodically scanned the slide and jotted down his findings in a neat hand, letters diminutive and crabbed. One side of his brain recorded his findings, and the other side rambled on as it had a hundred times before. "I've got to come up with a project that no one else can possibly replicate. Something so ingenious that I can work at it for years if necessary and no one else can steal the damn thing from me before I finish."

He would not remain the forgotten man, taking on assignments from other scientists, performing the more or less routine chores which someone had to do but which were usually relegated to younger, or less talented, researchers. No, he would not stay forgotten. The drive for recognition, for status in the scientific community, for a personal victory which would transcend anything that had ever been done before, pushed incessantly at his very being. He would do anything, risk anything, to achieve the goal. Someday the inspiration would come, and he would be ready for it, and would sacrifice everything for its completion. *Everything*.

Chapter 2

The room in which the man and woman sat was large, Victorian in design like the rest of the house, but simply furnished. Originally it had been filled with elegant draperies, sofas and armchairs, end-tables, coffee tables, and oil paintings. Butlers had padded on slippered feet and maids had lived in.

Now the solid oak floors were hidden by wall-to-wall carpeting, the furniture was late Weiboldt's, and the paintings were all gone. Actually, the decor fitted the occupants better than more extravagant fittings. A fire crackled in the fireplace, and from time to time the woman put down her paper, got up and carefully placed another log of maple or oak upon it. The man scarcely moved except to turn the pages of the magazine he was reading. The man, John Reynolds, lay in the easy chair with his feet outstretched on an ottoman, his head propped up with a small hard pillow. He smoked his massive churchwarden pipe, and on his nose sat a pair of rimless half-glasses.

Across the room, Sylvia sat almost bolt-upright, reading a newspaper. She was thirty, just a few years younger than her husband, and almost as tall. Never a candidate for homecoming queen, she was nevertheless

9

attractive. Her dark brown hair was somewhat touseled, for she had just come in from outside with an armful of wood, but it was usually carefully combed. Her eyebrows were neatly plucked and trimmed, slightly arched, but so dark she needed no artificial pencilling to outline them. Steady grey eyes flicked down the columns of print with speed-reading rapidity. She was dressed in a long, wooly nightgown and bathrobe.

John Reynolds sudddenly became more alert, more attentive to his reading. Whereas before, he had been skimming quickly through the pages to pick out the highlights, he now read carefully, ever more slowly. At the end of the article he paused, then leafed back to the beginning and re-read it.

The entire scenario flung itself across his brain almost in the same second his mind comprehended the author's meaning. He slumped in his chair, pipe hanging precariously from slack jaws, glasses tipped foward onto his nose, pupils wide but eyes vacant. His glance shifted quickly, guiltily, toward his wife, as if she could have looked through her paper and read the thoughts threading his mind.

How many other scientists, trained as he was, would grasp the significance of that article? Any? And if they did, would they follow it through as he knew he must, if he were ever to have peace of mind again? Was it likely that any of his co-workers in the university laboratory would even *read* the piece? So. They were all too oriented to the cell itself, to the micro-anatomy and micro-physiology of unicellular life. They were too intent on finding the agent responsible for wild, uncontrolled, cellular proliferation, for cancer, to be attracted to such philosophizing in a natural history magazine, written for laymen at that.

He reached for his notebook, always close at hand, and began to write down the plan which had flashed through his mind just minutes before.

The child first—
Most expensive, probably—
Most dangerous, certainly—
Must be newborn—

He stroked his mustache, musing. Should really be black, he thought, but not in today's world. White then.

Settled: white.
Next, the . . .

He continued to write for some minutes, then looked over what he had written. The toughest part would be to get the baby. A white, intelligent newborn human baby. It would be the best of all to get her by Cesarean section, not yet human-touched, human-fondled, human-fed. No memories, however distant and time-dwindled, of the touch of soft hands and purring oohs and ahs. Not even an infant-addled recollection of soft bed, and softer paper diapers to be dredged from the never-lost subconscious at some critical moment.

Silvia put down her paper and announced she was going to bed. "Coming, John?" she asked.

He shook his head without looking up. "Not quite yet."

"Like a nightcap, dear?"

He started slightly, adjusted his glasses to the tip of his nose so he could look over them, and stared at his wife.

"It's bedtime, John," She picked up the newspaper, folded it neatly and replaced it on the sofa.

"Uh, no, dear, not tonight. Or not yet anyway. Thanks."

"New idea burning the brain cells again?"

"Sort of," he answered, smiling thinly. He scratched his bald pate and ran his fingers through the long hair over his ears.

"Goodnight," Sylvia said.

"Goodnight," he answered.

She was not offended by his brusqueness, did not give it a second thought. Some nights he was like this, almost oblivious to her. Actually, she was pleased to see him so absorbed, for he had been like this so few times during the last year. She knew him well, had always idolized him for his genius, and was willing to accept him on his terms. He had been a good husband—kind if not loving, adequate, if not skillful as a lover (matching, she admitted, her own restrained libido), and when he called from the lab to say he was working overtime, she knew he really was.

When she was gone, Reynolds pushed his glasses back on his nose, and slumped further in his chair. He made notes in a tiny hand on the ruled notepaper, easily writing two sentences between each blue line. In his mind he turned over the varied problems he would face if he were to actually execute the plan. Before long, he began thinking of the plan as an experiment, then finally as the *Grand Experiment.* By the time he went to bed he knew he would do it—needed only time, a little luck, patience, and no regard for the cost in human terms to himself, Sylvia—and two others.

Chapter 3

Next day, in the small office next to his laboratory, he leaned back in his swivel chair, put his feet on the desk, smoothed down his mustache with a finger, and gazed out the window at the cold white facade of the University Hospital across the street.

"Doctor Reynolds?"

He had not heard Jan come into the office and the look he turned on her was hard, almost brutal.

"Don't you ever knock?"

She fingered the edge of her loose-fitting maternity blouse and stammered, "Your door was open and I could see you weren't busy . . ."

The harsh glint left his eyes as he remembered that her husband was overseas in Germany and she was desparately trying to save enough money to join him before the baby was born.

"Come in, Jan. I was thinking and you sort of startled me. What can I do for you?"

"It's just that Dr. Stevenson wants the notes you made up for him yesterday—that is, if they're ready."

"They're ready. Not annotated, but he may not need that yet."

"I'll take them and let you have them back when he wants more."

He handed her the manila folder and she turned to leave.

"Jan . . ."

"Sir?"

"You haven't been out to see Sylvia in quite a while. . . ."

"No, it's been months."

"She misses you. I'll have her call you and we'll have you out to supper some evening."

"That'd be fun. I really do miss those walks in the woods we used to have."

"The maples are turning color already. Blackcaps almost gone. Hazelnuts on every bush along the drive." He smiled, and she thought again fo the warm human being hidden somewhere inside that scientific automaton. The smile faded, and she knew she was dismissed. If she had been a wild animal, she would have smelled fear as she left. Outside the office she half-closed her eyes, shuddered involuntarily, and shifted her manila folder under her elbow so it wouldn't be stained by her moist fingers.

He walked slowly around the community hospital, keenly aware of the bustle of people. Cars, buses, cabs. People strolling, ambling, or hastening through the doors of the emergency room and front entrance. Nurses, orderlies, interns, doctors in business suits or white coats. Old people, canes tapping the concrete. Young people, glowing with energy. White faces, black faces, ashen faces, lined faces, hopeless faces. An ambulance rumbling, roof light glowing, siren-whine groaning through contralto to silence, backdoors flailing, attendants jumping, stretcher wheels falling and locking in place.

He was in a residental area several miles from the University Medical Center. The small hospital, about two hundred beds, was community-owned and non-

14

profit. He was not known here, could be just another patient on his way to the out-patient clinic, or perhaps a doctor savoring the warm, fall sunshine before making morning rounds.

He went in the front doors, stood gazing around him for a moment, then purposefully strode to the receptionist's desk and bought a local newspaper. He sat down, read the sports pages, the editorial pages, then turned casually to the record of births the previous day. There had been three babies born in this hospital the day before.

He memorized the name and address of the father of one child and tossed the paper on the chair beside him. An elderly couple across the room looked up from their papers and then resumed reading. A child sitting on the floor almost at his feet stared up at him, but his father was engrossed in a paperback. Reynolds sighed as if bored, got up and sauntered toward the main hospital corridor, then ran up the stairs to the maternity ward on the second floor.

Swinging doors confronted him, and alongside them a sign read, "Babies shown at 12 AM and 7 PM. Fathers please register with ward clerk." He pushed through the doors and moved down the short hallway to the counter desk where a green-clad girl was talking to a very nervous young man.

"Yes, sir," she was saying. "The doctor said he would come right out when the baby's born. Why don't you have a cup of coffee down in the waiting room?" She glanced at Reynolds with an amused smile and then added unnecessarily, "Expectant father."

The young man grinned and said, "First one," and went off down the corridor to the coffee room.

"What can I do for you, sir?"

"I'd like to see David Rose's baby if I could."

"Are you a friend of the family?" Her attitude indicated

15

a sudden but subtle reluctance, perhaps almost hostility.

"Yes, don't you do that for friends?" He could feel the sweat break out under his arms and trickle down his back, and he knew his face was flushed.

"Not usually. But I guess it's all ᵣight. Especially since Mr. Rose is down there at the viewing window now."

She pointed down the long corridor to a half-dozen people standing before a plate-glass window, pointing, laughing, gesturing.

Reynolds turned quickly on his heel, muttering he would come back some other time, and raced down the stairs. He could feel her eyes boring into his back, and wondered if she had already picked up the phone to call the hospital security guards. Once on the street he forced himself into an orderly but rapid walk to his car, started it up and pulled quickly out into the traffic.

Well, he thought, I found out what I wanted to know. That way is out. Should have known. But what now?

For the first time since his idea had come to him he sensed the enormity of the risk. But it would be worth it, and he had to go on. *Somehow.*

As he drove across town to his office he pondered the problem. A red light halted him, and he watched the pedestrians crossing in front of him. A young woman, bulging with child, waddled across the street. If only she knew the benefits to science, she would *give* him her baby and be thankful of her contribution. And then she was gone, and the faint flicker of an idea flitted through his mind and was snuffed out when the light changed and a horn sounded impatiently behind him.

He stood with his back to the dark living room, eyes somber and unseeing as they looked out onto the moonlit snow covering the lawn. Drifts had obscured the usually sharp outlines of the privet hedge, and swirls of snow skidded down the driveway. The maples were bare, black, gaunt, spector-like in the bright night. A cold moon, quarter-waned, threw the shadows of heaving branches onto the house. Two steady headlight beams threaded through the darkness as a car approached, stopped in front of the house, and a huddled, bulky woman climbed the steps and rang the bell.

The lights flicked on in his room and in the hall Sylvia threw open the door with a cry of greeting.

"Jan, come in before you freeze to death."

"Thanks. I really should have stayed home. I thought once or twice today the baby's coming." She laughed nervously, a tight smile creasing the frosted stiffness of her upper lip. She shook out her hair and handed her coat to John.

"Now, wouldn't that be fun?" he said. "The very first baby born in our house."

Sylvia's look told him she didn't think it a bit funny, but Jan seemed actually amused.

"Now that would be something," she said, her smooth stride across the living room belying her extra weight. "But you're not a doctor! Not an MD anyway. Ph of D."

"Mmm," he mumbled, pulled a pipe out of his pocket to hide his irritation, and filled it.

"We're *so* sorry you didn't get to Germany in time for the baby," Sylvia said, and sat primly, schoolmarmish in contrast to the lively and lovely beauty of her husband's laboratory technician. Jan eased herself onto a straight-backed chair of uncertain vintage, and waved off with a slender hand John's offer of his easy chair.

"No, doctor, I'd probably never get up. Probably just as well being here, Sylvia. You never really know what kind of a doctor you'll get overseas."

John grunted. "Probably a better chance of a good one!"

Jan laughed. "Maybe."

Slyvia smiled conspiratorily. "What's it going to be, a boy or a girl?"

"As long as it isn't a chimpanzee, I don't care what it is," she answered. "Ronnie or René, Francis or Frances, who cares?"

John could feel his fingers tighten on the arms of the chair and the muscles of his abdomen tensed in a painful contraction. In his mind's eye he visualized again the ungainly figure of the pregnant woman crossing in front of his car at the stoplight. *Karma.* An act of God. Call it what you will, he suddenly knew his Grand Experiment was about to begin.

"A little sherry, Jan?" he asked.

"Yes, but not too much. Tonight may be the night."

Yes, tonight will be the night, Jan, John Reynolds thought, when you and I will be immortalized with Lorenz and Tinberger, yes, even with Darwin and Mendel. But your name will never be known, must never be known. It is for *me* to be the creator and for you to be forever unknown. For *my* name to be on everyone's lips and yours to be buried so deep in my subconsciousness that someday even I will not remember it. Moreover, you yourself will never know, must never know, what part you played in the greatest drama unfolded on earth since sapient man evolved from speechless ape . . .

Chapter 4

Outside the house a cold blast of arctic air rattled the dry brown leaves of the old oak and a few broke off and fluttered to the ground. The storm windows of the ancient house shuddered spasmodically and an almost human keening emanated from the power lines under the eaves.

Rented years ago by the newly-married Reynolds as a temporary home until something better could be found, they had come to love the house and finally bought it. They renamed their home "Standing Oaks." It stood almost at the center of a twenty-acre hardwood stand, private, isolated, perfect for the honeymooners then and even more perfect now for the life they preferred to live: she in harmony with the woods around them, with her flowers and vegetable garden, he in complete dedication to his career as a micro-biologist at the university, thirty minutes away in the city suburbs. He had a small laboratory in the old butler's pantry where he could work on projects independent of his work at the university. His private lab had been equipped slowly and painfully with sophisticated expensive instruments, including the best light-microscope money could buy, micro-surgery tools and instruments. His dream was to own a scanning electron microscope, but the cost was still prohibitive for a private individual.

A log in the fireplace burned through and the fire settled with a soft whoosh. Silvia Reynolds opened her eyes and looked across the room, first at her husband slumped in the easy chair and then at the girl stretched out on the sofa. We should wake her up and take her home, she thought, but she looks so comfortable. Almost drugged.

And *he* must *really* have an idea this time, she thought, his eyes so bright and his concentration so complete. She was used to his brainstorms, and had learned to respect them. For ten years she had watched these periodic phenomena and knew that from these flashes of fireside inspiration had evolved some of the most intricate experiments and some of the most startling advances in the science of micro-biology. Sometimes he would rush into his laboratory without a word and spend half the night peering into his microscope or filling his notebooks with cryptic notations which would bear fruit months or even years later.

His brother laughingly called him the "mad scientist," but she did not consider him mad. At least not in the sense of being deranged or psychopathic. Perhaps in the sense of being disciplined, devoted, even possessed, yes. But not demented.

He looked up, bemused, unseeing, then caught her eye and corners of his crinkled for a fraction of a second before unfocusing again.

"Shouldn't we wake her up, or put her to bed, or something, John?"

"No, let her sleep."

"It's nearly bedtime. And she said she might be going into labor."

He pushed his glasses down on his nose so he could see her better. Could he ever keep this project from her? *Should* he? Could she help? Could he do it *without* her?

"Well, I'm going to bed," Sylvia announced and stood up.

He made up his mind.

"I don't think you should, Sylvia."

A gust of wind shook the house and a puff of smoke exploded into the room from the fireplace. The girl turned restlessly on her side, exposing a long slim leg. John scarcely noticed, but Sylvia crossed the room and pulled the afghan from the back of the sofa, threw it over the girl, and tucked it in.

She sat down on the end of the sofa and put Jan's feet in her lap.

"What do you mean, John?"

"I need that baby, Sylvia."

"You need . . ." she started, her eyes widening in horror.

"Listen," he said, and the words tumbled out in ever-widening circles as he described the intricacies of the plan.

She listened, mesmerized by the droning voice, the howling wind, the flickering firelight, the handsome black eyes, the gentle posturing of long slender fingers. The irrational became rational, and the impossible possible and she knew she could do it when he pleaded, "And I need *you* to help, Sylvia.

"The room's ready," he added, and she nodded, knowing now the reason for his long hours in the basement for the past three months. She stroked the girl's leg in her lap, then gazed into her sleeping face, knowing instinctively that never again would she be able to do so.

"What do I do?"

"What I tell you."

"Yes." She stood up. "You've already drugged her."

"Yes, in the wine."

"When did you know?"

"When she said she didn't care what she had, as long as it wasn't a chimpanzee."

"I saw you change."

21

"Did *she*?"

She pondered. She smiled wanly. "No, I don't think so. She's used to your moods."

She knelt in front of the fire, both knees down on the hearth, hands out, fingers splayed to the warmth as if the room had suddenly chilled. She placed both hands alongside her cheeks, fingers tingling, temples twitching as her jaws tightened spasmodically. I mustn't cry now, she thought, mustn't mock his genuis.

When she turned, he was gone. His shoes clicked softly on the solid oak floor of the corridor to his lab in the old pantry.

The girl, Jan, scarcely moved when the long needle slipped silently into the flesh of her arm. It was the moment of irrevocability, the point of no return. Five units of pitocin were circulating in Jan's body, and soon would begin to act upon the huge, muscular uterus. From then on, the organ would act on its own, and in a few hours disgorge itself of the tiny human burden it had lovingly clothed and fed for so long.

"It's got to be a girl," Sylvia whispered.

"I know. It will be. It's got to be." He set in the easy chair near the fire, smoking his pipe, watching the girl on the sofa. With each contraction, her uterus lifted upwards, straining against the waistband of her skirt—hard as steel but gentle as a lover's hand, pressing downward, wringing itself out.

He was Semmelweis now, Aesclapius, Hippocrates, J.B. Murphy, Falls, Schweitzer, all the great physicians gathered together in one frail man, tenderly coaxing out the circle of black baby's hair, watching it grow steadily larger, stretching the maternal tissues to whiteness, rotating slowly to slide between the bones fore and aft.

Suddenly it was there before him, and he was Adam up to his elbows in milky water turning bloody and dirty yellow and Abel lay before him on the white sheets, but no,

22

not Abel, nor Cain either, for it was a girl, and her name was Penelope. He watched her face, flaccid at first, still nurtured by the pulsating blue-white cord wrapped once around her scrawny neck. He clamped the cord, cut it and quickly disentanged it. The face contorted, eyes tightly shut, eyelids greasy with the same cheesy material which covered her body. Her mouth opened tentatively, her chest convulsed rhythmically, ineffectually, then expanded with an audible wheeze.

The room was filled with the raucus cries of the newborn baby and Sylvia wiped tears from her eyes with the back of her cotton-gloved hands. "Oh, John," she said. "Can we?"

His fingers bit into her arm. "Don't ever say that again!"

He had to say that, for the same question had come to him, and he knew they must *never* ask that question. They must discipline themselves as they had never done before, must shunt personal feelings aside, must maintain a scientific calmness and detachment now and for years to come. Seldom before had two people been entrusted with a more awesome task in the pursuit of pure science.

"All right, John." She felt again the power of his voice, his eyes behind the rimless glasses, his mind. "All right John, I won't."

Methodically, ritually, as if he had done it a thousand times (he had never done it), he wrapped the baby, extracted the placenta, injected another five units of pitocin, massaged the hard shrunken uterus through the flabby belly wall, then stood back while Sylvia cleaned Jan and the mess on the sofa.

Women's work. Would it always be? Had it always been? Could this baby's offspring help solve that riddle? Other riddles? Conundrums that could not be solved even at Delphi, in the rock-strewn, barren hillsides of

23

ancient Greece? It was this hope—certainty?—that allowed him to take a young woman's firstborn child from her.

His motives were the purest that the ivory towers of scientific research could envision. From this stratum in Harvey's mind came the concept of the circulation of the blood, from Newton's mind the concept of gravity as a definable force, from the mind of Galileo the concept of the sun as the center of the universe. The other motives were more shadowy, less clearly defined. These would always have indistinct margins, overlapping borders: family love, social consciousness, religiosity. These could always be overriden by diamond-hard, sharp-cornered scientific thought.

Jan moaned and her head rolled back and forth on the sweat-stained pillow.

"Don't let her roll off the sofa," John cautioned. "I'll give her a long-acting barbiturate that will keep her asleep until morning. We've got work to do."

After he had given the injection, he lifted the baby carefully and held her at arms' length.

Walking carefully so as not to awaken her, he carried Penelope downstairs to the specially prepared room where she would live for fifteen years.

Chapter 5

In a dark corridor outside a lighted basement room, Sylvia Reynolds sat on a high stool, a half-smile on her lips. Entranced, she watched the antics of a little blonde girl through a one-way window. The girl, Penelope, now three, twirled faster and faster, her long hair trailing behind her. Her perfect, naked, little body blurred with motion. Suddenly she stopped, swayed gently back and forth, dizzy with merriment, and toppled to the floor. Her rump bounced on the heavily padded green carpeting and she lay still for several moments, blue eyes wide open.

Sylvia pushed her hands into arm-length gauntlets which projected into the child's room just below a long narrow window, and gently clapped them together. Penelope turned her head and looked at the cloth covered fingers, then raised her own hands and tapped them together.

"Thank you," she said slowly, in a musical little voice, giggled merrily, and jumped up. She ran easily to the hands, then stopped before touching them, knowing this was now forbidden. The hands made the silent signs, "Good, Penny, very good." Sylvia withdrew her hands from the gauntlets, and continued her bemused observations. The little girl sat on the floor and began building a house of blocks.

"She's thriving," John Reynolds said from behind Sylvia, and Sylvia jumped slightly at the intrusion of the penetrating voice.

"Yes," she answered, her voice almost devoid of emotion. Slowly, agonizingly, she had come to accept what she saw before her now as she watched the little girl playing with the blocks. The child's home was a rectangular room, ten by twenty, eight feet high. In one corner was a small, galvanized iron sink placed on the floor. Into it flowed a steady stream of cold water which overflowed into a concrete trough leading to a large drainhole in the floor. Penny used the water for drinking and washing, and used the trough as a toilet. The sink was small enough that even as a toddling infant she had not been in danger of drowning in it.

At one end of the small room was a door, made entirely of one-way glass, and recessed so cleverly, without an inner knob, that it did not look like a door. The Reynolds used this door as a watching point, and when Penny was asleep, slipped things into the room when necessary. She had never seen her captors, and so far had not even questioned the arrangement. She was happy, well-fed, warm, and had never known any other life.

Sylvia remembered now, as she watched the little three-year-old, how she had taken care of the infant just a few years ago. She had been placed in a small, glass-walled incubator similar to those in a newborn nursery, except it had no top. One of the sides slipped in and out easily so the child could be fed and bathed. There was the one-way glass just above the gauntlets, which also slid to one side when milk bottles and cleaning cloths were introduced into the room. At all other times the handling of the baby had been done by means of the gauntlets. And, of course, extreme care was exercised that Penny was asleep when the window was opened.

Sylvia let her thoughts slip back through the years, knowing that John stood behind her, waiting for her to say something.

"Do you remember, John, how she was as a little baby?"

"Sylvia," he said sternly. "I thought we were all through with that."

"It doesn't hurt, John. Not now. I'm committed with you. Committed so thoroughly that a little reminiscence won't matter. *Do* you remember, John? We knew she had to be fondled, loved, petted, or she would never develop at all. She would have died, would have wasted away to nothing, and then would have died of no obvious illness. Just would have died for want of love."

Until lately, Sylvia had never quite given up the idea that someday John would relent, would soften his obsession and would bring the Experiment to a halt. But there had never been any sign of regret. In fact, he had grown even more single-minded, and now she knew she had no choice but to follow his example. It was too late.

"Do you remember, John, how we used to handle her, cuddling her and stroking her to ease her crying, feeding her, doing everything except taking her out of that room and clasping her to our breasts. God, how I used to wish I could break down those horrible barriers which separated us and rock the little one to sleep in my arms."

"Yes, I remember," John said, "and I remember how I told you that you were driving yourself crazy by identifying so closely with Penny that you'd never be able to do what we both knew we'd have to do someday."

She nodded, tears coming to her eyes and dropping unnoticed on the concrete floor of the basement corridor. "And I told you, I can still remember the exact words, 'Don't you see, John, I'm her mother—she may not be my baby—but I'm her mother, and there's no other way I can be unless you forbid me to see her at all.' And you didn't want to do that. Even then."

But for a while she *had* made a gallant, valiant attempt to remain aloof, shielding herself against the inevitable heartbreak which would result if she became too involved in the life of the doomed Penelope. But it had proved impossible. The baby had cried and she had fed her, dirtied herself and she had changed her, fretted for attention and she had tickled her.

"It's time for a movie, Sylvia."

Sylvia brushed the tears from her eyes and pushed her hands back into the gauntlets. She clapped her hands and Penny looked up.

"Turn around and look at the wall, Penny," Sylvia spelled out in Ameslan.

Obediently, the little girl scrunched her bottom around on the carpeting and sat facing a silver screen which was unfolding at the other end of the room, covering a large blackboard and a tray of colored chalks. The movie projector was outside the room, the lens recessed into the wall.

As John readied the movie, Sylvia remembered Penny's second birthday, almost exactly a year before. It had been an exciting day for the Reynolds, for it was then they began teaching the little girl to talk. She had been walking for about six months. The lack of outside stimulation and example had retarded her growth in both mind and body. She didn't sit until about eight months, didn't crawl until about a year, and didn't even try to walk until almost eighteen months. But the Reynolds had not been worried. They knew she *would* grow, would mature, and they knew they had time to teach her what she needed to know.

On Penny's second birthday, Sylvia, with John watching anxiously through the one-way glass door, had said, "Penelope." The child had stopped in mid-stride on her way to the water tank. Her eyes had widened in suprise and she looked toward the wall from which came the strange sound. A speaker was hidden in the motor housing of the mechanical screen. At the same time, Sylvia had pushed her arms into the gauntlets, and with a finger crooked she made the signal, "Come here." Still without complete understanding, Penelope had walked towards the hands which had fondled her and washed her for two years.

Sylvia had tapped her on the chest and said, "Penelope." Then she had made the hand sign for "P" and tapped her on the chest, again repeating softly, "Penelope."

Penelope's mouth had opened slightly, then her lips had come together in the puff position and she almost verbalized the first letter of her name, but ended only with a brief soundless expulsion of air as if gently trying to blow out a candle.

But Sylvia had been elated. It was the first of many long steps in teaching the child a few words which she would need to know if she were to become what John and Sylvia intended her to be.

Sylvia had turned the child around and pushed her gently away from her, saying at the same time, "Go." The child had turned slightly, looked over her shoulder at the hands in their cotton gloves, and said clearly, "Go?"

"Yes, *go,* Penelope."

"Go," she had said, and had run toward Sylvia's hands.

"No, *go,*" Sylvia had said and pushed the child away again. This time the child had run off, laughing delightedly, and turned for approval. The hands had clapped softly and withdrew.

Slowly, ever so slowly, the vocabulary had been

enlarged to include the common nouns and verbs which the child would need to function in her limited environment. She had mastered the words easily. With each spoken word, Sylvia had demonstrated the sign for that word, using the American Sign Language of the Deaf, Ameslan.

Turning a rheostat on the wall beside the projector controls, Reynolds darkened the room. He flicked the switch on the projector. A half-grown chimpanzee jumped from the ground onto a wooden "jungle-gym" and swung crazily from strut to strut. He leaped down, rolled on the ground, tickling himself, grinning ferociously, scratching, rolling over and over. Penny at first sat as if mesmerized, then tried to imitate the little chimp. She rolled about, giggling and scratching, tumbling over, all the time trying to keep her eyes on the ape on the wall. Sylvia laughed outright, but Reynolds watched silently, moodily, thinking ahead in time twelve years when there would be a real chimp in that room. Until then, Penny would have to be satisifed with movies of the only other living creature she would ever see.

The chimp leaped up in a small tree, hanging there by one hand and one foot, scratching his belly comically. Penny looked around for something to climb, and when she couldn't find anything, she fell down on the carpet and lay there, curled up in a tight ball, ignoring the movie.

Viciously, Reynolds switched off the machine. "Why in the hell does she always do that?" He stumped up the stairs and Sylvia turned the lights back on. The little girl did not move.

Sylvia pushed her hands into the gauntlets, picked a cookie off a shelf inside the room and said softly, "Penny!" The little girl turned her head to the side, saw the cookie and slowly crawled over on her belly toward it.

Pathetically she tried to reach it without getting up, and couldn't. Finally, with a deep sigh of aching reconciliation and acquiescence, she stood up and took the proffered morsel.

Despite the isolation, and despite the deprivation of stimuli, Penny did grow mentally and physically. By the time she was five, she already had an Ameslan vocabulary of over 1,000 words and could communicate quickly and easily with the Reynolds. She could also talk to them in English, for it was important to the Experiment that she know how to speak. As she became more and more proficient in oral language, it became necessary to forbid her to use it all the time, for it did come easier than signs, particularly when her hands were full. But it was extremely important that she not forget Ameslan.

Once or twice a week, after Penny had begun to learn Ameslan, Reynolds showed a movie of a chimp using the sign language. He was careful to edit out the footage which showed the human teacher, and Penny of course assumed that the chimp was talking to another chimp or perhaps to her. She occasionally glanced at the gauntlets in the wall when she saw the chimp use a sign she didn't know. Either John or Sylvia was always there, and quickly explained in sign language or in English what the new sign was.

The nursery incubator had long before been removed, during the night, cautiously watching the sleeping Penny on the floor. It was the only time either of the scientists actually entered the room during those first five years. Everything else that needed to be introduced into the room was quickly pushed through the sliding window above the gauntlets, always when the child was sleeping, and always with extreme caution. Several times the child had rolled over and looked in the direction of the window just after it was closed, but she never gave any indication that she had seen it open.

Except for the mild mental and physical retardation, the child seemed to thrive in her isolation, unaware of the fact that she was but one of two billion other animals in the species *sapiens,* genus *Homo.* She knew nothing of trees and parks, oceans, lakes and rivers, mountains and rolling wheatfields. She had never seen a city street teeming with other people, nor had she seen a cow or a horse, a cat or a dog. She had seen movies of a chimpanzee, and sometimes rubbed her own smooth white skin when the chimp picked at the long black hairs on his arms or legs. If she wondered why the gauntlets spoke to her in English and Ameslan while the chimp spoke only in Ameslan, she never questioned it. If she wondered why she was white and hairless, and the chimp black and hairy, she never asked. There might have been a thousand things about which she wondered, but if so, she did not verbalize them.

She did not ask for roller skates for Christmas. She had never seen a pair, had no shoes to put them on, had never heard of Christ, and did not know that several hundred million children waited anxiously once a year for skates, and sleds, and books, and bikes. She had never thrown a football or a snowball. She did not know rain, nor sunny skies, nor had she ever watched the moon rise red in the east while the sun glowed orange in the west. She had never caught a bluegill on a worm, nor skinned her knees playing hopscotch.

John Reynolds knew this, but he preferred not to think about it. He was, however, a changed man. He continued to work at the University laboratory, mechanically performing his assigned duties. He no longer pursued new ideas down the long corridors of his brilliant mind, nor tinkered in his home laboratory into the small hours of the morning. He sat, bemused, for long hours, in the chair by the fire, thoughts ranging from ahead in the consummation of his Great Experiment, to the time when questions would be answered which so far had hardly dared to be asked. Sometimes he read from his scientific periodicals, but skimmed everything but the new material dealing with chromosomal inversions and translocations, evolution in humans and chimpanzees, regulatory mutations, genetic manipulations by chemicals, and chromosomal banding techniques. These he read avidly, notating the articles, copying out the important parts into a growing compilation of such information in his notebook.

"Are we really so different from the chimp?" John asked Sylvia one night. "Is there a uniqueness about us which we can be proud of, which separates us so distinctly from the genus *Pan*?"

"Thomas Huxley didn't think so," Sylvia answered.

John eyed his wife curiously.

"Surely you remember," Sylvia said with a smug smile, "when he fought the battle of the hippocampal gyrus with Richard Owen?"

John smiled, then laughed outright, one of his rare and beautiful laughs. "Yes, now I do. Over a hundred years ago, wasn't it?"

Sylvia nodded, a little put out that he remembered the incident.

"He proved," John continued, "that all apes do indeed have a hippocampus, while those animals lower on the scale of evolution don't. But just what importance do you think that has?"

Sylvia was quiet for a moment, contemplating her fine white fingers. "I think that that is *just* what you're trying to prove in this experiment which has consumed our lives."

"Go on."

"You are trying to prove that there *is* a continuity between *Homo sapiens* and the rest of nature. You are trying to prove that Stephen Jay Gould was right when he said that the only honest alternative is to admit the strict continuity in kind between ourselves and chimpanzees."

"Do you think I can?"

"Do you?"

"Yes."

"Then, so do I."

John considered this for a moment, then said, "And do you think we're going about it the right way?"

"Is there another?"

Chapter 6

He sat alone in the narrow prow of the small boat, his hair flowing along his head, bald pate shining in the moonlight. Ahead, on the horizon to the north, the big dipper lay upside down, pointing toward a pole-star forever invisible at this latitude, a few degrees south of the equator. In the south, the Southern Cross flickered brightly in the pollution-free air of East Africa.

The steady hum of the small outboard engine drowned out all other sounds as they crept slowly along the dark coast. John Reynolds did not know exactly where they were, but from time to time the coastline on his right receded far enough to be invisible even in the bright moonlight. Then, almost without warning, a dark bulk of headland would loom so close he felt he could almost touch it. But the pilot did not slow his craft, nor appear at all concerned. He knew there were no rocks, only white sand beaches paralleling the rocky headlands, farther inshore.

John had seen it all in daylight. He and the black skipper had run along the shoreline just the day before, the engine at full throttle, eating up the twelve miles from Kigoma, Tanzania, to the Gombe Reserve in less than an hour. John had posed as a tourist, interesting in seeing the Chimpanzee Reserve from afar, but afraid to go ashore.

Tonight, at a speed of three to four knots, the trip would take several hours. John didn't mind. He welcomed the chance to slip his mind out of gear, to ruminate for a little while, alone with himself. He thought back over the past few weeks, marking time in the new Safari Hotel in Arusha, waiting for the radio message from the ethologists at Gombe that his quest was over. He spent the time walking about Arusha, bargaining with the woodcarvers for a few statues for Sylvia, absorbing the flavor of a town caught midway between the historical Tanganyika of Livingstone and the envisioned Tanzania of Nyerere. On concrete walks he rubbed shoulders with Waarusha herdsmen, and dodged Mercedes Benzes and Land-Rovers along with the German and American missionaries. From the bougainvillia-draped patio of the hotel he stared almost straight upwards at the snow-capped peak of Mt. Meru and knew that it still was home to the gods of local tribesmen.

Tonight, he knew those people were unimportant. All people, everywhere, were but a facade. What they did, what they said, how they lived out their alloted span, everything they thought and all they believed they understood: all a false front for the real undercurrent of life to which John Reynolds would soon hold the key.

He remembered the exact words from his notebook, written almost five years before as he had sat with the magazine article in his hand which had given him the idea for his Experiment. He could not have forgotten it, for he had read it a thousand times while he worked out the details of the plan which is a few days would be one step closer to fruition.

"Next, the chimp—
Only one logical place—Gombe
Goodal and von Lawyck probably gone by then—

36

Chimps will still be there—maybe with other ethologists
    doing work—
Contact: Probably Hemingway's son in Moshi—''

That had been five years before. Now of course, the
ethologists *were* back in the Reserve, without Jane, and
of course without Hugo. And Hemingway had referred
Reynolds to Nairobi. Nairobi had jumped at the chance
to be of help to a fellow-scientist, even without knowing
just exactly what his experiment entailed. Reynolds had
given them a pseudonym, John Foxxe, accompanied by
several pages of documentation of his qualifications,
which, if they had bothered to check, would have been
seen to be outrageously forged. But it had worked, and
here he was.

The scattered pinpoints of light, campfires on the
hillsides, abruptly ceased. Reynolds knew they had passed the broken coastline where the tribesmen could live,
and had reached the southern boundary of the Gombe
Stream Reserve itself. He knew they were about halfway
to the camp, for in daylight he had seen the change from
jutting promontories to densely wooded mountains cleft
by deep valleys. It was the rainy season, so no fishermen
were on the beach, no temporary huts dotted the white
sands.

The throbbing of the outboard was soporific,
mesmerizing. The gentle heave of groundswells in the
big lake rocked his body with the synchronicity of a
metronome, the hand on the cradle, and he dozed.

He awoke as the prow of the small skiff grated on the
beach. Black hands reached out to pull the boat onto the
sand and a voice called out of the darkness. ''Is that
you, Dr. Foxxe?''

''Yes, yes. Who is it? And why don't you have any
lights?''

A giggle, girlish and musical, erupted almost beside

37

him. "Why, you said this was top-secret. No one must know you have come."

"Yes, true, but could there by anyone around *here* who would know or care?"

The first voice, male, young and strong, answered, "Not bloody likely, sir, but we didn't want to take any chances. Come alone then, we've a bit of a hike."

Firm hands steadied Reynolds as he stepped out of the boat. "My gear?" he asked.

"Not to worry," the girl answered, "Makala will bring it along to your room."

For a half hour they trudged through soft sand, then Reynolds could feel the land rising slowly as the beach gave way to a hard-packed path. He could see the lights from several small buildings in the forest, and heard the dull rumble of a small generator. The forest itself was silent and eerie.

His guide threw open the door to a small cottage and led the way inside.

"Welcome to Gombe, Dr. Foxxe." He pronounced it "Gome-bay," and Reynolds smiled inwardly, knowing now that he had mispronounced it for five years or more. "I'm Peter Cudlipp, and this is my wife, Mary Ellen."

"Pleased, I'm sure," Reynolds answered.

Cudlipp was a tall, thin man, under thirty, with long blond hair and a clipped mustache. His wife was tall and lean, with pixie-cut hair and an elfin smile. They both were deeply tanned.

Cudlipp eyed Reynolds with an amused smile playing about his lips. "So you've really come all this way just to pick up a chimp?"

There was no answering smile on his face or his voice as Reynolds answered, "Seems so."

Cudlipp glanced at his wife and then took the suitcase

from the wiry black man who had carried it from the boat.

"Your bedroom is in here, doctor. You'll find everything you need, I think, for tonight. We usually breakfast together around eight, but there's no need for you to get up that early tomorrow. I'll ask . . ."

"I'll be there, Dr. Cudlipp."

"Peter, please, if you don't mind, too far from civilization to be formal," Cudlipp said. "And we call my wife Meg, to remind her of her more carefree days when she was just Mary Ellen Gardiner." There was a twinkle in his eyes as he put a hand under his wife's elbow and guided her to the door.

"Goodnight, doctor," Meg said, and stepped out into the darkness.

"Goodnight," Reynolds answered.

"The generator will go off in about a half hour, doctor," Cudlipp said. "Will that give you enough time? If not . . ."

"That'll be fine. Thanks."

"Tomorrow, then. Goodnight."

Reynolds nodded.

When the screen door swished to, Reynolds sat down on his narrow cot and opened his suitcase. He took out pajamas, bathrobe, toilet case, slippers, placed them neatly on the cot, and undressed. When he had changed to pajamas and bathrobe, he put on the slippers, sat on one of the meninga-wood chairs and put his feet on the table. He got up again, filled his pipe, lit it with a slow rolling motion of his head while he kept the match steady, then sat down again with feet on the table.

The lights dimmed, went up, dimmed again, then went out. The generator stopped, and total silence ensued. Gradually Reynolds recognized that it was not a total silence after all, for muted forest sounds could now be heard. The rustle of the wind in the tall trees, the restless chattering of a dry palmetto by the window, distant nightbird calls, and from the beach a gentle slapping of waves on sand. He would have stepped out for a moment but for his fear of the unknown darkness. These fears were probably groundless—still he did not want to be carried off by a hyena or a leopard. He puffed. his pipe in the darkness until he realized he did not enjoy it when he couldn't see the smoke wreath from his nose or mouth. Had he never smoked the pipe in the dark before?

Chapter 7

Reynolds cowered in the shadow of the old barn and watched Jan's distorted face hurling epithets at Sylvia, her long hair twisted in ringlets about her face, dirt smudged around her eyes, lips curled back in hatred. Then she tossed her head in agony and screamed—and screamed. Reynolds threw back the covers and sat bolt upright in his cot, slowly sensing that he was in the Gombe cottage. The unearthly screech trailed off, started again, and was joined by a chorus of barking, yapping sounds that Reynolds had never heard before.

He ran to the window and saw Peter and Meg Cudlipp racing across the compound toward the edge of the forest. Quickly changing into shirt and slacks, Reynolds put on his shoes without socks and sprinted across the packed earth to the edge of the clearing.

Peter motioned him to be silent, and he crept up to the bushes behind which Peter and Meg were crouched. Peter pointed. Stalking through the forest was a huge chimpanzee, the small body of a baby baboon clutched in his dangling right hand. His left hand touched the ground for balance from time to time as he lumbered toward a large rock.

Around him was a circle of chimps, some staring at him, eyes wide, hair standing on end, others loping along beside him trying to clutch at the baboon. The baboon infant was still alive, struggling frantically, whimpering sounds coming from his throat. Around this circle ran four big baboons, dancing and cavorting

41

and making lunges at the chimp carrying the infant, roaring hoarsely.

The chimp stood upright, grasped the infant baboon by both feet and smashed his head against the rocks, killing it instantly. The chimp glanced down at the infant, then swung it again, the head bursting open this time and splattering brains over the rocks. Instantly the other chimps clambered on the rock and licked the brains and the blood until the rock was clean.

The chimp then climbed a tall tree, settled itself in the highest branches and began to tear the flesh out of the belly and eat it. Several other chimps climbed the tree and begged for food, but the big chimp pushed away their hands and continued to eat. A loop of gut fell from the infant baboon and one of the chimps reached up and pulled it down, eviscerating the infant completely. The intestines draped around the lucky chimp and he scampered through the branches to another tree where he and several others began tearing the guts to pieces and eating slowly with handfuls of leaves pulled from surrounding trees. The four baboons just disappeared.

Reynolds returned slowly to his cottage and sat down on his bunk. He wasn't sure which was worse, the dream he had been having or the scene he had witnessed in the forest. He knew from Goodal's work that chimps sometimes kill other animals and eat them, but somehow the description in the book seemed to have little in common with the sight he had just seen. Would the chimp he was taking to his laboratory have somewhere within him the instinct to kill? Could be, Reynolds, somehow cull the tendency? Did he want to?

At breakfast, Peter watched Reynolds curiously, then asked. "That little episode in the forest this morning didn't bother your appetite much, doctor?"

Reynolds smiled wanly. "Not too much, I guess. You've seen it before, I suppose?"

"A couple of times. Rather gruesome, what?"

"Yes, but part of their normal behavior? You didn't interfere, I noticed."

"God, no. That's not our job. Watch and make notes. Even these so-called 'tame chimps' aren't really tame, just used to us." He paused, toying with the food, then looked up.

"So your coming here bothers some of us—no, not your coming—your *purpose* in coming. I dare say that distinction should be made."

Reynolds was silent, waiting for Cudlipp to continue.

"We do wonder, doctor," Peter said, "about your need for a *newborn* chimp. Chancy business, I'd say. Very difficult to raise a newborn in captivity."

"I know. I've studied the problem for years. Everything I could get my hands on."

"You know then that one must sometimes kill the mother to get the baby? Or if you don't, sometimes the mother will literally mourn for months? Become depressed and irritable. If a chimp baby dies the mother will keep it with her for days, even after it has begun to smell and attract flies."

"Yes, I know."

"Can you tell us," Meg asked, "just what kind of work you are doing, doctor?"

"No, I'm sorry."

"Odd," she mused.

"You'll learn of it someday, Meg," Peter interposed, "and then we'll all be famous." He grinned and returned to his toast and marmalade.

"Yes," she said to Reynolds, "I suppose you know what you're doing. It's just that we have such an attachment to all these chimps. Know them by name and all of that."

Yes, Reynolds thought to himself, I know what I'm doing. And it'll make all this look like child's play.

43

Someday they'll gasp with astonishment, and chide themselves for even suggesting that he didn't know what he was doing.

Reynolds met with Peter Cudlipp in the small office he shared with another ethologist. File cases lined the walls and minila folders were scattered over both desks. Prominently displayed in a small book case were Goodal's *In The Shadow of Man,* and Goodal and van Lawyck's *Innocent Killers.* Two of George Schaller's books lay on the same shelf, *The Serengeti Lion*, and *The Mountain Gorilla.* Other ethological studies, well-thumbed and dog-eared, lined the shelves, among them the books of the father of modern ethology, Konrad Lorenz of the Max Planck Institute in Munich. Reynolds spotted two he had read years before, *King Solomon's Ring* and *On Aggression,* and an ethology text by Irenaus Eibl-Eibesfeldt.

Cudlipp watched Reynolds scanning the book shelves. "Are you interested in ethology, doctor?" he asked.

Reynolds answered casually, not looking at Cudlipp, "No, not really, only as it applies in my own field." Had he been on the edge of a trap? Surely Cudlipp had read the forged papers which had been forwarded to the Gombe Stream and knew that ethology definitely wasn't his forte.

"Well, let's get down to business," Cudlipp said, and pulled a file toward him from a stack on his desk. "This is the entire record of observations of the chimp we know as Tempest. She's eleven years old, and has never been pregnant before. We know her ancestry from our old records, but she was mounted by several males the first time she went pink and so we do *not* know exactly who the father of your chimp is."

Reynolds' face reddened, and his mouth hardened perceptibly. "Doctor Cudlipp, I specifically instructed you to have the lineage of my chimp clearly documented. This may very well be the most important single experiment in the history of mankind, and I can't afford to take chances."

Cudlipp bit his lip to keep from saying, "We all think *ours* is the most important," and calmly answered the charge. "We seldom if ever know the father, doctor. Even when a dominant male forces a female to accompany him into the forest when she is pink, we know only by inference that he is the only one to have impregnated her. We do know that each of the chimps who mounted Tempest is a normal, healthy, adult male, and I'm afraid that's all we can do. Now, if you don't want Tempest's baby, we'll all breathe a deep sigh of relief when you're gone."

Reynolds nodded. "Go on," he said, but the veins in his forehead throbbed for several minutes.

"We also know that Tempest was aggressively reluctant to be mounted by her brothers, and none of our staff ever saw them have sexual relations with her. Again we can't be entirely sure."

Reynolds opened his mouth to say something, then closed it again resolutely.

"Two days ago, Tempest delivered a normal, apparently healthy, male infant. She brought him into camp yesterday for the first time." He grinned, then laughed aloud. "Too bad you couldn't have been here. You would have loved it. It was wild. Since it was her first baby, the other chimps really had a fit. She wouldn't let them come near her, and we were afraid a few times that the youngster would fall off when she scampered into a tree for seclusion. Older mothers usually just lay the newborn on the ground beside them and the rest of the chimps can resolve their curiosity by

45

poking it gently, or even grooming it, but the new mothers usually keep everyone else so far away that they don't get a chance to do so. Anyway, the baby's here. Now, all we have to do is get it without killing Tempest or getting killed ourselves.''

"You've got a plan?" Reynolds asked unemotionally.

Cudlipp was silent for a moment. "You don't really care how we get the chimp, as long as we get it, do you?"

"No."

Cudlipp sighed gently. His eyes rested on Jane Goodal's *In The Shadow of Man,* and he remembered the tenderness with which she described mother-child relationships in the chimps she was studying. Not so, this man Reynolds. He needed a male, infant chimp for his work, and it was unimportant how he got it.

"Meg will get the babe. Tempest trusts her. Probably will let her come closer than anyone else. May even let her fondle the child. Meg will cry for the next week, but then she's scientific, too. God, man, this had better be important."

"It is."

Cudlipp nodded. He knew it was. It had to be, or he wouldn't have gotten such explicit orders from the Director. But this man Foxxe, he was inhuman, more inhuman than the chimps themselves. He probably wouldn't shed a tear if he had to steal a human mother's baby.

Cudlipp nodded again, and moved to the door. Reynolds remained seated, but through the window he could see several of the Gombe Stream staff seated on a the ground well away from the main group of buildings, notebooks in hand, watching the chimps in their mid-morning grooming rituals.

"Meg!" Cudlipp called.

Mary Ellen appeared outside the door, where she had apparently been waiting for the summons.

"Now?" she asked.

Cudlipp nodded.

Reynolds got up quickly and walked to a window. He watched Mary Ellen, and Cudlipp watched him.

Meg sauntered slowly through the bushes and small trees edging the open compound behind the feeding station. She disappeared, but within a few moments she reappeared and with her was a young female chimp holding a newborn baby to her breast. From the newborn's abdomen hung a slightly withered placenta, and from time to time it bounced on the ground and jerked at the youngster's belly. Neither baby nor mother seemed to notice.

The other chimps in the area stood and stared at the mother and newborn baby. A young male chimp bounced up and down, then shuffled slowly toward Tempest. Tempest slowed, stopped, then turned and walked submissively toward the male. The male pursed his lips in a loud "Hoooo," then dropped his lower lip and opened his mouth widely, uttering a raspy, panting "Waaaa." He repeated this several times, and Tempest answered him with the same ritual, except that her sounds were more like grunts and pants, then submissively touched his side. She turned around and presented her rear in the basest form of submission, but when the male attempted to reach out and touch the baby, she whisked it away.

The male pant-hooted loudly, then ran to the nearest tree and noisily climbed it. For the next few minutes he went leaping through the trees, calling loudly and almost continually, while the other chimps, except for Tempest, watched him curiously. Tempest, finally frightened, cowered beside Mary Ellen, and this seemed to act almost as a signal to the adult males who had been

47

quietly observing the interaction. They leaped into the trees, bouncing and jumping from tree to tree, hanging from branches and screeching loudly.

Gently, carefully, aching with apprehension, Meg grasped the newborn chimp and pulled it slowly away from Tempest. Tempest scarcely noticed until the babe was actually gone, then her face split in a ferocious grin of fear and she reached out spasmodically for the youngster. But Meg was gone, running at top speed for the closest of the small cottages.

It was all over, now just a postscript, anticlimactic. After the years of planning, the letters back and forth, the logistical nightmare in timing, John Reynolds sat down on the chair beside the window and breathed a deep sigh of relief. Cudlipp looked at him pityingly, but Reynolds did not notice. It was too great a moment to share with anyone who could not know the significance of that moment. John Reynolds bowed his head, not in prayer, but in obeisance to the destiny which now stretched before him.

The screeching, wailing, and thunderous roars which shook the camp for the next hour did not penetrate John Reynold's brain. He tuned it out, reveled in his self-imposed seclusion, and felt the holy light of immortality within him.

Chapter 8

It was infinitely easier to raise Hermes than it was to raise Penelope. Penelope had to be strictly isolated from all human contact, but Hermes merely had to be isolated from other chimpanzees. The Reynolds modeled his home after Washoe's in Reno: a small house trailer, a completely fenced in back yard where he could romp and play, and later on, complete run of the Reynolds' house.

Actually the infant Hermes was treated as a member of the family from the start. He had to be fed frequently, about every three hours at first. iust like a human baby. Reynolds used human milk, obtained . from the LaLeche League, and little Hermes thrived on it. Chimp babies in the wild live on mother's milk almost exclusively for the first two years, then continue to suckle their mothers for over four years. During the first few years they are extremely dependent on their mothers, and sleep with them every night. Up to the age of five or six months they are protected by their mothers from all contact except their own siblings, so Sylvia maintained her vigil with the youngster day and night for half a year.

From the very first, Hermes clung to Sylvia, usually by the hair, draping himself around Sylvia's neck while she did her housework or sat in long vigils at Penelope's window. His little fingers and toes entwined themselves in her hair and the fabric of her dress, loosening only when he awoke hungry. He whimpered pitifully, then louder and louder until Sylvia shifted him around to her breast and fed him from the bottle.

Also at six months, Hermes took his first unsupported steps. He had been able to stand upright, holding Sylvia's hand, since the age of two months, and had been able to move around on Sylvia's body, if she held him securely, since the age of three months. But the first time he actually broke physical contact with her was with that first step at six months.

Sylvia described those first steps to John when he came home. "It was at once frightening and delightful," she said. "For six months I've lived with that little ape hanging somewhere on my body—usually around my neck—and all of a sudden I couldn't feel him! I was lying on the sofa, and he was standing beside me, one hand gripping my arm, and then he let go. I looked up, and there he was, several feet away, his lower lip hanging down in that silly little grin he gets sometimes. All of a sudden he just collapsed and sat there, the goofiest look on his face. He looked around at me and the grin changed to a frightened look and he crawled back to me and I pulled him up on the sofa and hugged him."

"About time he had some playmates, then," John said, his face immobile, almost hard.

The smile faded slowly from Sylvia's face, and she scratched Hermes behind the ears. "Yes, I guess so, John."

"Also time he began to learn a few Ameslan signs."

"Yes, John, it is."

"Who'll we get to play with him? Any of your friends have small children?"

"What friends, John?"

Without answering, he crossed the living room to his chair, filled his pipe, lit it, and blew the smoke into the air. He nodded his head a couple of times, studiously avoiding her eyes, acknowledging without rancor or unhappiness that they no longer had any friends.

"John," she said cautiously, "what about Penny?"

He almost spit the pipe out of his mouth. "My God, are you crazy? Let them grow up as brother and sister?"

He slumped in his chair, letting his glasses ride down on his nose. Sylvia ran her fingers through her prematurely graying hair, then wiped from her forehead the beads of perspiration which had popped up through the deep flush on her face and neck.

"Let's think about it awhile, then, John," Sylvia said quietly.

"Not much thinking to do, Sylvia. We've got to get at least one child in here every day so Hermie will have someone to play with, groom, and so forth. Maybe . . ."

For just a few seconds Sylvia had the sickening feeling that John was contemplating another kidnapping. Her heart pounded furiously and her stomach muscles tightened. Her mouth was dry and she could not speak.

"Just maybe," John continued, "we should adopt a child or two."

"And raise him in this menagerie?" Sylvia cried, her hands clutching the little chimp so hard he awoke and started to whimper. "No, John, it wouldn't be fair to *any* child to live here."

"You don't think we'd be good parents?" His lips were drawn back in a smile, but his voice was bitter, and the skin on his face was drained of blood.

Sylvia knew there was no real need to answer. She was now 35 years old, caught up in a nightmare from which she would never awaken. Her once lustrous hair was dull, going gray, and had not been handled by a beautician for five years. Her eyes, once gray and bright and laughing all the time, were clouded, almost colorless, melancholy. Her former prim, but nevertheless trim young body now sagged with too much fat. Her clothes

51

were drab. She was old. Old and weary. She was mother to a beautiful little child who had never seen her and nursemaid to a chimpanzee. Could she be a good parent?

"Answer that one yourself," she shot back at him, and stuffed a bottle in Hermes' open mouth.

For a moment she hoped he had been hurt just so she would know there was a glimmer left of the John Reynolds she had married. But that young John Reynolds was gone, ever gone, irretrievably replaced by the brilliant scientist who had meditated by the fire and caught a thunderbolt of inspiration from the sky.

"We'll find someone," he said.

And he did. A week later he announced that a young technician at the lab had been overjoyed to find a place for her three-year-old to stay during the day so she could continue working full time.

"She knows about Hermie?" Sylvia asked, and stroked the back of the little chimp draped around her neck.

John tugged at his collar and glanced sideways at Sylvia. "She knows. She says she loves animals and thinks it's just great that her little Sandy can play with a real live chimp!"

Her pupils dilated widely in apprehension, Sylvia asked, "Sandy?"

"Sanderson Wheeler the second."

"My God." She collapsed into a chair. Penny's mother would be coming twice a day to that house. Monstrous. She couldn't stand it. How could John be so insensitive?

"Jan," she began, and fought for control of her voice, "Jan Wheeler hasn't been here for over five years. Not since . . ."

"No, but I've seen her almost every . . ."

"And she never called."

"No."

"And now she wants to bring her *baby* out here?" Sylvia's eyes widened in horror.

"He'll be all right."

"Oh, I know. I know *he'll* be all right. But what about *me*? I've got to greet her every morning and give her back her child every night. And every time I do I'll think of . . ."

"Sylvia!"

Tears streamed down her face, and her fluttering hands found a handkerchief and wiped them away.

But he would not be swayed.

"She never suspected a thing, you know, Sylvia. She believed me when I said the baby was stillborn, and she accepted both the birth and death certificates without question."

"I know that, John. She *trusted* us."

He was not only unswayed, he was unperturbed. As he had done a thousand times before, he crossed the room and sat down with his pipe and magazines. While he lit his pipe and pushed his glasses back onto his nose, Sylvia sobbed once or twice and ran to her room, flung herself on her bed and her whole body shook with the heartaching grief of frustration and fear. Hermie did not even wake, but sleepily crawled off her back and snuggled under her arm.

For almost three years the child Sandy was the constant companion of the chimp Hermie. They gamboled on the lawn in the summer and in the trailer house or the main house in the winter. They romped, ran, and chased each other around the small sapling in the center of the fenced-in yard. Hermie climbed the tree, swung from the small branches and hit playfully at Sandy with his arms, or hung by his feet and grabbed at Sandy as he ran by. They groomed each other, Sandy running his fingers through Hermie's long hair, picking at invisible nits and dust, Hermie scratching and tickling Sandy under the arms and along the back of his neck. They wrestled, Sandy usually the winner because of his greater weight. They strutted around, showing off like all little children do, swinging their arms, stamping their feet, pirouetting until they became dizzy and fell to the ground in a tangle of black and white arms and legs.

When Hermie was about nine or ten months old, he began the first attempts at making a nest to sleep in. He would climb part way up in the tree, bend over a couple of small twigs, and try to lie down. Usually he succeeded only in making himself more uncomfortable, and would jump up after a few seconds and scamper down again. Neither the tree nor he were big enough to make an acceptable sleeping nest.

At about the same time, Hermie became playfully interested in climbing on Sandy from behind and would simulate copulatory movements with his pelvis. This was normal behavior for his age. If he had been in the wild, and had been around female chimps at the time of their estrus, he would have done the same thing, at least until the female tired of the game and brushed him off. But Sandy instinctively disliked this activity and Hermie soon gave up.

John Reynolds was satisfied. Hermie was going to be normal. Penelope was maturing also, living out her days in the total seclusion she had always known.

Sylvia taught Hermes Ameslan, slowly and laboriously, one sign at a time, and by the time he was three he could use several hundred signs correctly. Although they never had what one would call conversation, they could "talk" to each other enough to communicate wishes. Hermes could ask for food, and could indicate his desire to play with some item which was not visible. Sylvia could tell him to climb the tree, and he would, or she could ask him to get something in the house, and he did. In time, Sandy also was able to "talk" to Hermes, and it was actually comical to see them sit knee to knee telling each other something. Even somber John Reynolds would watch with a twinkle in his eye.

Sylvia and Jan Wheeler seldom said more than a few words to each other when they met each morning and evening. They commented on the weather, and exchanged other impersonal remarks, but seldom did they even talk about the boy and the chimp, even when something interesting had happened. If Jan wondered about this, she never said anything. She knew that her relationship with Sylvia had been altered by something, but she did not press to find out what it was.

Late one cold winter day, Sylvia took Sandy and Hermes with her shopping. When she returned to her car, it wouldn't start. Anxiously she looked at her watch and realized that Jan Wheeler would be arriving at the house in less than fifteen minutes. By the time she found a friendly old farmer with jumper cables, and got the car going, it was already a few minutes after five, and Jan had arrived at Standing Oaks.

Jan was puzzled when no one answered the door, the first time in over two years that no one had been home when she came to get Sandy. She tried the front door, and found it locked. She went around to the back and found it unlocked. Pushing the door open, she stepped into the kitchen. No one. She called out and received only an odd echoing in the big old house.

The back door blew shut with a slam. She jumped, startled beyond reason. What's wrong with me? she thought. She knew there was nothing to be afraid of. Sylvia was probably upstairs with Sandy and Hermie, and John would still be at the lab.

She looked into the living room, then pantry-lab. She stood at the bottom of the stairs and called again. Still no one. They could be asleep upstairs, and she climbed the stairs slowly, curiosity now rising. She opened the doors one by one and looked in.

No one.

She retraced her steps downstairs, looked out the front window and saw no one on the lawn, although she didn't expect they would be out there, cold as it was and almost dark.

The basement door was locked but the key hung beside the jamb. She opened it, knowing this was one part of the house she had never seen. A tremor shook her and she wondered why. She could feel her heart beating against her ribs, and her breathing was short and raspy. She held onto the railing and peered into the darkness.

She felt along the wall for a switch and found none. Strange. But there was a faint light coming from the far end of the basement, enough to see the steps after her vision dark-adapted. A long, oxygen-hungry sigh escaped her, and she breathed deeply, listening to the thud of her heart.

She started down, drawn by invisible hands, responding to external forces she could not have defined if she had had to. There was something down there she had to see. A presence. Her eyes were bright and staring, her pupils wide and black, but she did not hear the back door open.

She reached the bottom step and saw that the light came from a long horizontal window only a few inches wide. She forced herself to walk to the window and look through it.

The little girl, now almost eight, was lying naked on the floor, giggling uncontrollably, watching a movie of two young chimps rollicking in a small room. The chimps chased each other around the room, sommersaulting, hitting and biting each other in play, occasionally leaping onto a small junglegym where they swung from bar to bar, all the time laughing.

But Jan did not watch the movie. And she did not laugh. She watched the little girl, blonde and fair, beautifully proportioned. Jan's mind flicked to a picture in her father's album of a little girl of eight or nine, lying on the beach in Florida, red-and-white rubber ball clutched in one arm and a puppy in the other. In the picture, the little girl had long blonde hair and blue eyes, and was tanned a golden brown. The little girl in the room was pale and ghost-like in comparison, but it was the same girl.

Chill fingers of ice stroked the middle of her back and froze her lips in a silent scream—as hot fingers of steel closed around her neck and squeezed and squeezed and squeezed.

Chapter 9

"Tomorrow," John said.

Sylvia nodded.

They both had aged prematurely in the fifteen years since they had brought Penelope to the basement room. He was 48, but his face was deeply lined and his bald head was mottled with the brown spots of advanced age. His hair was almost white, and he had let it grow long so that it hung down to his shoulders. In a rare moment of levity, Sylvia said he looked like Benjamin Franklin, only skinnier. John took it as a compliment, and pushed it a step further saying, "His inventions were merely mechanical, mine will be of the very matrix of mankind."

"How poetical," Sylvia had answered sharply, and John had thrown her a leaden look.

Sylvia was only three years younger, but in many ways looked older than John. Her almost white hair was thinning, and would have resisted attempts at improved appearance even if Sylvia had tried, which she didn't. She had grown fat in the years after Jan Wheeler's death, but then she had slowly lost all she had gained, leaving her skin wrinkled and leathery. Loose folds of skin hung from her upper arms, and her neck was prune-like and scrawny. Only her eyes retained some semblance of her youthful vigor, and even they were frequently dull and lifeless.

But if John looked older, he still maintained the youthful single-mindedness of purpose which had prompted the Grand Experiment in the first place. In fact, sometimes his eyes lit up with the old fire, particularly as he thought ahead to the day when he would be able to resolve some of the questions which had troubled philosophers for the entire history of the world.

"Do you realize," he said to Sylvia one night, "that in a few short years we will be able to sit down with this creature, this hybrid being, and ask it questions, and get answers, and *know* without doubt what it is like to be a chimpanzee, or at least part chimpanzee? We'll know who's right, the animalists or the humanists, whether or not the sub-human species regard themselves as having a language, whether they have an inherent dignity which they can label as such, whether or not they can think *conceptually,* or only *perceptually . . .*"

"What do you mean, John? Do you *really* think any species below man can actually conceive of objects that aren't really there?—of *concepts*?"

"Conceive of them? Yes, I think maybe they can. Verbalize, no. They don't have words for right and wrong, just and unjust, infinity and eternity. But can they conceive of them? I don't know. Nobody does, and that's *my* genius. I'm going to be able to answer that question. And you will, too. Right here in this house."

Right and wrong, just and unjust, infinity and eternity. Words. Symbols for concepts. The humanists, like Mortimer Adler, claimed that man does not have the right to assign the power of conceptual thought to animals below man. The animalists (a gross and easily misinterpreted word) claimed that until it is *proven* impossible, man must not assume that animals below him are incapable of conceptual thought, must not assume them to be capable only of perceptual thought.

Tomorrow, she thought, tomorrow is the day John has been looking forward to, and I have been dreading, for almost fifteen years . . .

She stood up, absent-mindedly brushed her hair back over her ears, and walked through the pantry-lab to the kitchen. She unlocked the basement door, steeled herself for the inevitable flood of searing memories, and started down the stairs. She stared straight ahead, seeing once again that day seven years before when she had found the basement door ajar, had known what she would find down those dark stairs, and had known what she would have to do. And she had done it, her ears ringing with screams which never came, her lids tightly closed over eyes reddened with tears, her strength almost unequal to the brutish task forced upon her by a will stronger than anyone's she had ever known. When it was done, she had sat down by the body, exhaustion engulfing her, a mindless shell of the whole woman she had once been and could never be again.

Twice they had murdered. Once, a newborn babe, who was not yet dead, and then her mother, who was. And twice they had gotten away with it. So far. John, coolly assessing the odds, without imagination, but with a scientist's cunning, had simply driven the body along the river route Jan normally took to Standing Oaks, placed her in the driver's seat, put the car in neutral, put her foot on the accelerator, threw the car into gear and stepped back. The car had careened across the road, bounced off a tree, and plunged into twenty feet of water. No questions had ever been asked.

When her foot hit the basement floor, Sylvia shook off the gruesome imagery. She took her place behind the long, narrow window through which she had watched Penelope for countless hours.

She looked at the girl as if for the first time. The changes had come so gradually, as they do with all growing things, that Sylvia had scarcely been aware of them. Now, the day before the culmination of their long vigil, she was able to see what she hadn't before.

The girl had matured, of course. She was still naked, but had never known clothes or shoes, and was therefore not aware of her nakedness. Like Adam and Eve in the garden, no one had ever told her she was naked. She had never seen people with clothes on, and would not have known what to do with clothes if they were suddenly thrust upon her. Her skin was alabaster white, her hair silvery blonde and very long. She was small, no more than 4' 6'', perfectly proportioned, but slightly plump. Like a tree dwarfed by lifelong confinement to too small a planter, she had not fulfilled her genetic promise. Her hands were small, but the fingers were thick and clumsy from long disuse.

But it was her face that Sylvia now saw clearly for the first time. No longer fresh, alive, and beautiful, as it had been during those early years, it reflected rather the haunted look of the insane. Penelope's features were still the same, bone structure good, with high cheekbones and modeled nose. The skin was healthy, though so pale that the blue veins showed with remarkable clarity. But it was her eyes that were different in a dramatically disconcerting way. They were the pale blue of a frigid northern sky in January, rimmed with almost indiscernable white lashes. There was incomprehension in them as she glanced around her, at the one-way window, the gauntlets, the blackboard and the motorized screen.

She was sitting in the middle of the room, legs straight out in front of her, back arched, slowly pulling straws from the broom she had been taught to use to clean the room. As she disengaged a straw, she threw it toward the fountain and drain in the corner. It spun like an arrow and dropped onto the pool, then floated in circles until it was carried into the drain and out of sight. Penelope watched it until it disappeared, then, without apparent emotion, pulled another straw from the broom and threw it also. It fluttered almost immediately to the ground and Penny picked it up and threw it again. It went a little farther, but still far short of the drain. The girl shuffled on her bottom to the straw, threw it, and this time it gained the pool, swirled a few times, and disappeared.

She continued until the broom was entirely destroyed, then lay on her back and stared at the ceiling. She closed one eye, then quickly opened the other. A small flicker of a smile played at the corner of her mouth. She closed the other eye, then quickly opened the second one. Again she smiled. For almost an hour she played this game, then seemed to doze, her face lax and mouth partly open. For a moment she looked like any little girl drowsily whiling away a boring raining afternoon.

"Sylvia! Come up here, I want to ask your advice on something." John's voice came from the kitchen, and from the past. Mesmerized by the little girl's hypnotic-like activities, Sylvia knew she must be dreaming, for John had not asked her advice on anything for over fifteen years. She flushed happily, and waited for the dream to continue, fitfully aware that if she could think about being in a dream, she must actually be awake.

"Sylvia! Where the hell are you?"

It was not a dream and John was calling her. She bit her fingernail as she had done thirty years before when she had to prove to herself that she was awake. She shook her body like a dog, brushed her hair back from her eyes, and climbed the stairs.

"Yes, John?"

"We've got to decide whether or not to tell Penny that she's going to have company tomorrow."

"We?"

"Yes, we. You know the girl better than I do. Far too well, as I've told you a million times. Well?"

"She should be told."

He nodded his head. She knew that if he had disagreed he would have pressed her relentlessly for her reasoning. And she might have had difficulty putting it into words. But somehow she didn't think it right to suddenly place another creature into that small room without warning Penelope. She had never seen any other three-dimensional animal. She had been watching movies of chimps since she was a tiny infant, and she used three-dimensional objects daily. But Hermes would would immediately begin to rough-house with her, probably frighten her with his attentions. She had never been touched by anyone or anything, except for the gauntleted hands of Sylvia and John. She had never looked anyone in the eye, had never felt a hairy hand on her arm or thigh. Yes, it would be frightening, even if she were prepared.

"What about Hermie?" Sylvia asked.

"What *about* him?"

"Are you going to tell *him*?"

He looked at her as if she were an idiot. She cringed as if she were, then continued, "Shouldn't he know he's going to visit a new playmate in a small room in which he's never been before? Shouldn't he know that she is to be his new bride, his first and only mate?"

"Are you mocking me?"

"No, John," but she knew she was, and couldn't stop. "If there isn't a possibility that he can understand all that, why are we doing this at all?"

She may have been deriding him, scoffing at his seriousness, making light of two murders and fifteen years of hell, but if he suspected it, he showed no sign.

He walked to the window and looked out on the lawn where Hermes lay scratching his belly with one hand, the other hand grasping his two feet together tightly. As he watched, John felt the touch of Sylvia's arm against his as she leaned forward to watch the chimp outside.

"You've been a good mother to that chimp, Sylvia."

"Hmph," she snorted, not knowing whether to take it as a compliment or not.

"He's imprinted on you, you know."

"I know."

She *had* been his mother. She had fed him as an infant, had allowed him to follow her around endlessly as a "toddler," had applauded his attempts to climb and build nests, and, like his real mother would have done, protected him from the frequent outbursts of temper from John. His adolescence had been similar to a teenage human, frustrating and trying. In the wild, he would have been stabilized by his mother, showing her respect and going to her aid if she were threatened or attacked by another chimp. If he were offered a banana, he would have stepped back and let her take it.

During the last couple of years, Hermes had followed the pattern of adolescent chimps in the wild. He frequently disappeared for hours at a time into his trailer house, grooming himself, eating by himself, seeking the aloneness that is the hallmark of the individual (human or chimp) who is trying to put himself into the order of things.

Anthropomorphizing the chimpanzee is obviously fraught with trouble, but it did seem that Hermes was slowly breaking away from Sylvia, but did not yet know where he belonged. In the wild, he would have begun gradually to spend more and more time with the adult males, gradually being accepted, but always being maintained in his proper place in the social hierarchy. His rise on the dominance ladder would have been determined by his intelligence and determination.

In the uncontested society in which he lived, he did not have to prove himself. If he wondered why Sanderson Wheeler had never come back after that cold shopping trip, he could not ask anyone. And no one told him, at least in terms he could comprehend. Some children had come to play for a few days or sometimes for a few weeks at a time, but they did not know Ameslan, and their mothers did not like the environment for their youngsters for any prolonged period of time.

The Reynolds went out onto the lawn. Hermie ran toward them, bouncing and screeching, lower jaw hanging open showing his teeth in what the Reynolds had come to recognize as his "play-face." He stopped a few feet from them and looked at John. When he had been a youngster, he knew he could get away with almost anything with John, but now he was old enough to be afraid of offending any male of higher rank. John sat down on the ground. Hermie ran to Sylvia and leaped into her arms. She sat down beside John, and gradually Hermie slid onto the ground, presented his rump to John, and allowed him to groom his back and shoulders with light pats and scratches.

John picked up the chimp, not an easy task since Hermes now weighted almost forty pounds, and set him in front of him. Hermes instantly grinned, knowing a talk session was coming.

"Maybe," John said to Sylvia, "maybe you'd better tell him."

"Nonsense. You're the ranking male here, and Hermie knows it."

Slowly, in the American Sign Language of the Deaf, John Reynolds told Hermes that he was to have a new friend.

"Tomorrow," he started.

"He doesn't know that word," Sylvia interrupted.

"What will he understand?"

"Try 'after night.' "

"After-night-you-to-to-small-room-meet-friend-not-like-you-not-chimp . . ."

65

"Why did you stop?" Sylvia asked.

"He won't get that."

"Perhaps not. Tell him anyway."

"You're telling *me* what to do?"

Once again she stifled the burning rage that welled up within her, as she had countless times in the past. She had never been able to stand up to his overpowering personality, even in their younger, happier days. Now it would serve no purpose at all and would only stretch to the breaking point the tenuous love they had for each other. His will was her will.

She knew it and he knew it.

He stood up stiffly and stalked off, his sandals slapping angrily at his heels. Hermie looked after him, slowly comprehending that the talk session was over for the day.

Hermes signalled goodbye, a grin of fear spreading across his face. He glanced anxiously at Sylvia.

She tried to master her emotions, tried to hide her hate, but she was not quick enough and the chimp saw it, recognized it and ran screaming into his trailer house.

Sylvia buried her face in her hands and sobbed.

Chapter 10

The ticking of the clock bludgeoned the predawn silence with the metronomic regularity, yet it was only half as loud as Sylvia's heart as she lay on her side, watching the first streaks of daylight creep down the oak tree outside their window. She was not sure she had slept at all. Perhaps she had dozed fitfully from time to time, perhaps not.

The pretty little face of Penelope as an ingenuous toddler had appeared on the dark ceiling of the room, and she had caught glimpses, there in the hush of the great house, of the older Penny, twirling in circles on the green carpet. Penelope's whole life unfurled before Sylvia's agonizing gaze, wringing her dry of emotion, and she hardly had the strength to cry. She saw again the struggle Penny had had with Ameslan, trying to fit it into her secluded little world, then growing old too soon as the dreadful boredom of her isolation weighed down upon her.

Today her isolation would end. She would meet another creature for the first time. How would she react? With fear, driving her into a corner where she would cower from the predictable antics of Hermes? With joy, seeing another being for the first time? With immediate animal love, taking Hermes to her in the rapture of mating?

Not for the first time did Sylvia wonder just how she herself wanted Penelope to react. For years, as she had anticipated this day with dread, she had nerved herself to accept the inevitability of it. The two would meet, and after a time—perhaps a few hours, perhaps a few weeks, they would mate. They would set into motion the scenario which John had envisioned on that long-ago evening in the dim past when Sylvia's life had formed a pleasant pattern of gardening, flower-arranging, shopping, entertaining, traveling. When she and John themselves had been lovers, excitedly telling each other the important—and not so important—events of their day. When there had been laughter in the house. When there had been love. When love had been there.

John stirred restlessly and rolled over to look at the clock on the night-table. He reached out and shut off the alarm before it could ring. Fifteen years before he would have touched her tentatively, testing to see if she were awake, and if she were, he would have made love to her, and they would have lain there for a few moments in each other's arms, acknowledging without words the strength of each other's love.

Sylvia reached out to touch him, but he was already throwing back the covers and on his way to the bathroom. She sighed, knowing that today of all days he would hardly be in a mood which hadn't surfaced, except briefly and habitually, for all those years since Penelope had come to live in their basement.

John came out of the bathroom, sensitive fingers brushing the long white hair back over his ears.

"Come, Sylvia, it's time," he said and slipped on a bathrobe and moccasins.

Knowing this was her last chance to protest, and knowing she never would, Sylvia accompanied him to the trailer house and woke up the sleeping Hermes. He leaped into her arms, almost knocking her down with his enthusiasm. She set him on the floor and took his hand. With her free hand she signalled for his attention and in Ameslan said, "We go to see a friend."

His comical monkey-face split into two halves with a grin that made Sylvia laugh in spite of herself. Even John smiled.

"It's going to be all right, Sylvia," he said, and took Hermes' other hand. The smile faded slowly and Sylvia knew he had surprised himself with this sudden outburst. "It's got to be," he added, and looked at her with undisguised fear.

Penelope was still sleeping, curled up in a tight ball against the far wall. The room was almost dark, lighted only by the small bulb above the door at the end. Sylvia wiped her wet palm on the back of her skirt as she took her position at the long window above the gauntlets. Her mouth hung open, her breath coming in short, choking gasps. Her heart was thudding with such power that there was a staccato puff of air from her mouth with each violent beat. She felt dizzy and knew she would faint if she did not control the hyperventilation of her lungs and brain. With one long inspiration she forced herself to hold her breath until the dizziness had subsided and she was in control again.

John stood at the door, Hermes jumping up and down beside him. John flashed the Ameslan sign for "Quiet," and Hermes squatted on the floor and waited. John could see into the room as well as Sylvia, but he waited for her signal to open the door and let the chimp into the room.

She signalled "O.K." and he opened the door, and Sylvia flicked on the lights.

The chimp stopped abruptly when he comprehended that John was not with him. He looked anxiously around, a grin of mild fear beginning at the corners of his mouth, his upper and lower teeth showing, but his jaws clamped tightly together. The scream which usually accompanies the grin of fear had not started yet, but was not far off, when he noted Penelope lying against the wall, still asleep.

This was a new game and he liked the looks of it. His fear dissolved, his gaze riveted on the little girl. In the wild, he would have already developed his stalking abilities, creeping up on an unsuspecting rodent or other forest animal, or perhaps on a sleeping playmate.

Closer and closer he crept, sliding along the green carpet on his rear, right hand supporting his torso, left hand waving in the air for balance. Sylvia was alarmed, knowing that if the girl were suddenly awakened she would be terrified. John watched the tableau coolly, aware that the girl should not be awakened suddenly, but confident he could prevent it.

When Hermes was about five feet from the girl, John spoke through the loudspeaker, sharply but not loudly, "Penelope!" Hermes looked around him, unable to discern the source of the voice. Penelope rolled onto her back, eyes open.

"Sit up, Penny," John said soothingly. As she did so, she saw the chimp.

The success of the entire experiment depended on Penelope's reaction in the next few moments. If a numbing fear overcame her and she withdrew into herself in a panic, she might never recover enough to accept Hermes into her solitary life.

John knew all this. He knew the moment had come when the Grand Plan, his Life's Work, had reached its height or its depth. In the next few seconds he would be king or beggar, lord or slave, god or mortal. He knew this. And he waited.

Sylvia watched open-mouthed. She glanced sidelong at John, knowing what was going on in his mind, wondering if she knew her man well enough to predict what he would do if Penelope leaped up in a frenzy of fear and they had to somehow entice Hermes out of the room. She wondered, too, if *she* had the courage to shout at Penelope to fight off the intruder, to stand up against Hermes and defend herself and her little world against an outsider. She licked her lips, now as dry and parched as if she stood in the equatorial sun from which this beast had come.

Penelope smiled.

Tears oozed from Sylvia's eyes and ran down her cheeks and dropped slowly onto the concrete of the basement floor. She knew now what she had really wanted, and she knew it was too late.

Penelope slowly moved from a sitting position onto her hands and knees, long blonde hair framing her face and streaming onto the floor in front of her. Hermes did not take long to accept his new playmate. He jumped up and down in front of her, grinning ferociously, screaming with good humor. Soon they were wrestling and playing, tickling each other in the ribs, and chasing each other around the small room.

They played for hours in the way that chimps play. They found mock battles, wrestled, groomed each other, splashed water, leaped against the wall and bounced back at one another like professional wrestlers on the ropes. They laughed, and screamed, and giggled. Hermes looked around periodically, perhaps for something to climb, and then leaped onto Penelope's shoulders. She grabbed him by the neck and threw him into the air, then tried to jump on him but he was still too little to bear her weight and they crumpled in a tangle of arms and legs.

John and Sylvia watched with intense fascination. John was serene, more relaxed than he had been for weeks. He stood with feet widespread, hands supporting his body on either side of the door as he leaned forward to peer through the one-way window. From time to time he would look toward Sylvia, smile or wink or wave a hand. He was more than happy, he was ecstatic. It showed in every movement of his body.

Sylvia, too, seemed more contented. And indeed she was, but to a lesser degree than John. She had overridden the first wave of sadness, knowing deep within her that she must accept the inevitable. And, for her, the inevitable was that John willed. So she rejoiced that Penny now had a playmate, and was able to at least temporarily find some happiness of her own. In Sylvia's mind spun the words of the old Doris Day favorite, "Whatever will be, will be."

John moved quickly to her side, reluctant to be away from the window for more than a few moments at a time. "Sylvia," he said, "you know the drill from now on. One of us must be here, wide awake, to watch Hermie and Penny every minute of the day and night."

"I know, John. But at night, too? Do chimps ever mate at night?"

"Rarely, as far as I've been able to read on it. But in the wild, a male and female chimp will often disappear for days at a time when she's pink. Who knows whether they mate at night or not. They never sleep together in the same nest, but that's probably more because a double nest is so hard to build. Besides, these aren't two chimps. And they may stay awake after we're gone, or wake up before we're back in the morning. We just can't afford to miss it."

"Couldn't we just take Hermes out at night?"

"After Penny's asleep? Huh-uh. Too risky. Besides, it may not take too long."

The vigil lasted for almost three months.

The first day and night were easy. John napped in the afternoon while Sylvia sat on a high kitchen stool at the long window above the gauntlets. Then John watched from the same vantage point all the first night while Sylvia slept. She brought him down some breakfast in the morning and while he ate he described the night's happenings. In fact, nothing had happened. When he had turned the lights down, both Hermes and Penelope had curled up in a ball and slept the whole night through. While they slept, John passed two days' rations through the window, bananas and pears and raw meat. Bananas, he claimed, were a nearly perfect food. Only baobab seeds were better, but he admitted laughingly that they were a little hard to come by.

During the next few days, John and Sylvia established an unvarying routine. Since John could not afford to lose his job, as uninteresting as it had become for him, he took the afternoon hours until after midnight and Sylvia took the night and day shifts, then slept when John came home.

For Sylvia the novelty of seeing Penelope and Hermes playing together soon wore off. And for weeks they did little else but play. Sometimes they did become digusted with each other, tempers flared, and they fought with teeth and fingers. But always they made up, usually with a pat on the head or a human-like pounting of lips at each other. Then they would groom each other, Hermes running his leathery fingers through Penny's hair, Penny picking at Hermes' long glossy coat with her rough, stubby little fingers. Never once did Sylvia see anything which even closely resembled an amorous interest.

John never tired of watching the two. His glistening eyes stared through the glass with diligent attentiveness to every move, watching for the slightest indication that they might be becoming interested in each other sexually. He was aware that in the wild state, male chimpanzees pay little attention to a female who is not sexually "ready." The estrus cycle re-occurs once a month, as it does in the human, and is evidenced by swelling and pink coloration of the genital area, which in the chimp is very obvious because she presents these parts when she

73

walks or lies down.

But Penelope obviously would never do this. Wryly, John thought about somehow trying to paint her little bottom, but this was simply out of the question. He could only hope that this was not the only signal given the male by the female. Or perhaps the two would mate in play, her actions accidentally or purposefully stimulating him to the act.

As the weeks passed, Sylvia came to loathe her voyeurism. She began to concentrate rather more on the social interaction between the two playmates. She noted that without any doubt they were able to communicate with each other. John had done his work well in insisting that both know Ameslan. At first, Penelope talked too fast on her hands, not really comprehending that her new friend could not "read" her hands as well as John and Sylvia had done. In fact, she often spoke orally to the chimp for several minutes before she realized he was paying her no attention whatsoever. Then she would signal to him in the classic handwaving movement of the deaf until he stopped what he was doing and watched her hands. Gradually she slowed down to a speed which Hermes could understand. She dropped out of her vocabulary the abstract words she had learned and began using only the symbols to which the chimp could relate.

Outside, the hazelnut bushes along the drive again hung heavily with ripening fruit, the leaves of the white oaks reddened and then browned, and the sugar maples flamed briefly and threw a crimson carpet onto the ground, the red cedars covered themselves with tiny blue-berry-like cones. The tall grasses in the meadows were pounded flat by the cold wet winds, and the struggling red-pine seedlings stood out green against the somber landscape.

The floral world of the great Midwest prepared itself

for winter, turning in upon itself in order that it might not succumb to drifting snow and numbing cold. Each plant, on stage for the briefest moment as Time measures time, knew instinctively what it must do to recreate itself next spring, and if it didn't, its line would cease to be. Those plants which did react just right would live to procreate others with the proper genetic code to withstand the next onslaught from a harsh world.

Inside, the ebb and rip of evolution's tide was being caught at its highest point. A master molecular biologist had finally caught one of those thunderbolts which had been flung at him for so long. He was about to match the genes and chromosomes of Earth's two most advanced animals, was close to his goal of hybridizing *Homo sapiens* and *Pan troglodytes*.

At what price?

"Don't ask the price," John had once said to Sylvia. "When there's a prize that's priceless. If you've got to ask the price, you can't afford it. I can pay the price, whatever it is. Can you?"

Chapter 11

The monotony of the basement vigil began to wreak a subtle change in Sylvia's attitude toward her self-imposed captivity. For one thing she realized she was a captive audience, unable to leave the basement, much less the house, unless John was there.

But even more important, gradually she was able to accept the two individuals in the small room as playmates, increasingly able to ignore the fact that they were so disparate in their outward appearances.

In her eyes and mind, the girl became more chimplike, the chimp more human, until there was a blending of personalities which Sylvia found progressively difficult to distinguish. Like the small-town Minnesotan who has seldom seen a black man until he is transplanted to a larger city or the south, and then realizes that his original prejudices and fears were unfounded, so Sylvia little by little came to realize that her early revulsion was dissipating. Imperceptibly her repugnance melted away, and she began to watch the scene with a detached, even scientific attitude.

John's perception of the drama—and he often did think of it as a set-piece, a play under his direction—had always been that of the scientist. Following in the traditions of original basic research, he had put into motion certain biological laws which would eventuate in an unpredictable result. Or at least in one sense the outcome was unpredictable: no one knew *exactly* what would happen. But John knew that if mating did not occur spontaneously, he would have to go to the next, much more difficult alternative: the artificial creation of the fertilized egg which he needed for the successful conclusion of his experiment.

As Sylvia's scientific curiosity was aroused, she recognized that she was pitifully ignorant of cellular anatomy and physiology. She badly needed more background information to help her understand what John was trying to do. She tried reading some of John's scientific articles, but the material was so full of words she scarcely knew, or knew not at all, that her progress was slow. She stumbled over "homologous proteins," and "deoxyribonucleic acids" and had to look up such commonly used words as "alleles," "electrophoresis," "genetic distances," and "congeneric species." Even her college work did not prepare her for understanding discussions of regulatory mutations, point mutations, and gene rearrangements.

She had to have help.

Far from the antagonism she half-expected, John was sympathetic, even elated, that she should want to know what he was doing. After fifteen years of passive acquiescence to his work, she finally was developing a real desire to understand it.

"Where do I start, Sylvia?" he asked. "I've thought and read of little else for fifteen years and I wasn't unversed in the subject before that."

"I know, John. Perhaps you could begin with what got you started on this crazy scheme in the first place."

They were in the basement. Sylvia sat watching through the long window, John sitting on a wooden kitchen chair tipped back against the wall a few feet from the door through which he had ushered Hermes. He sat with his eyes closed. It was after midnight, time for Sylvia's shift, and time for him to get to bed. His half-glasses still sat on the end of his nose, where they appeared to be in imminent danger of falling off.

He opened his eyes and looked at Sylvia when she said

"crazy scheme," then realized that this was indeed a milestone. For, in years past she would not have dared to use that term. Paradoxically, now that she *could* use it, John knew she had made the turn toward accepting the "crazy scheme." Just as a considerate person will not even jokingly call a really stupid person a "stupid idiot," but will readily use that term when referring to an intelligent friend, so John knew that Sylvia's ability to call his scheme crazy was tacit admission—that she no longer considered it crazy.

"Well, it was that article in Natural History that got me to thinking. I wondered, and asked myself this question: if we really want to know whether we differ from chimps in *kind* or just in *degree,* why don't we try to hybridize *Homo* and *Pan,* and then see if we as *Homo* are really unique, or do we just differ from *Pan* in degree? With me, so far?"

"Yes, go on."

"All right, but you'll have to stop me if you don't get the gist of what I'm saying. I know you've been reading, but what you've learned I don't know." He tipped the chair forward, turned it around and sat on it backwards, his arms resting on the back of his chair. He lowered his chin to his hands and sat quietly for several moments. Sylvia looked at him to see if he might be dozing, but he was wide awake, as alert as if he had just awakened in the morning from a long sleep.

"First of all," he continued, "you've got to realize that it is now possible to compare *Homo* and *Pan* in many physical and biological ways. You can estimate very closely the genetic distance—that is, the difference between the two species in inheritable traits—by rather exact biochemical methods. You can compare the cellular proteins *exactly* by three basic methods—electrophoresis, immunology, and sequencing techniques—and you can compare the nucleic acids by annealling techniques . . ."

"You just lost me."

"Not important. Just remember that the methods used are very exact and not open to varying interpretations. Now, *Pan* and *Homo,* chimp and man, have been compared by all of these methods and—to quote King and Wilson—"the intriguing result is that all the biochemical methods agree in showing that the genetic distance between humans and the chimpanzee is probably too small to account for their substantial organismal differences.""

"Organismal differences?"

"The differences in anatomy, physiology, behavior, ecology."

Sylvia's eyes widened. "You're saying that . . ."

"I'm saying that the genes of the human and the chimp are as similar as those of sibling species of other organisms. Sibling species, if you don't know, are species which do not differ significantly morphologically, but function as spearate and reproductively isolated populations in nature. Now, it's clear that we're *not* siblings of the chimps, but the overall genetic distance between us is less than we average for sibling species!"

"I'm beginning to comprehend."

"Not yet you're not. Let me enlarge a little on the organismal differences. Are we anatomically similar to the chimps? Only in the thorax and arms. We differ substantially in brain size, anatomy of the pelvis and feet and jaws, and the relative lengths of limbs and digits. Furthermore, we differ radically in posture and locomotion. We get our food in vastly different ways, at least most of us do. And last, but obviously not least, we differ enormously in our ability to communicate."

He stopped speaking, for Sylvia had suddenly begun to concentrate intently on the occupants of the small room. John jumped up, whispering, "What's happening?"

Sylvia relaxed, and slumped back on her kitchen

stool. "Nothing. For a moment I thought . . ."

John looked through the window, then returned to his chair. "Some day . . ." he muttered.

"Where was I? Oh yes. Evolutionarily speaking, it's clear that *Homo* and *Pan* have a common ancestor. That is, *Homo* didn't evolve from the chimp, nor *Pan* from us, but both of us evolved along different lines from the *same creature*. In terms of anatomy and adaptive strategy, we as humans have developed much more rapidly than has the chimp lineage. But, mark *this* well: at the macromolecular level, chimps and humans *have* evolved at similar rates."

In a manner mockingly reminiscent of the classroom, Sylvia turned and said, "Illustrate, please."

"Easily. For example, we know from the studies I mentioned earlier that the cellular albumins of the human and chimp are equally distinct—immunologically—from the albumins of other hominoids, that is the orangutan, and the gibbon. We know, too, that the DNA's—deoxyribonucleic acid—the carriers of genetic information—in chimps and humans differ to the same degree from the DNA's of other hominoids. In other words, we know that *Homo* and *Pan* are not only remarkably similar, but they are different *in the same degree* from the gorilla and orangutan and gibbon."

"Whew, well I asked for it, I guess."

"Don't you . . .?"

"Oh, yes, I understand. And maybe now I can say I'm beginning to comprehend?"

The corners of John's mouth turned up and there was the ghost of the long-ago kind of smile in his eyes. Sylvia felt the stirring of a love she once had had for this complex man.

"Yes, I guess you can," he said.

She flashed him a smile which made him wince visibly. There *is* a man there, Sylvia thought, beneath that icy facade. Somewhere, deep down inside, locked up with a thrown-away key, was the man she had married, the man who had once walked with her through the snow-laden pines, who had shaken snow down her neck and then dug it out with warm fingers and kissed her wet ears and blew his warm breath on her cold neck. So long ago.

"Since the contrasts," he continued, "between organismal and molecular evolution are so great, we can only assume th at the two processes are mostly independent of each other. Therefore, and this is the basis for all we are doing here, *therefore,* we made the assumption that the *regulatory mechanisms* in the two species have mutated—changed spontaneously for no apparent reasons—during the course of evolution. And it is the diverging mechanisms *regulating* anatomy, physiology, behavior, and ecological adaptiveness, which have caused the marked apparent differences between *Homo* and *Pan.*" He paused to see if she were still with him. She nodded.

"Go on," she said.

"Almost done. Mutations of the regulatory mechanisms may occur in two ways. One, they may be 'point mutations'—one type of nucleotide substituted for another in the so-called 'operator genes,' those which effect the production of proteins but not the sequence of the animo acids."

"I can't say that I fully understand that."

"Not necessary. We aren't going to deal with the point mutations in Hermes and Penelope. What we *will* deal with is the second way that regulatory mutations may occur—the changes which have occurred in the *order* of the genes on the chromosomes."

He was the professor in the classroom again, his finger stabbing the air to make his point. It was as if he had been waiting for this chance to expound his theories. Sylvia was no longer his audience. He was at the podium of a large lecture hall, the geneticists and anthropologists and biologists of the world all sitting foward in their seats to catch his words. Where had he come from? they all asked themselves. Why haven't we heard of him before?

"There are four ways in which the genes on a chromosome may change. One: inversion, that is, the gene turning upside-down so that it attaches at its other end. Two: translocation, or the moving of the gene from one place to another on the chromosome. Three: an actual loss or addition of a gene on a given chromosome. Four: the fusion—growing together—or fission—separating—of chromosomes themselves.

"Now, we know from banding studies of the chromosomes that since the lineages of *Homo* and *Pan* diverged there have been at least eight inversions, two translocations and one chromosomal fusion over five or six million years."

His finger wrote in the air once more, and then came down. He was back in the dark basement of Standing Oaks, his wife seated on a kitchen stool watching a blonde girl and a chimpanzee playing in an almost bare, lighted room.

"And you're going to change that?"

"In one sitting. I don't know how long it will take me, but I'm going to turn those genes around, and re-attach them, and the new cell will live and grow, and we will have a new creature, never before seen on this earth."

"But you can't, what's the proper word, *un*fuse that one chromosome, can you? And what will happen if you don't?"

"I know I can't. But that's a chance I'll have to take."

Chapter 12

Slowly Sylvia climbed the basement stairs, fumbled briefly with the key in the lock, crossed the kitchen to the wall-phone and dialed a number she knew well.

When John answered she said, "You can come home now."

Excitedly he asked, "You're sure?"

"How can you *not* be sure with something like this?"

"I'll be there in fifteen minutes."

He slammed the receiver onto its cradle and called to his assistant. "I'll have to leave you to finish this titration. Got to run. And I won't be back today, probably not tomorrow either. Think of something to tell the boss."

Even while he ran across the parking lot in the windy cold of the early winter afternoon, he was able to calculate that Penny was indeed mid-cycle. Somehow Hermie must have known. How could he? Was there an aura, a subliminal odor, which stimulated the species *Pan*? Teenagers of the species *Homo* obviously had no way of sensing what Hermes had sensed. For if they could, it would be reasonable to assume that high-school marriages and abortions would be less common.

He ran the back stairs three at a time and threw open the door. For the first time in three months Sylvia was in the kitchen when he came home.

"You're absolutely sure, Sylvia?"

She nodded her head, and sipped slowly from a steaming cup of black coffee. "Want some?"

He shook his head. "Tell me about it."

"Not today, John. You'll have to take my word for it. Someday, maybe, but not now. You'll just have to take my word."

He rushed past her, through the open basement door, and down the stairs. Hermes and Penelope sat facing each other, rolling a ball back and forth across the carpet. Well, John asked himself, what did I expect? That they would be cuddled in each other's arms? He smiled grimly.

He threw his coat and tie on the basement stairs and opened the door to the small room which once had been the coal bin. Flicking the light switch, he stood in silent contemplation. The room had been transformed into a miniature operating theater. In the center stood an old, cream-colored operating table which had been junked by the University Hospital years before and had stood in the storeroom waiting to be thrown away. Over the table was a discarded set of operating lights, now renovated and usable. In the corner was a small oxygen tank on a rolling stand.

John stood quietly for several moments, surveying the material on the tables. Ether, ether cone, knee straps, bottles of sterile water and saline, pHisohex, zephiran, sterile gloves and paper gowns in pre-sterilized wraps, small bottles of morphine and atropine, sterile syringes and needles.

He was not an unexperienced tyro about to perform his first operation. He had done hundreds. All on female dogs. It had gone badly at first for his only background in surgical technique was cat dissections in college biology. And there had been times when he had botched things so badly that he had to sacrifice the dogs long before he had completed the procedure. But he kept trying, and eventually he developed a proficiency which would have surprised a trained surgeon. There was no paucity of stray female dogs.

He was also no stranger to the anatomy of the human female's pelvic organs. Anatomy books and atlases were easily bought in the university bookstores. Post-mortem examinations were done daily in the university morgue, and John was a frequent attendant, receiving not only invaluable information on the details anatomy of the cadavers, but also the plaudits of the physicians who complimented him on his interest in the clinical aspects of practice. This recognition as an interested primary researcher eventually brought him invitations to witness all sorts of operations.

He did not pick and choose. He went to all he could, watching carefully the movements of the surgeon's hands, cataloguing in his precise brain the intricate steps which maintained sterile technique. Of special interest, of course, were gynecological operations, and these he watched with particular attention to surgical detail. Recognizing from the start that most of the operations were terribly gross compared to what he would have to do, still be learned from them what he could.

As he stood in the old coal bin, he knew he was ready. He also knew he did not have long to dally.

He climbed the basement stairs at a trot. Sylvia had finished her coffee and was rinsing the cup in the sink.

"I'm going to need you now," John said, "more than ever before. Are you going to be o.k.?"

She turned to face him, tears brimming over in her eyes. "Yes, John. I'm fine. Just tell me what to do until I get my mind back in gear."

"First, the seconal in the milk."

"Two grains? Three?"

"Better make it three."

She took the carton from the refrigerator, poured a glassful and added a tablespoon of malt. From a bottle on a top shelf she took two red capsules, broke them one by one into the glass and stirred for a few moments.

"Shouldn't I heat it? She likes it warm."

"Not enough time. She'll drink it."

With John leading the way down the basement stairs once more, Sylvia carefully followed him to the long window above the gauntlets. She placed the glass on the kitchen stool. John watched the two inmates of the room, then slowly turned down the lights with the rheostat. Slightly surprised, Penelope looked up, then signaled "Goodnight" an Ameslan to Hermes. After long years in a contrived environment, she had developed a conditional reflex to the lighting. Hermes had not, and he continued to roll the little ball around on the floor while Penelope retreated to her favorite sleeping place, curled up, and within a few minutes was fast asleep.

From his post by the long entrance door, John signaled "O.K." to Sylvia. She put her left hand and arm deeply into one gauntlet, slid the window slightly open with her right hand, and passed the drugged milk into the room. Quickly she shut the window, and inserted her right hand into the other gauntlet. She nodded to John.

He slowly turned up the lights until they were as bright as they had been before. Hermes scarcely noted the change, since he had not been perturbed by their absence, but Penny stirred restlessly, then awoke as from a long sleep. She rubbed her eyes, saw Hermes still playing with the ball, and crawled quickly to him on her hands and knees, eyes bright and face smiling.

"Penny," Sylvia said.

The girl stopped, stood up, and walked slowly and wonderingly toward the gauntletted hands. Sylvia held the glass in her left hand, and with her right hand signaled to the now alert Hermes, "Not for you. For Penny." Hermes bounded up and down, screaming in rage, but did not try to take the glass. Penelope reached out, took the glass, signaled "Thank you," and sipped it slowly. Once or twice she held the glass away from her with a slight grimace, but continued to drink it.

She handed the glass back when it was empty, then returned to her play with Hermes. Sylvia and John watched. Gradually she lost more and more interest in the roughhousing of the inexhaustible chimp, and when she sat down, John again turned off the lights. Sylvia withdrew her arms and sat on the stool, bemused as ever at the power of the barbiturates.

They waited for an hour. Twice John got up and went into the old coal bin, but Sylvia sat silently on the kitchen stool. All of the old doubts paraded before her mind's eye, and all of the reasons for scotching the whole sheme reappeared in full color. Once she looked up to see John standing before her, arms akimbo, eyes boring into hers. She felt for the thousandth time the power of his will over hers, and she nodded to him. "Don't worry," she said.

John stood at the long door. He reached for the knob, took a deep breath as if to fortify himself, and opened it. Sylvia laughed out loud when the dark form of the chimp hurtled out of the darkness into John's arms, then careened off his chest to the floor and leaped gleefully up the basement stairs. They let him go. He could not go far, and even if he did, he was probably of no further use to them.

John turned the lights up slightly so he would not stumble over playthings on the floor, picked the girl up in his arms and carefully carried her to the operating room across the hall. She squirmed just a little, but did not awaken and lay still on the table while Sylvia placed the canvas restraint just above her knees and around the table and buckled them in place. John secured her wrists in the leathers on either side of the table.

He seated himself on the small revolving stool, turned around to the table behind him, and drew up a cubic centimeter of atropine sulfate, a dose of 1/150 of a grain. Sylvia squeezed Penelope's upper arm until a vein bulged in the lower arm, and into this John slowly injected the atropine. Within a few minutes, Penelope's face flushed a slight pink.

"I think she's ready, Sylvia," John muttered. He placed the guaze-covered ether mask over Penelope's face and began dripping ether onto it. Her breathing stopped almost immediately as the irritating gas penetrated her windpipe and bronchial tubes. But she could not hold it for long, and every time she took another breath, she breathed in the heavy fumes of the drug.

From time to time, after her breathing became regular and deep, John shone a penlight into her eyes, "Look here, Sylvia," he said. "Her pupils are quite small now, just slightly smaller than normal. They should slowly get larger, to about normal size, and then's when we've got to be careful. Here, you take it for awhile. I've got work to do upstairs."

Reluctantly, Sylvia took her place on the metal stool and continued the anesthetic.

John clambered up the stairs, mind at ease for the first time in months. Like a student whose cramming is over and only needs to execute the examination, he went straight to his laboratory, switched on the light and peered intently around the room for a few seconds. Carefully he removed from the drawer in the desk four tiny glass needles, drawn to a very fine point and slightly curved at the tip. He placed them on a small perforated metal tray. From the same drawer he lifted out a felt-lined box two hair loops, then capillary tubes with fine hairs sealed in the ends, and placed them alongside the glass needles. He placed the try in the small pressure sterilizer, sealed the door, adjusted the timer, and turned on the current.

From the refrigerator he removed two tiny, square agar dishes and a small sealed bottle of a balanced salt solution. These he carried to the kitchen. The agar dishes he placed on the table, the vial of solution in the oven, and set the knob on 120 degrees. He stood for a moment reflecting, concentrating—then, satisified that the oven was working and that he had done everything he could do at the time, he returned to the operating room.

Sylvia was crouched in the classic position of the anesthetist, her left elbow resting on the table, hand holding the ether mask tightly on Penelope's face, her right elbow also on the table, that hand holding the ether can slightly tipped so a steady drip of ether fell on the gauze mask.

Penelope's breathing was heavy and regular, and she seemed to be in a deep sleep. Her long blonde hair, oily and dirty on her head, but clean and shiny near the ends, streamed off the end of the table into Sylvia's lap. Beads of perspiration dotted her forehead above the ether mask. There was a faint animal smell about her, of dried urine and feces about her orifices, of armpits never deodorized or shaved, or teeth never brushed or gums massaged.

John scrubbed her lower abdomen with pHisohex soap for ten minutes, rinsed it with sterile water from a bottle, and with long bold strokes painted the entire abdomen with tincture of zephiran. With the skill of an operating room nurse, he opened the packs of drapes and surgical instruments on the table, carefully pulling down each corner and inverting it to expose the contents without touching them. He then scrubbed his hands and forearms, dried them cautiously holding the towel at arm's length away from his body. With Sylvia's help, he maneuvered into the sterile paper gown and latext gloves.

Sylvia poured a few more drops of ether onto the gauze and covered Penelope's face with it. Then she helped John slide the instrument table over the end of the operating table. From it he removed four sterile paper drapes and placed them over the girl's body, leaving only the lower abdomen exposed.

John picked up the scalpel and Sylvia checked the girl's pupils for size. It was, for John, a holy moment, though he would not have called it that. Like Michelangelo climbing the ladder for the first time to the ceiling of the Sistine Chapel, like Bach sitting at the organ with fingers upraised before striking the first chord of a new cantata, like Darwin stepping off the Beagle onto the Galapagos Islands, yes, like thousands of men before him who had sought out truth in the kaleidoscopic welter of false gods on this earth, John Reynolds picked up a scalpel and placed it, cold steel and razor sharp, on the bare skin of the girl-goddess, Penelope.

Chapter 13

It was three o'clock in the afternoon, four hours after Sylvia's call to John at the lab, when the scalpel slid slowly down through tough white skin from navel to mons pubis. Skillfully adept, John clamped subcutaneous bleeders and left them to clot spontaneously between the jaws of the hemostats. He separated the muscles in the midline with a single smooth stroke of the second scalpel, and grasped the shining blue-white peritoneum with two curved forceps, and cut in between them. The surgical defect sucked air softly and the peritoneum lifted gently away from the underlying small bowel.

"Fix the light, please."

Now with the gentleness of a mother washing her baby's eyes, John slid his right hand deeply into the pelvis and felt blindly for the left ovary and Fallopian tube. Upon finding them, he just as carefully lifted them through the coils of small intestine until he could see them clearly.

Deliberately and calmly he packed away the bowel with his left hand, holding them with a cloth-like, paper laparotomy sponge, and peered anxiously at the small white ovary in his fingers. Its surface was smooth, unbroken, glistening. Gingerly he allowed it to drop back into the pelvis.

"Not that one." He removed the sponge, and the small bowel fell back in place, each loop undergoing an irritative, reactive peristalsis as it sought to regain its normal position.

Just as painstakingly as before, he slid his fingers into the pelvis on the right side and thoughtfully sought out the right tube and ovary. He lifted them into view, packed the bowel away again, and stared at the ovary. A small, dark red spot was immediately apparent on the surface of the otherwise hard white organ. A streak of dark blood stained his finger as he carefully ran it over the spot of the ovary.

He nodded to himself, then for the first time looked at Sylvia at the head of the table. "She's ovulated, alright. From the right side. I can see the ruptured Graafian follicle, still unsealed."

He placed a Kocher forceps across the Fallopian tube at its junction with the uterus and let it slide into the abdomen to its normal position. Taking a sterile towel from Mayo table, he placed it over the entire incision.

He stripped off his gloves and gown and threw them onto the floor. "Be right back," he said, and bounded up the stairs to his laboratory. The sterilizer had shut itself off and the red light was out.

In the kitchen, the oven light was also off, indicating that the proper temperature had been reached. Using an asbestos glove, he slid the materials out of the oven, and strode carefully yet quickly down the stairs.

He placed the bottles on the table behind Sylvia, rescrubbed his hands and put on sterile gown and gloves. Penelope slept peacefully, her breathing deep and regular.

"Everything o.k. at your end, Sylvia?"

"Seems so. Her pupils are good and her breathing is satisfactory, don't you think?"

He nodded and stripped the towel off the incision. Reaching into the pelvis, he cautiously pulled the Kocher into the wound and placed two more clamps on the broad attachements of the Fallopian tube.

He placed clamps between tube and ovary, then along

the filmy, ligamentous attachments of tube to uterus, then with scissors resected the tube above the clamps.

He held out a small glass beaker toward Sylvia, and she filled it with solution from the heated bottle marked "lactated Ringer's solution." Carefully John placed a tie around each end of the Fallopian tube and dropped it into the Ringer's solution.

Now, working as rapidly as he could, he closed the entire abdominal incision with through-and-through sutures of heavy nylon to all layers—peritoneum, muscles, subcutaneous fat, and skin.

"Stay with her, Sylvia. Let her come up to a normal deep sleep, but at the first indication that she's waking up, give her an injection of morphine sulfate. Use your own judgment, but you'll probably have to use rather heavy doses to keep her under, probably fifteen or twenty milligrams at a time. You won't need any help with that, will you? If you do, come into the lab as quietly as you can. I'll be unable to leave, but we can talk."

"Any idea how long you'll be?" Sylvia asked.

"None."

With extreme care, he climbed the stairs, knowing that he carried the lifeblood of his entire career in his hands. He backed into the laboratory, pushed the door widely open with his buttocks, then swung the door closed with his foot. He sat down on his chair for a moment to quell the rising flood of fears and to give his hands a chance to stop quivering.

Slowly the adrenalin stopped flowing and John became once more the cool research scientist, about to perform just another experiment in his long career. He opened two sterile towel packs and laid one on top of the other on the work table beside the microscope. With sterile lifting forceps he extracted the Fallopian tube and ovary from the beaker of Ringer's solution and placed it on the towels. Opening another sterile pack, he extracted a pair of tiny dissecting scissors, a small Adson's tissue forceps and a small but powerful hand lens, and laid them on the towels alongside the tube.

He opened the sterilizer, and with an abestos glove pulled out the perforated metal tray and laid it on the towels beside the other instruments. Concentrating for a moment, he considered calling Sylvia to help him for a few minutes, but thought better of it, and put on sterile gloves.

With great care, mindful of the fact that the object he was searching for was about 100 microns (or 1/250th of an inch) in diameter, about the size of a grain of sand and therefore visible to the naked eye, he slit the Fallopian tube from end to end. With the hand lens held close to the opened tube, he scanned slowly from the fimbriated end of the tube to the narrow proximal end. Once he paused, went on, then returned to the same spot. With the lens held in his left hand, he reached for a hair loop and gently laid it alongside the object of his search—the ovum shed only hours before by Penelope's right ovary.

The ovum adhered quickly and solidly to the hair loop. John transferred the capillary tube to his left hand, and reached out blindly for the tiny agar dish. He positioned the dish on the sterile towel, placed a drop of sterile warm Ringer's latate solution on the agar, and transferred the ovum to it. Turning slightly sideways, he slid the agar dish under the lowpower objective of the microscope.

Switching on the arc light, he settled himself behind the binocular eyepieces. With the first, low magnification of 5X in the eyepiece of 10X in the objective (a total of 50 power), the ovum could be brought directly into the center of his field of vision with only minimal manipulation. Gradually he increased the power to 200X in the objective and zoomed the eyepiece from 5X to 10X for a total magnification of 2000 power.

As he did so, he recognized at a glance that he did not have a moment to lose.

The mature human egg is about 100 microns in diameter, that is, one-tenth of a millimeter or 1/250th of an inch. In diameter it is the largest cell in the body, although some others are much longer, particularly those spinal column nerve cells whose axones and dendrites extend from the spine to the tips of the toes and fingers. The ovum therefore appears huge compared to the spermatozoon which has a head only about ten microns in length and a tail sixty microns long. In volume, the sperm is only about 1/50,000 that of the egg, but there are about 300,000,000 in each ejaculate.

Normally the sperm takes only a few hours to swim from the vagina through the uterus, and out into the Fallopian tube. There they encounter the egg which has been ejected by the ovary into the end of the Fallopian tube and carried down the tube by a current created by the sweeping action of millions of tiny cilia and by the muscular constractions of the tube itself. If fertilization takes place, usually within a day, the new cell passes slowly through the tube in about four days, and developes as it goes. By the time it reaches the uterus it is ready for implantation in the wall of the uterus.

As John fine-adjusted his microscope, he saw the egg was ringed by tiny sperm trying to penetrate the cell membrane. A few had already made their way into the *zona pellucida*, a clear translucent zone twenty microns thick which surrounds the real cell membrane and probably is a protective shield for it. None had penetrated the cell itself.

He settled down to wait. Meanwhile, there were things he needed to do. Periodically glancing into the microscope, he drew his micro-manipulation instruments close to the binocular microscope. From his left he pulled in the heavy instrument which bore a microscopic probe on the end of a flexible shaft. The probe itself had been sterilized and was protected by an easily removed cover. From his right he pulled down an equally heavy instrument which contained his dissecting tool, a spatula-shaped micro-scalpel, also on the end of a flexible shaft which could be manipulated by remote-control knobs for fine movements.

The two micro-tools were mounted on arcs which moved in such large circles that they completely eliminated the faint tremor which is present in even the steadiest operator's hands. On each flexible shaft were mounted two large, serrated knobs at right angles to each other, and with these the micro-tools were moved a micron at a time. Since they could move only in two dimensions, the stage under the microscope was also especially constructed so that it could be moved upward and downward a micron at a time with a fine-adjustment knob.

Then, with a patience matched only by nature photographers and deer-hunters, Reynolds waited.

Chapter 14

Alert, tense, yet strangely filled with an inner peace that only absolute committment can bring, John Reynolds awaited the onset of a process first described by Oscar Hertwig in 1875 in the reproductive cells of the sea urchin, a marine animal whose eggs and sperm normally unite outside the body. John knew what to expect for he had thoroughly studied this monumental work and the many, many other corroborative experiments since then.

But when he saw it happening, he was at first almost overwhelmed with awe.

One of the spermatozoa had managed to wriggle through the cell membrane and was lying inside it. It lay there for a moment, as if tired from its exertions, and perhaps it was. At the same time, and without visible change in the cell membrane, the other spermatozoa outside the cell gradually fell away, one by one, and none tried further to penetrate the cell. A chemical barrier, as yet unexplained by an biologist, had been erected instantly, and the remaining sperm were rendered impotent.

The minutes ticked by and still the sperm in the cell remained immobile. Slowly then, nearly imperceptibly, tiny lines began to radiate out from it, spreading out into the surrounding egg cytoplasm until the sperm (now called the male pronucleus) appeared as the center of the multipointed star.

Like Columbus on an uncharted sea, or Neil Armstrong on an untested moon surface, or Christian Barnard clamping and removing the first human heart, John Reynolds knew he was entering an undefined and unexplored area of human endeavor. He knew that once the male and female pronucleus had fused, he had less than an hour in which to complete his micro-surgery.

Should he begin the operation now, while the nuclei lay far apart? Would they go ahead an fuse, after having been tampered with? Or would they merely go about their business of procreation? He didn't know. And there was no way for him to know. This was one of the problems which he had turned over in his mind countless times in the past years, and he had never been able to make the decision.

As in every other decision which one makes as he goes through life, it must be made at the time the alternatives present themselves. If, afterwards, an unfavorable result occurs, then he may say he should have done it a different way. Then he may use what doctors only half-jokingly call the retrospectorscope, but at the time of decision he can not avail himself of the crystal ball. Nor can he legitimately use the often-wrong hunch, or the much maligned, oft-touted, extra-sensory perception.

He sat and waited. He thought of the girl on the table downstairs and the chimp roaming the house. The cells under the microscope did not in any way resemble those two huge creatures, yet they were the same. One sprang from the other, created by it, unknowingly carrying its own immortality in its miniscule molecules. Each pronucleus with its 23 chromosomes and uncounted genes represented not only the individual which it had now left behind, but the new individual which it would soon create. As surely as the fledgling leaves the nest, as finally as the child leaves the home, the sperm and egg had abandoned their milieu and struck out into an unknown which they could not envision or comprehend.

While he waited, John studied the chromosomal structure of each pronucleus. He wished for the tremendous magnification the scanning electron miscroscope gave, but could not be used because no cell could live in the vacuum necesary for the proper operation of the electron 'scope. Besides, the maximum potential of the electron microscope (about 1,000,000 power) was possible only by means of photomicrographs, and no suitable technique had yet been devised to do microsurgery under such conditions. But John had studied the differences between the human and chimp chromosomal patterns, using the electron scanner at the university, and he knew what he had to do.

The chimp cell, before it halves itself to form sperm or egg, has 48 chromosomes, the human 46, except in genetic diseases such as "Mongolism," where there are 47. And John knew that the chance of recombination of the chromosomes from Penelope's egg and Hermes' sperm was extremely unlikely unless he could successfully correct the eight inversions and two translocations of genes on the involved chromosomes.

He thought he knew how to do it. He had studied the work of Chang, Boyer and Helling who had developed an enzyme which would literally cut through the genes as cleanly as a surgical knife. This was an important discovery, because some diseases are caused by the presence or absence of just one gene. The addition or deletion of that one gene could change the course of the individual's life.

Unfortunately, John could not simply add the enzyme and the proper genes to the cells he now studied under his microscope. He had to be much more specific.

He did not want whole-scale breakdown of the chromosomes. Instead, he merely wanted to selectively detach eight genes, one by one, turn them around, and reimplant them. In two places on other chromosomes, he had to "cut out" translocated genes, split two different chromosomes in the proper places, and insert the translocated genes into their new positions.

And he had fifty minutes or less in which to work. About five minutes for each operation.

John tensed as he saw the male pronucleus start moving toward the female, carrying its aster with it. Extremely slowly, nearly imperceptibly, it moved. Then it seemed there was a magnetic attraction developing, for the female pronucleus also started to move toward the male, though more slowly. As John watched with almost uncontrollable anticipation, the two nuclei nestled side by side and the astral radiations which had originally surrounded only the male pronucleus now spread out and extended through the entire cell. Scientists call this stage the monaster—or "one aster" stage.

With maddening slowness, the cell membranes between the two pronuclei broke down and the nuclei began to fuse into one cell. The chromosomes began to arrange themselves around the middle—or equator—of a spindle-shaped configuration. It's now or never, John mumbled to himself. If they were every to be altered, and rendered capable of recombination, it would be now.

He dropped the microscope stage down, well away from the objective. Taking a sterile pipette, he inserted it into a sterile bottle of enzyme, aspirated a tiny drop, and placed it directly on top of the barely visible cell in the agar plate. Quickly he raised the stage, and anxiously focused on the cell. Only a slight progression had occurred. Now, an unbearable tension rose in John's mind and body. He was nearly immobilized by it, and took a deep breath to relax.

Blindly he reached for the manipulator knobs to his left and maneuvered the probe slowly and painstakingly up against the first chromosome he needed to alter. With the manipulator knobs on his right he maneuvered the spatula-shaped "knife" over the exact spot on the chromosome from which he intended to cut the inverted gene. Releasing the knife controls, he grasped the control of the microscope stage and slowly, ever so slowly, lifted the cell toward the knife blade. A tiny, invisible bit of enzyme had clung to the blade, and when it touched the chromosomegene attachment, it caused an immediate cleavage of the gene from the chromosome.

John almost cried out with joy, but restrained himself because he knew he had a long, long way to go. He dropped the microscope stage two microns away from the enzyme-coated blade as quickly as he dared, then with infinite patience used the probe controlled by his left hand to turn the gene around and reimplant it on the chromosome. It adhered in perfect position as if it had always been there.

For a few seconds, John watched with wonderment and awe, realizing that an almost religious ferment had engulfed him. Without taking his eyes from the binoculars, he wiped his perspiring hands on his thighs. He did not have to check his watch. He knew he had taken more than the allotted five minutes to perform the first operation. But he would take less time with the others. He knew now he could do it.

And he did do it. In less than forty minutes he operated on the ten chromosomes, inverting eight of them and relocating the other two. Meanwhile, division of the chromosomes into two distinct clusters was occurring, half of them going to one pole and half to the other, reforming there two separate nuclei.

His work was done. He felt exhausion creeping through his body and his eyes ached from the hour long vigil at the binoculars. He wanted to see the first cell division, and knew this would occur within minutes, but he raised his eyes from the miscroscope, slumped back on his chair, and rested.

When he looked through the binoculars again, perhaps five minutes later, two asters had formed at either end of the reformed nucleus, now containing the paried 46 chromosomes and the one extra chromosome from Hermes' spermatozoon. Almost absently he wondered what genes that extra chromosome carried, and if it would affect the growth and development of the hominid he had just created.

Now an indentation of the cytoplasm between the two asters appeared, and formed a cleavage furrow which continually deepened until the entire cell separated into two identical halves, each a perfect replication of the original cell and each nucleus containing identical chromosomes and genes.

He had been upstairs for two hours. Gravely he thought of the moment when he had wondered if he could tell Sylvia what he planned to do, and then as quickly had wondered if he could do it without her. She was still down in the basement, keeping silent watch over the sleeping Penelope. She had missed the culmination of all their work, their heartaches, their loneliness, yes, and the breaking of the rules of men and God. But he would tell her about it in great detail, and if there was ever another time . . .

God, he broke off, another time?

He moved wearily to the wall switch and turned on the lights. With great care he removed the agar dish from the microscope stage and placed it carefully on the sterile towel. With the hair-loop he meticulously transferred the blastomere from the agar onto the slit Fallopian tube and carried it gently to the basement.

He answered Sylvia's questioning stare with a curt nod, almost as if he had just checked the parking meter and found there was still time left. He laid the sterile towel containing the tube and blastomere on the back table, scrubbed his hands and put on a sterile gown and gloves. With a heavy scissors from the instrument table he cut out the stitches holding Penelope's surgical wound together. Gently he separated the edges, watching the girl for signs of pain. She was still highly narcotized and still had some circulating ether, although most of it would have been detoxified and eliminated by the lungs.

Carefully he reached into the left side of the abdomen, lifted up the end of the left Fallopian tube and grasped it with a long forceps. Sylvia slid her hand under the towel on the back table and presented the split tube and its microscopic burden to John, and he lifted it out without touching the towel. He laid the tube on the instrument table, took a hairloop from the sterile back table, and picked up the blastomere. Holding the fimbriated end fo the tube gently with forceps he tucked the blastomere well down into it.

Now he carefully sewed up the abdominal incision in anatomical layers—peritoneum, muscles, subcutaneous fat, and skin. the girl stirred restlessly a few times, but did not awaken. Sylvia sat poised with the ether can and mask, but did not need to use it.

John lifted the girl up in his arms and carried her back into the room in which she would live for only another nine months. He placed her in her favorite position against the far wall.

"She's breathing alright, I think," John said, "but I'll stay with her for a while just to be sure."

"I'll stay with you."

"No need."

"I want to. You can tell me what you did."

So they closed the door, and with Sylvia perched on the high stool as she had for about 1300 hours before,

John told her. He narrated the story in a flat monotone voice devoid of emotion, but Sylvia could detect the underlying surge of nerves stretched taut with wonderment, awe, almost with bewilderment. Long before he had finished, she had lost the thread of his description, but she didn't mind, because she sensed what this coup had done for him. No matter what happened now, even total failure from this point on, she knew that something extraordinary had happened to her husband. She knew that whether or not a new form of life had been created, John Reynolds had been re-created in a different image, had undergone the transformation which always befalls the artist when he has accomplished something of earth-shaking importance.

When he had finished, he turned from the window and slowly climbed the stairs. Sylvia wept.

Chapter 15

A car door slammed in the driveway and when Sylvia looked out the kitchen window she could see the jauntiness of John's gait, could see the youthfulness with which he pulled open the garage doors and drove inside. The back door opened, closed with a bang and John stood before her, eyes sparkling even more than when they had first met almost twenty years before. Then, almost as if he were embarrassed by his enthusiasm, he took her gently by the shoulders and kissed her on the cheek.

"Hello, hon, anything new downstairs?" he asked.

"No, not really." She reached up behind his head with both of her hands and pulled his lips down to hers. She let him go and said, "Thanks for the roses. That was awfully sweet of you."

He mumbled a disclaimer and disentangled himself from her arms. "I've forgotten more than my share of your birthdays in the last fifteen years! What's for supper?"

"Wildebeeste stew!"

"Again?"

She laughed and returned to the stove as he ambled into the living room while filling a pipe. She could hear him kicking off his shoes, then riffling through the papers to the editorial page. From there he would go to the sports, and finally the comics. He rarely read the front page. "Just the same old things happening to different people," he had explained many times.

He called to her from the living room, "Where's Hermes?"

"With Penny," she answered and waited for his explosion. For several seconds he was quiet, then she could hear him padding across the carpet on stockinged feet, and knew he was standing behind her in the doorway.

"She's too far along to be playing with that chimp, Sylvia," he said in a level monotone. Without turning around she could feel the fire in his eyes burning the back of her head.

"She's all right. She can take care of herself."

"Sylvia, I've waited too long . . ."

"*We*'ve waited too long . . ."

"All right, we've waited too long, and worked too hard, to risk that fool chimp kicking her in the stomach and ruining the work of a lifetime."

She turned to face him, hands folded at her waist.

"John, have you seen them together lately? He's so gentle with her. It's almost uncanny, almost as if he *knows*."

The cold anger slowly subsided from his eyes as he acquiesced to his wife's judgment.

"And she is *so* lonely," she added.

His eyes flashed again. "That was, is, and always will be, part of the game."

"I'll go get him," she said and started for the door to the basement.

"No, you might as well leave him till after supper. But this has got to be the last time."

"All right, John."

After supper, while he worked at his desk recording in ever more detail the first fifteen years of his Experiment, Sylvia unlocked the basement door with a key she now carried with her at all times. With her hand on the railing, she slowly descended the staris which by now, after thousands of trips, had become like a well-beaten trail through the jungle. Her hand knew every irregularity on the rail, her feet every worn riser. She no longer thought of *anything* when she went down, but pulled the curtains across the stage which had once felt the tread of her bare feet on the way to murder.

In the ten years that had gone by since that day, Sylvia had effectively blocked out the dreadful memory. Her mind, like that of all humans, had several rooms. Into one room, the living room, she invited anyone who might want to come in: the clerks in the shops, the gas station attendant, the paper boy. Into another room, the bedroom, she invited just John, whenever he wanted to come, for as long as he wanted to stay.

Into a third room she herself went, and she alone. It was in this room she steadied her mind, renewed her pledge to John's work, rationalized that the ends justified the means. In this private room she argued against the observation of C.S. Lewis: "obedience and rule are more like a dance than a drill, specially between man and woman where the roles are always changing." She knew her role was unchanging, unchangeable.

But there was a fourth room, and it was of this room that she was most afraid. Into the fourth room no one went, even Sylvia herself. From this room no one, nothing, ever came out, not even Sylvia's innermost being and buried thoughts. For if the room were ever opened, the ravages on her mind would have been more horrendous than the fate which overtook the world when Pandora took the lid off her jar of evils. And Pandora, even though created by the patron saint of Magicians, Hermes the Thief, and by the fire-god Hephaestus, and by the love-goddess Aphrodite, had been unable to quell the stench of diabolism nor staunch

107

the flow of malevolence.

And so Sylvia maintained a stern vigilance on this fourth room, and her unconscious mind hid the key.

She glanced briefly into the lighted basement room and then turned down the lights. Penny no longer reacted with predictable Pavlovian reflexes when darkness encompassed her home. She had noted rather early that Hermes appeared and disappeared when the lights were out, and she now sat patiently and curiously to see if she could solve the riddle. Hermes munched on a handful of lettuce leaves, glancing now and then toward the one-way-glass door at the end of the room. He also seemed aware that dimming of the lights usually meant that the door would open and he could escape to the kitchen or his trailer house in the yard.

Penny was gross. With her legs spread out in front of her, her belly almost rested on the floor. Dozens of garish purple streaks several inches in length marred the alabaster whiteness of her abdomen and flanks. Because of the extreme weakness of her abdominal muscles, she had to cup her hands under her abdomen and lift it up in order to move about.

She had grown fat, ugly, lethargic, a pitiful white grub of a girl. Sylvia, watching through the window, scarcely ever thought now of the pretty little toddler she had once been, nor even of the slimmer, though still animal-like, young teenager who had fallen asleep eight months before and had awakened unknowingly pregnant.

The glorious vessel holding John's Grand Experiment was hideously repulsive, an amorphous, repellent grub. Neither John nor Sylvia persisted in thinking of her in any human terms. John's earlier concern for her welfare was really for the unborn child. She was the nutrient broth, the agar dish, the egg yolk, on which the embryo grew. When she had fulfilled her functions, she would be thrown away. Somehow.

In the darkened room, her attention span had spun out, and she lay on her side, back to Sylvia, apparently sleeping. Sylvia watched for several minutes, then went to the long door and without looking more closely at Penny, opened it. Hermes dropped his handful of greens, scrambled noisily toward the wide open door, and Penny opened both eyes in startled amazement. With an agility which Sylvia could hardly believe, she rolled onto her hands and knees, spun around, and crawled frantically after Hermes. Her long hair trailed on the ground, her head bobbed up and down like a sea lion chasing a sea cow, and her eyes shone with a curious mixture of fear and anticipation. The corridor outside her room was lighted by two small unshielded bulbs, enough for Penny to see the enormous form of Sylvia standing there with her hands outstretched in mute denial.

Hermes scampered happily up the stairs and out of sight, leaving Sylvia and the little girl alone. In the few seconds since Penny had opened her eyes to witness for the first time another human being, Sylvia's mind raced with a multitude of conflicting thoughts. Should she let the girl out, comfort her, then push her back in the room? Should she slam the door quickly before Hermes got out, or should she let him out and then shut the door? Should she merely order the girl back into the room, and then shut the door? Should she say *anything* at all? Surely Penny would recognize her voice, after almost sixteen years. She would not confuse it with John's, since his was the only other voice she had ever heard. Or did it make any difference what she did?

"Penny!" she said with all the authority she could muster.

Penny stopped, panting furiously, and pushed back on her haunches, one hand balancing her like a football lineman ready to charge. Her eyes stared malevolently at the giant towering over her. Her jaws were clamped shut, a trickle of saliva coursing down one corner of her drooping lower lip. Her nostrils dilated. But she did not move forward.

Slowly Sylvia pushed the door shut and leaned against it, her whole body trembling with the monstrousness of the image of the white blob now settling slowly to the floor. She reached jerkily for the rheostat on the wall and slowly turned up the lights in Penny's prison.

Fearfully she climbed the stairs, knowing she would have to tell John. She closed the door at the top, locked it carefully, and slipped the key in the pocket of her dress. She crossed the kitchen, ran water in the sink until it was icecold, and washed her face and neck with a corner of the handtowel. Carefully she dried herself, took a deep breath to control the frantic beating of her heart, and went into the living room.

She stood there for several moments before John realized she was waiting for him to look up. When he did, he pushed his half-glasses onto the tip of his nose, took in her agitated appearance in one glance, and laid his paper down on his lap.

"She saw me," Sylvia whispered.

Disbelief hooded his black eyes. "She *saw* you?"

Sylvia nodded. "I thought she was asleep. I had turned down the lights, then waited like you've told me, until I was sure she was asleep."

"And you opened the door, and she *wasn't* asleep, and she *saw* you?"

She nodded again.

John folded the newspaper and laid it on the floor beside him. For a few minutes he sat immobile, arms stiff and hands on his knees. Once a thought came to him and he turned to speak, then changed his mind and pulled himself to his feet. He seemed bewildered, yet surprisingly unperturbed. Sylvia had expected rage, fury, even hysteria, such as he had evinced when the Milan scientists had upstaged him.

Then he turned suddenly, took the key from her, and clumped down the stairs.

When he returned, Sylvia still stood in the doorway, head bowed in abject despair. Instinctively she put out her hand to take the key from him, and watched him cross the room to his chair and sit down.

"She's quiet, Sylvia."

No reprimand, no torrent of insults, no strident accusations of stupidity. It would have been better if he had struck her, for then her guilt would have been punished and she could have sought his forgiveness. This way she was like a naughty child not knowing when or if she were to be spanked.

"Don't worry, Sylvia, she won't figure out what happened. God knows how many other hallucinations and delusions she's lived through these past years. This will just add an other to her collection."

A low moan of contrition and understanding escaped Sylvia's throat as she sank down to the carpet and leaned against the wall.

"It does sort of bring things to a head, though, Sylvia. We've got to come to grips with the next steps. We haven't talked much about what will happen to her afterwards. We've got to."

For the third time in as many minutes, Sylvia nodded her head and waited.

"Was she afraid of you?" John asked.

"Horribly."

"Do you think you could overcome her fears?"

"Overcome her . . . you mean?"

"I mean, go into that room and talk with her."

"Now?"

"No, not now. Tomorrow."

111

"Why, John?"

"She's got to get used to people someday. I thought we'd probably wait until after the baby's born, but perhaps the time is now."

"I see."

He was carefully stoking the churchwarden, tamping it ritually to the proper compactness with his thumb. In the light of the kitchen match his eyes glowed like a misbegotten viper's. Smoke billowed around his head and the bowl of the pipe glowed dull red.

"Do you, Sylvia?" he asked.

She scrambled to her feet and stroke around the room, shaking her head like a dog emerging from a lake.

"No, I *don't* see, John! I don't see why I have to do this. Why can't we just put her in an institution, tell them she's a niece or something who will need perpetual care? Tell them anything, just to get rid of her." Her voice was rising dangerously to the brink of hysteria and she was closer to losing control than she had ever been.

Like the coarse rasp of a pine-auger, his voice cut through her core of madness.

"Sylvia, sit down!"

Once more she shook her head, a lock of white hair falling over her eyes. She pushed it back with one shaking hand, and sat down opposite him.

"All right, John," she said in a level monotone, "tell me once more what to do."

Chapter 16

Sylvia stood quietly on the back porch in the early morning sunshine. June, she mused, and what is so rare as a day in June. Then, if ever, come perfect days, said Shakespeare. He didn't know about today. He didn't know about little girls kept locked in basement rooms for fifteen years, nor of misogyny perpetrated by two scientists in the name of Truth. He might have laughed, though, as the techniques used, for he himself frequently used plot and counterplot, fair means and foul, to bring about his heroes' and heroines' desired goals.

Sylvia glanced at the eastern sky as the sun was suddenly obscured. A light southeast wind blew warmly over her and the ice clouds ranging at 30,000 feet presaged a mid-afternoon storm. She shivered as her bare feet felt the dew-wet grass in the back yard. The sun appeared again and a spider-web shimmering with a million tiny drops shattered as she opened the gate to Hermes' yard.

He heard the gate-latch clang open and bounded out of his house with the wide-awake alacrity of animals and children. His teeth shone in a cavernous grin as he grasped Sylvia's hand and allowed himself to be led back into the kitchen. Despite her preoccupation with her day's assignment, she smiled wanly as Hermes made the sign for banana and sat dutifully at the kitchen table. Whatever else they had done, the Reynolds had trained him well.

She watched him carefully peel the upper half of the banana and eat it with noisy gusto. She was still not sure it was a good idea to take him in with her to see Penny. That had been John's idea. Suppose he sensed the fear which Sylvia assumed would emanate from Penny, and suppose he tried to defend the girl against the intruder, even if that intruder were his own "mother." She was no match for an almost full-grown chimpanzee. He could tear her to ribbons with those meat-eating canines before she could get out or before John could get in. She had thought it too much of a risk, but John had prevailed as usual. He thought he had good reasons why Hermes would be a good buffer in the tight situation they anticipated.

"Get John," she signalled in Ameslan, and delightedly the ape slid from the stool and scrambled sideways out the door. Sylvia turned and scanned the skies outside, noting that the aspens across the meadow south of the house were trembling in the freshening breeze. The sky was now overcast with translucent clouds, and the sun, when it could be seen at all, shone as though through a frosted glass. Premonition after premonition forced themselves one by one through her consciousness. The acrid looker-room smell of sweat filled the air.

Together, hand in hand, the three conspirators (one unwitting, to be sure) descended the stairs to the basement room.

"John, I've never been so afraid," Sylvia said, her tremulous voice punctuated by her rapid breathing.

"Nonsense. Nothing to be afraid of."

Penelope was still asleep.

"Shouldn't we wake her first, John?"

"Yes, I think so," John answered and slowly turned up the rheostat about halfway.

Penny opened her eyes slowly, lifted her head and looked around. She moaned softly, grasped her pendulous belly with both hands and rolled onto her other side.

John turned the lights all the way up, and with that Penny sat up and peered glumly about.

"All right, Sylvia," John said softly.

Sylvia took Hermes' hand, opened the door, pushed him inside, and took a step inside herself. John closed it quickly behind her, and remained there with his hand on the knob.

"Stay, Hermes," Sylvia commanded quietly but with vigor. "Stay." She held him firmly by the hand.

We don't have to do this, Sylvia thought violently, we don't *have* to. In a month she'd have been gone, unaware of the rest of the world, unaware of all that she'd missed in life. She'd be *gone*. She'd be dead . . .

The pupils of Sylvia's eyes contracted to pinpoints as she realized the awful truth. It had all been charades, all a great to-do signifying nothing; all their talk the night before about re-educating Penelope to society, about psychiatrists and social workers and halfway houses and a simple job in a factory: all had been one great big *lie*.

John had known it last night. He knew it now, standing outside the door pretending to be waiting for her to begin the process of reversing the irrevocable past. He might even be laughing as he watched her. She turned to look at the door, and saw only the flat, grey-brown glass mirroring an old woman holding the hand of an ape.

She let Hermes go and sank to the floor beside the glass door. She mustn't give way now, mustn't let the dull clouding of her mind pull her all the way into oblivion. Not now. She closed her eyes and saw again the quaking aspens and the dew-covered cobweb and the hazy yellow sun. She smelled the stink of phenol and the stale odor of urine, the reek of an unwashed human body.

She opened her eyes. Penny sat Buddha-like a few feet away, mouth hanging open, eyes peering intently from under fat-heavy lids and colorless eyebrows. There was almost pure curiosity, tinged faintly with just the hint of fear, in those pale blue eyes. She had placed her hands flat on the floor, tilting her body slightly forward, and

115

her long blonde hair streamed around her face onto the floor beside her hands.

Hermes, for once, stood awed. It was as if he at least partly understood the significance of the drama being played out before his eyes. He looked first at Penny, then at Sylvia, then back at Penny. Tentatively he touched Penny on the head, a long finger stroking slowly through the tangled matting on her scalp. She reached up, and irritatedly pulled the finger out of her hair.

"Hello, Penny," Sylvia said. What do you say to a sixteen-year old girl you've never met before? Sylvia thought. And it did seem as if they were complete strangers. The sixteen years were as nothing. There was absolutely no common ground upon which to build. Oh, there *were* things to talk about. How do you like your home, Penny? Is the food good? Do you like sweeping out your room every day, Penny? Did you know it's going to rain later today? Are you afraid of thunder-storms, or hail, or do you like to stand with your face to the skies and let the rain stream down your cheeks and neck? Or would you rather play in the snow and stick pieces of coal in a snowman's belly and sing "Winter Wonderland" to your boyfriend? Perhaps you'd prefer to sit in the grass on the edge of a stream and throw pebbles into the water and watch the ripplies drifting down over that big fat trout lying under the submerged log?

"Hello," said the girl, "are you Sylvia?" The fear was gone now.

No, thought Sylvia, I'm not Sylvia. Not the Sylvia you know. Not the Sylvia who handled you with arm-length gauntlets when you were a baby and longed to cradle you in her arms. I'm another Sylvia. I'm the Sylvia who ought not to be here at all, ought not to be staring at Penelope with startled recognition of latent humanness emanating from the over-fattened slug of a laboratory specimen germinating the fruits of sixteen

116

years of controlled isolation taking the son of a forest ape for husband groaning with pain at every movement stretching the skin of her belly till it split in vivid streaks urinating in the concrete waterfall spilling from the fountain . . .

Oh, God, no, I'm not Sylvia. She opened her mouth to scream and felt rather than heard the door open behind her and then did not feel the rough hands dragging her backwards through the door and did not hear the door slam and the lock click not the staccato beat of curses falling on her head like pellets of lead in the duckmarsh.

Consciousness returned slowly and just before it did she saw again those pale blue eyes staring into her and then she *did* scream. A long, piercing, reverberating, agonizing scream which carried into all parts of the house except that one place where it had originated.

So Penny did not hear it. Nor would she have known what it meant. She could not know that one tiny little crack had formed in the lid on Pandora's jar.

Sylvia's scream woke her and she had stopped screaming long before John Reynolds arrived and threw open her door ready to shout "Shut up" or some other endearing epithet.

She lay on her back in bed, fully dressed, the afternoon sunshine streaming in through the window. The image of Penny's face just a few inches from hers faded slowly, replaced by a blurred masculine face with drooping mustaches and hooded black eyes. She closed her lids tightly and pressed her fingers into the eyeballs until they ached. A tear squeezed out from each corner, then became a flood as her sobs shook the bed as she moaned, "Oh, John, I'm *so* sorry, so *sorry*. I tried, I really tried, but it wasn't there. The strength I mean. I wasn't strong enough."

His voice, when he answered, was neither condemning nor conciliatory. Just hard. Resigned, in the way he affected when he knew he had been deceived. "I thought there was more to you than that, Sylvia," he said in a flat monotone. "You really blew it, you know."

She rolled over on her side to avoid the black eyes piercing her defenses. "It was when she said, 'Are you Sylvia?' wondering, hoping, almost as if she had been waiting for me to come, like Cinderella waiting for her fairy godmother."

She sat up on her bed, groping for her shoes, and, not finding them, shuffled to the window and looked out. "It's not going to rain, after all, is it, John?"

Without turning to look at her, John answered, "It has already. Hours ago. You've been sleeping all day." His tone was not unkind.

"Yes, I see that now. There are puddles in the drive." She knelt before the open window and put her nose against the screen and rubbed it up and down like a child. "I'd like to go for a walk, John. Barefoot. And wade through the puddles. Oh, can I, John?"

John's eyelids lifted slightly and a brief flicker of fear scintillated in his pupils and was gone. He had spent the day in his study, ruminating on the early morning debacle, wondering just how Sylvia would be when she awoke. Now he knew. And he knew it was no time to be too soft, for if he showed weakness now, she would sense it with that awful sixth sense that she had in more measure than most women.

"No, Sylvia, not now. It's time for you to get supper going."

She stood up slowly, turned around and faced him, her nose black from the screen, her eyes round and fixed, her mouth slack and trembling slightly.

"Yes, John, it's time to get supper."

118

Chapter 17

In the hush of the coal-bin operating room, Penny's stertorous breathing was harsh and strident. Even the drip-drip-drip of the ether on the gauze mask could be heard between her respirations. There was an overwhelming sense of *deja vu* in Sylvia's mind as she hunched over the blonde head. In one hand she again held the half-pint of ether, in the other the ether mask on Penelope's small jaws. The fumes were visible in the still air, rising from the mask like heat waves over a concrete road.

Sylvia had not yet quite recovered from the episode in Penny's room. To all outward appearances, she was thinking normally, but from time to time she would sit down, interrupting whatever she had been doing, and appear to be musing, mulling over something very important. If John saw her do this, he spoke sharply to her, and usually she would start, then get up and return to her activities. Sometimes he would have to speak several times, or even shake her by the shoulders, before she would rouse from the fugue-like trance.

Now as she sat at the head of the operating table, John glanced at her from time to time to make sure she was fully awake and alert.

"All right at your end, Sylvia?" he asked her now.

"Yes, I'm o.k., and she's going down easily. When are you going to begin?"

"She still responds when I pinch her with the Kelley. I don't want her jumping off the table."

"The baby is getting a lot of ether, John."

"I know. I can handle it. I expect him to be sleepy."

They had talked for days about the details of the Cesarean section. John had been adamant that Penny was not to be allowed to go into labor.

"Oh, no," he had said. "That would really be taking a chance we can't afford. I want that baby's head round, not squashed like a watermelon, not pounding on the perineum for six to eight to ten hours trying to get out. I'm taking no chances on a brain hemorrhage, or a cerebral palsy, or any other labor-connected injury. I'm not taking any chances of a breech, or a disproportion between his head and Penelope's pelvis. Huh-uh."

So they discussed the anesthesia, the choice of instruments, the timing of the operation relative to Penny's stage of gestation, the suture materials, and a hundred and one other details.

Rather conspicuous by its absence was any further discussion concerning Penny's future after the operation was over.

John stood quietly beside the mound of white flesh tinted orange-red by the antiseptic paint. He held a straight Kelly hemostat in his right hand, and periodically he gently pinched the skin of Penny's abdomen. He was fully dressed in operating gown, hat, mask, and rubber gloves. A few grey hairs curled from his sideburns around the mask ties, and the long grey hair above his ears swept back below the cap to a ducktail on the back of his head.

His eyes were bright, glinting brilliantly in the cold white light from the operating lamp above his head. He looked happy. He also looked quite distinguished, the epitome of the successful surgeon, confidently awaiting the proper moment to begin his case.

He had ever right to be confident. He knew exactly what he had to do. The technical details of the surgery were so clear in his mind that he didn't even need to refresh his memory with surgical or obstetrical texts. His only concern was to resuscitate the baby if it didn't breath well at first and he wasn't really worried about that.

As he stood waiting, he didn't even worry about the external appearance of the baby. He knew what it would look like. It would look human in all respects. He had seen to that in the laboratory nine months before. Sylvia had voiced doubts, wondering if perhaps the baby would have some external marks of its dual interspecific heritage. John knew it wouldn't.

The name of the baby was preordained, derived by John through a clever play on words. Though not a classical scholar in college, John had nevertheless been exposed to Greek mythology from time to time in the course of his schooling. It had therefore been an easy research when he merely looked up the words *Homo* (man's genus) and *Pan* (chimpanzee's genus) in the library's mythology section. "Homo" was no one. "Pan" was an Arcadian deity who came to be worshipped thoughout the Greek world. His father was Hermes, his mother Penelope. Hermes was the tricky thief who on the day of his birth successfully stole Apollo's herd of cows. He was the magician, the king's herald who carried a magic staff with which to control nature, political power, even lovemaking. Penelope, his wife and Pan's mother, was an Arcadian goddess, and probably a different Penelope than the wife of Odysseus of Homer's *Odyssey*.

Pan, the offspring of this union, was represented in early art as bestial in shape, frequently having the horns, legs and ears of a goat. Later on, the human parts were much more emphasized and the bestial characteristics dwindled to a little pair of horns. He was represented as vigorous and lustful, a giver of fertility. He was concerned with the flocks and herds, not with agriculture, and therefore could make men, like cattle, stampede in "panic" terror. Like the shepherd, he was a piper, and a late legend represented him as the lover of a nymph Syrinx ("Panpipe"), who disappeared into a reed bed where Pan then made the first pipe from reeds. Like a shepherd, he haunted the high hills and could send visions and dreams.

"Pan," the curious mixture of man and beast, with a heritage from both, had been created. Created, not by the waving of a magic ward nor at the whim of an ancient Greek god, but by the delicate maneuvering of a micro-scalpel in the hands of a scientific genius, John Reynolds.

He stood now with more power than Zeus had ever dreamed of in his most halcyon days. He stood with a full-sized scalpel in his gloved hand, drawing a blood-red line on the nine-month-old brown scar coursing down the orange-white flesh. The flesh heaved once and was still, split asunder with the canny skill of a master technician. Down went the knife, up went the blood, down again went the knife and up again went the blood, till the wound ran with in and spilled onto the white sheets.

Blood washed in waves from mangled uterus and torn uterine arteries over the beautiful face of a boy named Pan (or was it the other way around—a creature Pan, named boy?), onto the surgeon's green gown and splashed in giant crimson drops into slippery puddles on the floor.

The reek of the abattoir mingled with the holy smell of ether amid the curses of the genius who had finally reached his level of incompetence. Sylvia, witness to more than her addled mind could any longer take, heard a roaring in her ears as if a godlike wind were roaring through a thousand giant pine trees, sloughing fitfully with a foretaste of death in the room masterminded to produce a new life.

And so Pan was alive.

And Penelope was dead.

Chapter 18

It was not a time for looking back, nor did he want to. Later he couldn't even remember shutting the door, and in fact hadn't. Sylvia, with tears streaming down her face, had come after him into the foyer, had watched him slog through slush and puddled water in the drive, and had slowly pushed the door shut. She stood for a few moments at the window in the old oak door, hands on hips, forehead against the cold glass. She could hear John, a few feet away in the living room, fumbling with matches to light his pipe. There was a scritch of a kitchen match on the under side of the coffee table, and between puffs, "Come away, Sylvia, he'll be back."

The boy, Pan—tall, lean and muscular—slowly sloshed through the melting snow into the cold March wind. He was hatless, and his long blond hair flowed in unruly waves along the side of his head and tapered low on his neck. His strong, handsome face was flushed a dark red, not entirely due to the raw, early spring weather. Periodically his eyebrows drew together in a contemplative frown, and his blue eyes squinted in concentration. There was too much to think about.

Unconsciously he toyed with the zipper of his powder-blue goosedown jacket, then zipped it up and stuffed his hands into the pockets. His tight-fitting blue-jeans, frayed at the bottoms and patched, were inadequate for the season, but he did not notice.

"Son of a bitch," he muttered, and kicked at a chunk of ice which had dropped from the fender of a passing car. Then a black, churlish smile tugged at the corners of his mouth. "No, not son of a bitch, son of a . . ." He couldn't say it. Maybe never could. The sullen look on his father's face and the anxious, reasoning smile on his mother's lips flashed before his eyes, and blotted out all other thoughts.

Slowly, but faster than he ever thought it could happen, he began to understand things he had always wondered about. "I suppose I had to know someday," he thought. "They had to tell me eventually. That was the whole idea, wasn't it?"

It was then that the tears came, and flowed and flowed until there was nothing more to cry about. It was the last time he ever cried.

All his life he had known that somehow he was different. *Really* different. Not just in the way everyone is unique, but qualitatively odd in his reactions to people and events. Even as a small boy he *thought* differently from his playmates.

He remembered now, as he shuffled in the soggy snow, the time when at the age of eight or nine he and three friends decided to climb one of the oak trees in the woods back of the house. The other three had gingerly worked their way from branch to branch, then hung on with both hands about halfway up, shouting to him to come down and quit fooling around. He had scampered to the very top, then had come part way down and started bending branches inwards on themselves to make a little nest. He had curled up in the nest and pretended to be asleep, oblivious to the cries of his friends. He remembered that at the time he thought it odd that his playmates were so frightened, where there was *nothing at all* to be frightened of.

Among other memories which came flooding back to him was the time he was lost, truly lost in the thickets and hardwood stands several miles from home. He had been only five of six then, and yet he had merely sat down on a log and carefully traced his course into the forest in his mind; by recreating his journey into the woods, he was able to slowly work his way out. And the amazing thing was that his mother had somehow managed to meet him halfway home.

When he asked how she knew, she simply shrugged and said, "Well, you're Pan, aren't you?" Finally one day when he was old enough, he looked up "Pan" in the set of children's encyclopedias. And then he began to understand.

Pan was the Greek god of the flocks and heards, and he carried a reed pipe which he played hauntingly to while away the days, and he could send dreams and visions to those he liked. His father was Hermes and his mother was Penelope. Pan was also the name given by some waggish, yet learned, taxonomist to the chimpanzee, but this meant nothing to the young boy at that time.

Now it began to make sense. And he understood. And at the same time that none of it made sense and he never could understand.

Never.

Now, at seventeen, he was lost again. Not in a forest which he could unscramble without a compass, but truly lost in a more intricate and infinitely more hostile jungle which had no game trails and tote roads or brushy streams which could, when followed, lead eventually to inhabited civilization.

But through the turbulence of his tortured thoughts he saw one thing very clearly. He could never go back to Standing Oaks, never return to that aging couple he had called Dad and Mom for so many years. He must exorcise them, like ghosts from his past, drain his mind of their presence like the oil from a crankcase, purge their pervading presence from the corridors of his childhood recollections. Poof! They would be gone.

Like that.

But they weren't.

His mother's tear-stained face and her last words to him rang in his memory like an ancient bell. "Pan, go take a walk, and think things out, then come back and we'll talk." He could not even blot out the remembrance of his father, with whom he had never been close, not like most sons with their fathers, nor could he forget those parting words, "Son,"—yes, he had called him "Son," one of the few times he had ever used that term—"go now, but come back to us. Come back, son!"

But he couldn't go back. Not now. Maybe never. And as the enormity of his decision suddenly crashed into awareness of all its implications, he stopped. He stopped, and sat down on the rail fence that lined the drive near its emergence onto the township road. And, if he didn't go back, what then? What then? Hammering, pounding—thundering in his brain went the question *What then?*

He stood up, brushed the snow from his jeans and felt where the cold wetness had seeped through to his skin. He walked out onto the township road and crossed to the other side to walk facing traffic so no one would offer him a ride. He walked steadily for an hour, away from home, away from the fields and forests he knew, away from those strangers with whom he had lived for seventeen years.

He took his wallet from his pocket and counted the few bills there. Less than twenty dollars. Won't buy many bananas, he thought wryly. Nor would it buy a bus ticket to very far. But, at the same time these thoughts went through his mind, he absentmindedly crossed the road and stuck out his thumb at the first car going by. It ignored him, but a few minutes later he was picked up by a delivery truck and carried twenty miles further from home.

Fifty miles more in a salesman's car, then a hundred with a university professor who would surely have known John Reynolds if Pan had identified himself, and finally a long haul of over two hundred miles in a hog truck on the way to market. South, and southeast, and then even more south, and the mountains of Appalachia were black and forbidding ahead of him in the warm wet dawn of the next day.

"Where y'all headed, kid?"

"Home, I think."

The trucker at first shook his head in confusion, then nodded knowingly as if this were what every seventeen-year-old did in the spring. He looked sideways at Pan, wondering if he should turn him in as a runaway, then decided against it. *This* one, he thought, ain't so much running away *from* something as *to* something, even though he mightn't know just what it was yet. Better leave him to work out his own way from whatever is bugging him . . .

Pan stepped down from the old farm truck and watched it lurch away, the squealing and grunting of the hogs obscenely noisy in the empty village street. When it was out of sight down the highway, Pan walked slowly along the sidewalk, wondering why he had gotten out here, still twenty miles from the city where the pigs were to end their days and where he might have found work. It was just six o'clock, too early for the shops to open but an all-night restaurant flashed a big E-A-T sign on the edge of town.

The donut was a quarter and the coffee a dime and he knew he would be hungry again in an hour. He was the only one in the restaurant and the waitress was getting ready for the breakfast crowd, making coffee and straightening the sets of salt and peper shakers along the counter. Without looking at her, Pan played a game he had perfected in hundreds of similar situations. Silently his mind spoke to her, and he could see the moment when his thoughts permeated hers. She hesitated almost imperceptibly, her hand above the counter, then moved again to lift a sugar canister to see if it needed refilling.

She turned to fill it, then looked straight at him. "Looking for work, Mac?"

He pretended mild surprise, then smiled. "Not quite broke yet."

She was fortyish, old enough to be his mother, her short black hair streaked with an occasional crinkly white strand. She wore an apron over a pink wash-and-wear dress, dirty white tennis shoes on bare feet. "Not what I asked," she said and filled a glass coffee pot from the forty-cup maker on the back table.

He stirred his coffee.

"Jed Schroeder's lookin' for someone to help him burn off his dove grass," she said. "Down in McWirter's coulee." She hesitated a moment, then added, "Don't pay much. Maybe ten, fifteen a day, and found. Don't last long either, maybe two weeks."

He paid her 15¢ and left a nickel on the counter. She looked at the nickel, then up at him, and put the nickel in her pocket. "Left at Butch's barber shop, 'bout five miles straight east. Ask anybody out that way."

He smiled, innocent, handsome, ingenuous; and she turned to the window and looked out. "Strangest kid," she thought, "and those eyes, so big and soft—most blue eyes are hard and bright—and looking right into my soul and knowing what's there 'fore even I do. Hope my Jenny don't get a look at him."

He turned left at Butch's and within a few hundred yards was in the country on a hard-packed, narrow, gravel road. A warm flower-scented wind drifted from behind him and he took off his jacket. Robins hopped in the low brush along the road, crows flapped lazily overhead on their way to feed, and fat grey squirrels darted up the backside of the oak trees on the sidehills. Dogwoods flowered in the shadows and the white patches of trillium were everywhere on the ground.

A few open fields and an occasional shack were scattered in the low hills, but the land was almost all untilled, perhaps untillable. The trees were mostly hardwoods, maple and oak and beech, with a few scattered cedars and pines. There were briar thickets and scrub oak jungles, and here and there were impenetrable tangles of vines and alders in the lower land between the hills. Tiny rivulets trickled from hidden springs and Pan stopped once to drink the ice-cold water.

The gravel underfoot gave way to clay and the road became a narrow track with clover and blue-grass growing in the middle. Thick brush lined with roadway and the tree branches met overhead to form a tunnel through the hills. The road began to climb, slowly at first, then a burst of steepcut switchbacks. The sharp slots of big deer criss-crossed the track and once Pan could hear the thudding of running hooves in a red oak stand.

He met only one other person, a young black on an old mule. A wave of the hand, a soft "Howdy," and he was gone and Pan was alone again in the warm sunshine.

A well-worn deer trail crossed the track at right angles and curved up the side of the hill. Pan followed it, and finally came out on top of the ridge where he could see for endless miles into the mountains. He sat on a stump and wondered if maybe he *had* come home.

Home. Home was an illusion, for he was Pan. "Well, you are Pan, aren't you?" his mother whispered in his ear. Yes, I am, he answered, and now I know who Pan is. Pan is the son of a beautiful young blonde girl named Penelope who died when I was born because her surgeon, "Dr." John Reynolds, my "father," didn't know how to stop the bleeding from her uterus. Pan is the son of a chimpanzee named Hermes, who was given to a primate research center seventeen years ago and may still be alive so Pan would be better off not knowing where he was.

John and Sylvia Reynolds had told him all this just yesterday, and they had expected he would accept it without a quiver, then go in to lunch with them and tell them all about how it felt to be part chimpanzee. Strangely, his first thought had not been one of fear and horror, but of his friend Paul Remsen. A few years before, Paul had come to him in tears, begging him to understand and still be his friend. "They just told me, Pan, that my Dad's not really my Dad after all, because Mom was married to someone else when I was born and then they were divorced and Mom married my Dad and he adopted me. Pan," he sobbed, "tell me you're still my friend even if my Dad's not my Dad!"

At the time, Pan had not been able to understand why Paul was worried about their friendship. What possible difference could it make? But in the following weeks he realized gradually that Paul had sustained a vicious blow to his ego. Pan knew, without being able to put it into words, that Paul felt he had been rejected by his "real" father, and was desparately afraid that this rejection would spread to his friends as well.

Now for the first time, Pan was able to fully empathize with the little Paul of so long ago. Was that not why he had hitch-hiked out of the country, why he had been unable to go home, why he had been afraid to go back to school and encounter his friends there? Was that not why he had climbed the deer-trail to this stump, and why he was entertaining the idea of staying there the rest of his life?

For he was indeed Pan. Pan of the flocks and herds.

The vigorous and lustful piper who haunts the high hills and sends visions and dreams to those he loves or hates. And he was *Pan troglodytes,* the cave-dwelling Pan, the tool-using, aggressive, highly-excitable, lovable Pan who is gifted in the arts of bluff and intimidation but who is also a killer.

He leaned forward on the stump, hands almost touching the ground, back arched and muscles stretched to their limit. He looked up into the sky through the newly-budding but still leafless canopy, his eyes cloudy and unseeing. Blood pounded in his brain and in his heart, and his mind shifted backwards in time—ten million years.

He stood in a stooped position, arms almost limp, open hands hanging near his knees and bouncing rhythmically against his kneecaps. His mouth sagged open, lower lip slightly pursed. Then his teeth came together with an audible, sharp click, and this lips thinned and the corners spread widely and were pulled downward in an inverted U, puckering the skin above his chin. His brows knitted together and the subcutaneous neck muscles—the platysma—pulled downwards in long arching strands.

He continued to look upward and then he spotted a long narrow branch just out of reach. He leaped for it, and it broke off with his weight. Now he hooted, and panted, and hooted again, bouncing up and down on the soles of his feet. He grabbed the branch by its butt-end and ran down the deer trail, dragging the branch in the dirt.

He circled the crown of the hill, stamping the earth with his feet and sometimes stopping to beat his hands on the ground. But always he kept running, around and around, then back to the tree where he had gotten the branch. Now scratched and bleeding from the thick tangles of briars and scrub oak through which he had raced, he sat, peering through the trees in all directions, obviously waiting for a response.

There was none. There were no other chimpanzees on the mountain.

He scampered down the tree, picked up the branch again and pounded and slapped his way through the scrub, hooting and panting in loud derision. He was the king of the forest, the dominant male, and everyone must know it by now. He climbed the tree again, higher than before, and dropped the branch to the ground. He watched it clatter through the branches and lie inert upon the smashed-down partridge pea and newly shooted fiddle-heads of bracken and fern.

Slowly, meticulously, instinctively, he reached out and pulled small branches to him and broke them under him to form a sleeping nest. He curled up and fell asleep while the late morning sun dried the blood on his lacerated arms and legs.

Chapter 19

He awoke, stiff and sore, in the middle of the afternoon. He opened his eyes gingerly to the glare of the sunlight streaming through the trees and stretched languidly along the thick oak limb beneath him. Awareness came slowly, then suddenly, and he sat up with a softly muttered, "What the hell . . ."

The broken-off branch lay directly below him where he had dropped it, and when he saw it he remembered with acute clarity all that had happened. Haven't done that in years, he thought, not since Mom told me I had to stop because it wasn't "proper."

But for the first time he recognized it for what it was—the charging display of the adult male chimpanzee. Now he knew why he had wanted to do it as a child, and why none of his friends did it, and why his mother wanted him to stop. They should have told me years ago, he thought. I would have understood better then, could have adapted, could have watched for other signs and symptoms, could perhaps have prevented this flight into nowhere.

Or maybe they could have withheld it all until he was older still. But no, that wouldn't have worked. They were also getting older, and his Dad had waited for all those years for the grand denouement, the moment for which he had sacrificed his life. And for which he had sacrificed other lives. For Pan sensed, yes, even *knew* without being given the details, that Penelope had to come from somewhere, and someone had been hurt deeply. Even more than he was hurt now.

He slid down the tree and sat on the stump where he had rested hours before. His beautiful blue jacket lay torn and rumpled in the dirt. What now? Back to the village? Look for McWhirter's coulee and Jed Schroeder's place?

Slowly he shambled down the deer-trail to the clay track. His usually neat blond hair was matted with blood and sweat, his striped shirt and blue jeans dirty and torn. Knowing he couldn't go back to the village in that condition, he turned left into the hills. At the first stream he stripped off his things, bathed in the cool water, and rinsed out his clothes. As they dried spread out on the bush in the hot afternoon sun, he lay naked against the broad bole of an aspen tree and drowsily brushed buzzing flies from his eyes and nose.

High in the sky a jet silently trailed twin streamers from fuselage burners, and then when it was almost out of sight the rumbling roar of its engines reached the earth. A partridge drummed a half-mile away, throbbing booms that slowly built a cresendo and ended in a straccto whir exactly like an old two-cylinder tractor starting up.

The thought came to him again: I *could* live here. Almost everything in the forest was edible if one knew how to use it. There were small animals which could be trapped, berries to be picked, leaves to be made into tea, tuberous roots to be dug, nuts to be harvested, and an endless variety of plants to be eaten raw or cooked. Quickly he ticked off in his mind the items he would need, and knew he could earn enough in two weeks to buy them. And when he needed something desparately which he couldn't buy, he could always visit the village at night and borrow it from someone who didn't appear to be too poor. He could do it.

He sat up straight, tucked his legs under him in a modified lotus position, then closed his eyes tightly.

Concentrating forcefully, he dropped a black curtain behind his eyes until the world about him was completely blotted out and all he could see was the infinite void of nothingness stretching between him and his mother. Sharp streaks of light crossed the dark draperies of his subconscious mind, twirling in kaleidoscopic contortions, then subsided into the soft glow of gold and orange and scarlet. Gradually, at first unrecognizable, then more and more distinctly, the face of his mother appeared on the screen of his mind and he knew he had reached her. He knew she had stopped whatever she was doing and was listening.

"Mother, listen!" They were not words, not even conscious thoughts, but more like echoes emanating from the bottom of a deep, dark, abandoned old well. They were not radio waves, not electricity, nor electronic ionizations of the stratosphere. They were not light waves, nor sound waves, nor any other known manifestation of man's intrusion into the science of communication. For he was Pan, and Pan used the power of his mind augmented by an inexplicable strength which had been willed him by Zeus, the god of gods.

"Mother," he pleaded, and she listened, "don't look for me, don't grieve for me, and don't forget that I'll always be your son and the son of Penelope. And please don't send you legions to find me, for they *would* find me, and destroy me. Do not betray me, my Mother."

And the wishes of his heart poured out across the mountains and fields into the sensitive and receptive inner world of Sylvia Reynolds. She heard, and understood the plea. And the dark, ruminating side of her son who was not her son was clearly defined for an instant and was gone as quickly as it had come. And though her son could no longer weep, she could, and did, until the tears were hot on her cheeks.

Pan breathed deeply, breaking the spell of almost five minutes, and with the breaking of his trance, his heartbeat increased from the slow thudding of once every two seconds—to twice a second—and then returned to normal. He straightened his legs, scratched idly at his skin which was drying in the warm sun, and looked around him.

Nothing had really changed, yet he felt more at peace now that he had communicated with his mother. Sometime soon he should try to reach his father, but that would be more difficult. Always had been. Some people just were not tuned in to his mind like his mother was. But he would try, and he would ask John Reynolds not to forget that Pan was still his son, and the son of Hermes, who was the true Pan, and who had bequesthed his son the legacy of animal bestiality. And Dad, he rehearsed in his mind, I must now live somewhere between the mythological Pan of the flocks and fields— and the bestial Pan of the caves. For now, *I* am Pan.

Yes, he was Pan, but he was also hungry. He dressed quickly, and struck off down the clay track in the direction of McWhirter's coulee. The sun was low, almost out of sight behind the low hills to the west, when he knocked on the unpainted plank door of Jed Schroeders's shack. A coon dog lay somnolently in the shade, one eye opening through a brown eyepatch, the other eye stuck shut with dried pus. Chickens scratched in the unkempt yard, rummaging between old tires, bits of twisted metal from long-defunct cars and machinery, rusted cans and buckets and utensils, and shreds of cloth torn from old shirts and pants.

For the first time in two days, Pan's face softened into a slightly wry smile as he waited for the door to open. He fully expected to see the black muzzle of a double-barreled shotgun poke out of the door, held by a modern-day Hatfield or McCoy. The door opened slowly and Jed Schroeder stood in the shadows.

He was a huge man, or at least had been once. Now he was just big, rounded of back and crippled in one leg. He dragged his left leg across the doorjamb, leaned against his crutch, and swung his good leg onto the porch. Pan backed away a few feet, giving Jed room to swing his limp leg forward again for balance.

Jed's face was old. Deeply-etched furrows on either side of his nose and through his cheeks spoke of strength of character and a long life of laughing. His brows were tangled, bushy, and now white like the thick crew-cut hair on his head. His face was clean-shaven except for a toothbrush mustache and a wispy goatee several inches long. He was the perfect picture of the retired, southern, country gentleman. Except that he was black.

"Didn't figure me to be black, did you, son?" His voice was deep, well-modulated, educated, but with the residuals of his boyhood still audible. He said "figger" for "figure," and "black" was a two syllable word, "bla-yuk." In his dark brown eyes there was the merry devilment of the sylvan satyr.

"No, sir," Pan answered with a smile.

"Born that way."

"Yes, sir."

"You're not from the South, are you, son?"

"No, sir."

In sixty years, Jed Schroeder had never yet been called "sir" by a white southerner.

"Here," Jed said, "sit down on the stoop. No, don't need any help."

He swung his lame left leg over the edge of the porch and with a powerful right thigh lowered his body to a sitting position. Pan sat down beside him, and they looked down the hillside where the setting sun was striking fire to the bare branches of the staghorn sumac and wild plum thickets.

Dusk was soft and sweet and filled with the rustling sounds of birds settling into their nests and the pungent smell of woodfire from inside the house. Except for the quickly asked and quickly answered routine of identification, their talk was of coon hunts, deerstands, rabbit warrens, grouse thickets, mink trapping. Pan mostly just listened, awed by the fund of nature lore stored in the black man's brain. Then slowly the mellifluous meanderings of the old man's monologue mesmerized Pan's tired mind, and he drowsed.

Jed noted the drooping eyelids and the slack jaw and suggested supper and a good night's sleep. There had been no need to verbalize the need each had for the other. They were like strangers on a desert track, one trading water and the other food. Or, like two enemy soldiers crouching in a shellhole in no-man's land, trapped in a hail of crossfire from both sides, one trading cigarettes and the other gum. The old man gave freely of his ancient wisdom, trading it eagerly yet ingenuously for Pan's youth.

Jed Schroeder was caretaker for the estate of a wealthy absentee-landowner. The tract consisted of over 10,000 acres of uninhabited wilderness, some of it arable and most of it not. It was managed entirely for quail hunting. Walking paths and jeep tracks had been bulldozed throughout the entire area, making an enterconnecting maze of hunting trails which could be used by the owner and his friends when they came down from the city.

Jed's job was to provide the best possible habitat for natural quail reproduction. This involved keeping the quail foods healthy and the undesirable flora under control. He sowed scattered fields with millet and rye, and planted hedgerows of multiflora roses and other cover throughout the range. Each winter he fired a different section of forest undergrowth so the lower, ground-hugging, quail-foods would have a better chance of developing. He supervised the raising of strong wild strains of quail to be introduced to the local conveys to maintain their numbers and their genetic superiority.

Most of the burns had already been done, but there was one job yet to be accomplished, the burning off of a heavy growth of "dove grass" in one of the owner's favorite hunting spots.

"What in hell is 'dove grass,' Jed?" Pan asked the next morning as they set out in Jed's old Ford truck.

"Don't know it's real name, Pan," he answered, scratching his short hair. "Just know that the doves love to flight into it in the morning and evening when they're migrating. But the boss doesn't like to hunt doves, and he's right about the grass cutting down on quail feed wherever it's found. We're going to burn it off these next couple weeks."

Crippled he may have been, but handicapped he was not. He used his crutch as a normal man would use a good leg, running the length of the field's edges with a five-gallon can, stringing a fine line of gasoline along it, then shouting orders to Pan as the flames crept through the foot-high grass. Pan raced from point to point with an old coal shovel, protecting the bigger trees, and a few bushes, all the time letting the gentle breeze direct the flames across the field. Rabbits bounded out of the grass, and a few quail flushed like feathered bullets into the shortstraw pines bordering the field.

The first field burned for an hour or more before Jed ordered Pan to begin snuffing out the leading edge where it threatened to spread into the pines. Pan dashed along the spurting flames, pounding them out with the flat of the shovel, then sprinted from place to place as smoldering clumps of grass burst into flame again. Finally it was out and the two men stood shoulder to shoulder watching the field for further signs of fire-life.

Pan was dripping with sweat, his long blond hair hanging almost straight down until he brushed it back behind his ears. Absently he picked ticks from his arms and flicked them into the field. The old man picked a tick off his neck, decapitated it with his finger nail and dropped the insect to the ground.

Pan imitated the black man, but wondering as he did so just what good it did to destroy a few small bugs when there were thousands of them left to breed anyway. He saw a tick on Jed's hairline, swept it off with his finger and crushed it. He saw another and then another and soon was running his fingers through the thick, closely cropped white hair.

"Sit down, Jed," he said quietly, his voice oddly resonant. The old man looked at his curiosly, but did as he asked. Pan knelt behind him and stroked Jed's hair, stopping occasionally to remove a tick or some insignificant particle of fire-ash or dirt. Silently he continued the grooming, his fingers working down Jed's neck, across his shoulders where the old blue workshirt stretched damp with sweat, under the armpits and finally down his back and under the heavy leather belt. Jed sat immobile.

Pan arched his back, crouched low to the ground, and crawled on all fours to the front of the old man. His hair hung across his face and he shook it back from his eyes. His eyes were blue in the light of the late morning sun, but the pupils remained dilated and vacant. He pushed his shoulder against the black man's chest and rubbed it up and down until Jed reached out and stroked his

140

head, then began to picke ticks and dirt out of Pan's hair.

Jed was staring now, wonderingly sensitive to the boy's needs, afraid of the spirits or whatever it was that had taken possession of the lad's mind, afraid not to groom him, reluctant to continue the charade. Playfully, Pan rolled away from him onto his back and grabbed at his feet with one charcoal-blackened hand. With the other hand he scratched at his belly and grinned, his lower jaw dropping away from his upper, showing the incisors and canines in his mandible. He giggled, whined, and flopped onto his hands and knees and presented his rear to Jed.

Suddenly, Jed had had enough. He pushed himself to his feet and drove the end of his crutch into Pan's buttocks. It was the wrong thing to do. Pan tore the crutch from Jed's hands, roared and leaped to his feet, arms hanging grotesquely from his shoulders. He bounced up and down, hooting derisively, and drew his lips back from his upper teeth in a hideous parody of a grin.

Lowering his head, Pan charged into Jed's midsection, knocking him backwards where he struggled for balance on his one good leg. In a bouncing, prancing rage, Pan circled, while Jed turned awkwardly to meet the expected rush.

But Pan was through with Jed and ran to a nearby pine and tore at a lower branch. It would not break off so he roared again in frustration and climbed through the limbs to the top where he sat in silent indignation for a few moments, then cracked the limbs into a small nest and lay down in it and dropped off almost immediately into a deep sleep.

Jed recovered his crutch and sat down on the ground, watching the sleeping boy in awe, trying to piece together what had happened. His own inner world was peopled with a host of dark revenants, but nowhere had he encountered such a spectacle of the devil incarnate, never had he seen the archfiend revisit the earth in such spectral form. He closed his eyes, squeezed them shut till the blood boiled in them and scintillating lightning flashes shot through them in painful arcs.

"Jesus, Jesus, elder brother of mine, Mary, Mary, Mother of God, come Jesus, come Jesus, come." He slumped to the ground with his forehead touching the ground like a Moslem in prayer, then straightened up, still on his knees, and brushed the streaming tears from his eyes.

Chapter 20

The road from the village was not strange this time as Pan strode rapidly from gravel to clay track through the arching trees overhead. The tunnel was darker now, the branches nearly in full leaf, but the robins were still there and the same squirrels poked merry little faces around the trunks of black oaks and stared at the intruder with frightened, inquisitive eyes.

With scarcely a look at the deer-track he had climbed only two weeks before, Pan climbed steadily to the crest of the hill and gazed somewhat pensively into the valley beyond. Jed Schroeder's shack lay nestled in the coulee on the hillside nearly a mile away, not mean and dirty from this distance, but picturesque and beautiful. A rooster's "Happy New Year" carried clearly to him on the silent spring breeze and reminded him of the morning following his second "fit" (as Jed termed it).

He had awakened on that day with the crowing of the cock, and had lain awake until Jed woke up and started pouring water into the old coffee pot. Bacon sizzled in the pan, eggs cracked and sputtered in the spattering grease, and Jed called softly, "Daylight in the swamp, Pan."

Wondering where Jed had heard the old wake-up call from the Wisconsin pineries, Pan had swung his legs over the side of the rough-hewn built-in-bedstead and slipped his bare feet into the wet, dirty tennis shoes on the floor. Without answering Jed, he had put on his shirt and pants and sat down at the table.

Years of schooling and a stint in the Army (where he had taken a fragment of shrapnel in his sciatic nerve) dropped away from Jed as he fell back into the argot of his youth.

"You be needin' a doctor, Pan."

Pan had looked into the dark brown eyes that stared, basilisk-like, into his. A streak of sunlight had caught Jed's left eye, constricting the pupil and highlighting the flecks of gold in his sclera. An omen? he wondered, an evil-eye in this humble shack, warning him? Against what?

"Maybe, Jed."

"You's got the falling fits, Pan."

Was it time to take another into his confidence? Would there be belief, or incredulity, or frank derision? He stared out the small screenless window at the flowering dogwood on the hillside. A flock of cedar waxwings pecked at the tiny, almost invisible real flowers of the tree (the big white "flowers" were actually modified leaves and not edible), then as if on signal flitted suddenly away and were gone. No, this was not the time, this probably not the person to confide in. There might come a time, but not now, not Jed.

"I'll go away, Jed, if you like."

Jed mopped up egg from his plate with a piece of bread, chewed thoughtfully, and said, "No need, Pan. Lots of work to be done yet."

For two weeks they had fought the grass with flame and shovel, and Jed went to the bank and drew on his boss's account and paid Pan $175 with no deductions for income tax and Social Security.

The door opened in the shack across the valley and Jed Schroeder came out and threw a basin of water into the yard. He stood there for a moment, wondering perhaps if Pan had used his earnings to get medical advice, and knowing he had not. No more had been said about the fierce aberration in the forest, and Pan had not fallen into a "fit" again.

Pan shifted his heavy pack to a higher and more comfortable position on his shoulders and started down the hill. He cut across country, avoiding the track which led past Jed's shack, following deer trails and the high ridges, bulling his way through tag alder thickets along the small streams which trickled down toward the big river in the valley. Grouse erupted from under his feet and bore through invisible holes in the thick woods. Twice he stopped to watch small does as they inspected him from near-perfect concealment in scrub oak thickets and then wheeled at the last moment to disappear like redbrown wraiths in the forest.

Ten thousand acres of uninhabited land. He could easily avoid the infrequent hunting parties which would invade the hills. Jed would know he was there, would see and recognize his spoor, would perhaps make abortive attempts to seek him out but would not try too hard, and would certainly not say anything to the landowners or anyone else. This much he knew from their two weeks together.

He came upon a walking trail, only a few feet wide, but free of trees and underbrush, and followed it as it would indolently through the hills. Occasionally he crossed a jeep track, double-rutted marks in the sand, and ignored them. He wanted to get as close to the center of the 10,000 acres as he could. This would give him almost a mile of wilderness in every direction, a mile through which no man could pass because the boundaries were posted. He would learn that territory as an animal would. He would know every hill, every trail, every stream. He would learn where the berries were in fall, where the dear ran when panicked, where the rabbits padded out their customary feeding trails, where the beechnuts and acorns fell in profusion, where the succulent shunk-cabbage and marsh marigold first appeared in the spring.

But first he had to find a place to live. It was not rock country and therefore it was unlikely he would find a cave. A crooked grin distorted his handsome face as he remembered that it was baboons who slept in caves and chimpanzees slept in trees. But he did not relish the thought of sleeping in a tree for the rest of his life. And would he really live here the rest of his life? And if he didn't, where would he?

When he judged he was near the center of "his" territory, he stopped from time to time to stand for long moments in contemplation of his surroundings. He knew exactly what he was looking for. Coming to a trail crossing, he noted that the path he travelled paralleled the base of the highest hills in the area, while the other ran straight down into the valley in one direction, and straight up the mountain in the other. He turned upwards. Outcroppings of limestone began to show through the thin overburden of sandy soil and in some places small but sheer cliffs made their appearance.

The lane narrowed, then disappeared completely. He turned around. Before him lay the country he had just traversed. Even at this height a few of the jeep roads could be discerned in the forest, although none of the walking trails showed. He judged he was three or four thousand feet above the lowest point in his territory. It was unlikely that any of the landowner's friends would have the desire or the energy to climb this high, and if they did, they would not leave the bull-dozed lanes except under unusual circumstances.

He pushed through the brush at the end of the trail and picked his way through the forest a few hundred feet to the very top of the mountain. It remained heavily wooded, primarily with oak and beech and a scattering of maple. In fact, it was so dense he could see no more

146

than twenty to thirty yards in any direction. He climbed a young beech tree, and even before he reached the top he knew he had found the perfect spot. Not a hundred yards away was a limestone facing about fifty feet high and a hundred feet long. Dense forest surrounded the facing, and clumps of brushes grew at the far end of the limestone.

He swung down from the tree, hand over hand, feet touching the trunk only for balance. Heavy cords of muscle stretched the thin fabric of his shirt and rippled in the mid-morning sun. His long hair was bleaching even whiter, and the two-week growth of reddish-blond beard was beginning to lie flat against his cheeks and chin. The canvas tennis shoes he had worn in the burns were blackened, frayed and beginning to come apart at the seams; they would not last much longer.

The campsite was perfect. He went to work at once with axe and saw. He selected two trees, ten feet apart and about four inches in diameter, tied a two-inch-thick sapling between them at a height of about four feet for the ridgepole of his lean-to, and made a frame of poles extending out from the ridgepole to the ground ten feet away. The open end faced the limestone cliff only a few feet away. He laid a newly purchased canvas tarpaulin on the frame, and held it in place with another frame of poles which he tied at top and bottom with heavy nylon cord. The free ends of the tarp which hung over both sides of the frame he staked firmly into the ground with sharpened spikes of oakwood.

He had a house. When he built his fire in front of it, the cliff would act as a perfect draft to suck the smoke up the hillside, yet reflect the heat directly into the lean-to. The canvas roof faced the east and would get the early morning sun. He was high enough to get any breeze that stirred the mountain-top, yet he was protected by the limestone facing on the west so he would not get the full brunt of cold winds in the winter. If necessary, he could erect a windbreak behind the lean-to to ward off any winds from that direction.

He laid another tarpaulin on the floor of the lean-to and threw his pack into one corner. Kneeling beside it, he emptied it out and checked his new purchases. There really wasn't much there, now that the tarps and axe and saw were out. He had bought two knives, one a long-pointed, stainless steep hunting knife in a heavy belt-sheath, the other a pocket knife with leather punch and coarse file in addition to the two blades of different sizes. He had bought two blankets, a compass, several coils of nylon of different sizes, two small cookpans, an iron skillet, half a dozen small toothless #1 1/2 traps for rabbit and squirrel, a five-pound bag of rock salt to be used until he found a natural salt-lick, several large steel forks and spoons, coils of thin wire of different sizes.

There ensued a period of tranquility in Pan's life which he would never have again. Perhaps the two quick outbursts of animalistic behavior a day apart had sapped the strength from the side of him which had evolved from Hermes. Perhaps the haploid genes from the chimpanzee, long controlled in the human environment of Standing Oaks, had merely burst out temporarily when unencumbered by strict human, parental control. Perhaps the more gentle Penelope would now guide the boy. Perhaps.

He was the Boy Scout on a survival hike, the *cheechako* testing himself in the pristine Alaskan wilderness, the adolescent Masai circumcision-candidate spending his year in the bush before the ordeal of the cold knife. He was a man, differing not in degree, but actually in kind from the animalness he shared with every other creature on earth. He possessed not only the power of perceptual thought, but of conceptual thought. He transcended the purely perceptual abilities of the animal, who deals thoughtfully with perceived objects, but who cannot put name-words to imperceptible objects, who cannot even conceive of imperceptible objects such as the solution to a mathematical problem or a chess game.

Pan was, for the time being, an historical, a *human* animal, able to accept transmitted and cumulative cultural artifacts from a previous generation. Possibly he could have survived without an axe and a spread of tarpaulin and even fire. As the son of Hermes he might have lived, but as the son of Penelope he lived a far richer, more comfortable life. From her he had inherited the ability to make tools for *future* use, to make tools which would make *other* tools, to make useless works of art which had no possible survival value. From her he had derived inherent dignity and inherent rights.

For almost two years Pan lived as the son of Penelope. He learned to recognize and use the wild plants and fruits which surrounded him on every side. In the spring he boiled dandelion greens in two waters to remove the bitterness; he picked the fiddle heads of the young ferns and boiled them with the early shoots of the skunk cabbage, then mixed in a few young leaves of the mustard plant for delicious taste; he peeled the shoots of the sumac and chewed on them raw; he boiled beechnuts from a hoard collected the previous fall, skimmed off the oil, and boiled the stalk of burdock in the oil; he made a soup thickener of wild violets (called "wild okra" by the Indians) and added it to rabbit stew.

In the summer he lived on the roasted roots of cattails; he searched out the trailing vines with flowers like morning glories and dug the twenty-pound roots of the man-of-the-earth and roasted them under a bed of coals; like the Pilgrims centuries before him, he watched for the pea-like, brown-purple flowers and violet-like odor of the groundnut and dug deeply for the thirty or forty tubers strung under the ground like potatoes; he dug the roots of the Jerusalem artichoke and the Indian cucumber; he cruised the swamp and pulled up by their roots the heavy bulrushes, then dried them to make a flour for baking into small cakes.

In the fall he ate raspberries, blackberries, blueberries, service berries, elderberries, and even the pucker-producing choke cherry. He collected the acorns of three oak trees—chestnut, post and white—saved most for the winter months, ate some raw, and made a delicious breakfast mush by grinding the kernnels, leaching in woodashes and water to get rid of the bitter tannin, then cooking slowly in the frypan.

It was in the winter that he, like all men and animals dependent upon the land for sustenance, struggled for existence. Particularly in that first winter, when he had little experience in survival and before he knew how much to hoard, he sometimes went days without a good meal. Then he would be lucky enough to trap a rabbit or a squirrel and for several hours slowly savor the delicious meat cooked in acorn oil. In that first winter he came to understand why the Indians called February the Hunger Moon, and learned to eat what they had: the white basswood buds|which cooked up into a mucilaginous but agreeable food.

Several times he almost gave it up. He told himself there was nor reason for this self-imposed exile, no good excuse for not walking off his hill to the highway restaurant, no need to stay away from Jed Schroeder's warm shack where there was a bed, flapjacks for breakfast, hominy grits and all the butter he could eat. Then he remembered why he was there. And he stayed.

His beard grew long and he cut it short with his skinning knife. His hair grew even longer and he braided it like an Indian or made a pony tail of it with a leather thong. His clothes wore out and he made new ones from the hide of a deer which fell miles from where it had been wounded by a hunter. His tennis shoes decayed and he went barefoot except in the very coldest of weather when he wore moccasins made from the same deerskin. His canvas lean-to thinned, and tore, and was replaced with bark layered like shingles on new saplings.

He learned his territory so he could walk or run directly from one spot to another without even thinking where he was going. He knew the location of every blowdown where he could disappear like a rabbit every time he heard hunters moving through the woods. At the first sound of shot or dog-whistles he smothered his fire, leaving only a few coals burning smokelessly in the corner of the lean-to. He had long ago used up his supply of matches, and had learned the art of maintaining a "coal-bank" which could be coaxed into a flame with a few pine needles of dry grass. His senses sharpened rapidly when he had to use them to survive. He began to see things he had never seen before, hear things which would have eluded him before, even smell that which would not have been noticed before.

He could foretell the weather a day in advance from the winds. A straight westwind always meant good weather unless it was slowly swinging to the southeast from the northwest, in which case it meant rain. A strong east wind, even in sunny weather, always meant a storm was coming, and a strong west wind meant clear, cold weather even if the day was rainy or snowy. A south wind meant warm weather, and he only needed to watch which way it was shifting in order to tell whether it was going to rain or clear up the next day. A north wind brought cold weather, and if it swung to the west it would stay cold and clear, if to the east, rain or snow.

There were moments and hours to rest, too, when he whittled on thin willow branches and made whistles and short flutes. He made a single-reed pipe by cutting a vibrating tongue in the side of a piece of narrow elder-wood and stopping up the end with mud. One day he made a double-reed pipe by pinching together one end of a freshly cut plant stem to give it a narrow aperture which widened and contracted when it was blown. These primitive pipes he played plaintively in the late evening hours when he sat in the glow of his warm fire.

Finally tiring of the limited range of these simple tubes, he constructed a much more complicated panpipe from canes he cut in the bottomland. With his pocket knife he cut them into twenty-one different lengths and then by trial and error he tuned them diatonically over three octaves, making the semi-tones by tilting them toward his lips. Then he fastened them together with nylon cord and the glue-like sap of the shortstraw pines on the hill above his camp.

He now had an instrument which was much more difficult to play, but which when mastered allowed him to simulate the keening of the nightwind, the soughing of the pines, the songs of birds, the drumming of partridge. Sometimes he just let his mind wander through the forested hills of his domain, and his lips played out the romance of running deer, tangled vines, scampering rabbits and soaring hawks. He eulogized the aging monarchs of the mountains and played in epitaph for the giants when they fell before wind and storm. Softly he traced the patter of foxes' feet, and with passion he called from his pipes the dreadful swoop of owls on their prey.

He spent the days with the busy-work of surviving, but there were those moments in the evening by the fire, or on the mountain resting after gathering firewood, when he could sit and think. He remembered the parting words of both John and Sylvia Reynolds, "Come back, son." He had never quite gotten around to try to reach his father through his powers of thought-projection, but he knew his mother well enough to know that she would have passed on that message he had sent so long ago. As the second winter passed, the days lengthening and the sun warming every living thing, he began to think of returning home. Returning to Standing Oaks, that is, for he considered his mountain-top home. It was here he had carved a deep niche in the eco-system. It was here he was in balance with the natural forces which governed the universe. Here, in the high mountain haunts, he thought he could drive down the heritage from Hermes into the dust and mud of forest trails and fern carpets and oakleaf mulch. In becoming more like an animal, he thought he could exorcise the animal from his chromosomes, could forever repress the translocated and inverted genes which John Reynolds had so cleverly transposed twenty years before.

He was wrong.

Chapter 21

Pan was sure that Jed Schroeder knew where he was. Many times he had sat silently in a tall tree or in the perfect concealment of an alder thicket and watched Jed studying the ground where he, Pan, had just walked. Jed would bend low, perhaps even kneel, to scrutinize a footprint, a broken-off flower stem, or a clump of crushed clover. Then he would straighten up, follow the spoor through the trees with his eyes, look around him, shrug his shoulders, and move on. Once he had even followed the trail up the mountain toward Pan's lean-to, but when he came to the end of the bull-dozed trail, he parted the bushes where Pan usually passed, sniffed the wind, and again with that characteristic shrug, turned laboriously on his good leg and stumped off down the hill. He knew.

One morning in late March at the end of the second year of Pan's hegira, he awoke to the sound of shotguns rattling in the valley a mile away. Quickly he rolled out of his blankets, scraped a few live coals from the fire into the frypan, and placed them in the corner of his lean-to. He covered them with one of his battered, blackening cooking pans, and laid his blankets over them. They would smolder there for hours, and Pan could add small pieces of charred aspen from time to time to keep the embers alive. When this was done he crept out of his

154

lean-to and climbed up and around the end of the limestone rockface and sat in the warm, early morning sun. Shots rang out again, and this time whistles blew the dogs in, and Pan knew there was at least one quail lying in the new ferns.

For three days Pan was confined to his mountaintop, afraid to descent lest the hunters accidentally run upon him. He had stood these vigils before, sleeping little, constantly alert for the sound of tramping feet and the even more dangerous roaming dogs. A ranging dog was always followed sooner or later by a hunter, and he dared not be found by one of the long-legged pointers. So far, none had even come close to his aerie.

On the third day Pan awoke at dawn, chewed on some shoots and chestnut-oak acorns, and climbed to his observation point. Long before he saw it, he heard the grinding gears of a jeep being incompetently handled on the track paralleling the base of his mountain. The jeep stopped, men called to each other in the forest, and Pan clearly picked out one voice urging someone to climb the trail to the top.

Quickly, yet stealthily, Pan returned to the lean-to and rolled all his belongings into a blanket, concealed the coals of his fire behind some rocks at the base of the cliff, and scurried back up the cliff to his lookout. On hands and knees he tunneled through the base of a wild plum thicket where he had hidden countless times before, and waited.

For at least an hour he heard nothing, saw nothing. Then suddenly he caught the unmistakable scent of a dog drifting in to him on the morning breeze. He knew the dog could not be more than a hundred feet away, because he could not have winded him further. In another moment he heard the pattering of the dog's feet in the carpet of last year's leaves, and a few seconds later the dog himself was crawling on his belly through the thicket toward him.

His namesake, panic, almost overcame him. The hunter would not be far behind, perhaps had already spotted the dog crawling into the thicket, and would be moving up toward it, gun at port arms, waiting for the explosion of rocketing quail out of the tangle of limbs and briars, knowing that no dog could keep a covey of quail pinned down in such a mess.

Hugging his blanket roll under one arm, Pan slowly backed out of the thicket on hands and knees. The dog stopped, groveled in the dirt, and moved forward again, tail wagging and jowls slobbering. Pan should have been amused at the dog's attempts to be friends, but he was not. He threw a stick at the dog, but the dog just grabbed at it and held it in his mouth gently as if it were a bird. Pan reached the edge of the thicket, turned to study the slope above him, and when he saw no one, sprinted up the incline to the dense stand of shortstraw pines. There he squatted on the ground, the cold sweat of fear dripping from him in rivulets. He knew the dog would detect the odor emanating from him and would know his prey was terrified. Not that the dog would be likely to harm him, but it would be unlikely to leave him now.

Below the rockface, off the north of his lean-to, Pan could hear the hunter scuffing through the leaves. A whistle shrilled, calling the dog. Pan could hear the dog stop, snort a couple of times in frustration, then run swiftly down the hill toward his waiting master.

Pan lowered himself to the ground and lay against his blanket roll. This was the closest call he had had, by far. He wiped the back of his hand across his eyes and flicked the sweat away. With considerable difficulty he took off his dearskin shirt, turned it inside out and lay it over a bush to dry. For half an hour he stood in the sun until the sweat had dried on his body, then threw the still-wet shirt over his shoulder, tucked the blanket roll under his arm, and walked back down to his lean-to. All day he sat in the lean-to, listening to the activity in the valley, heard the jeep start up and drive away, waited until he could hear no more, then as the sun set behind the mountain to the west he shouldered his blanket roll and started down the trail.

And again it was not a time for looking back. He was a man, not an animal, and never again would he be hunted like one. Or so he thought as he pushed through the brush at the upper end of the long trail to the base of the mountain.

The wind was beginning to pick up and Pan stopped to put on his shirt. He dropped his blanket roll to the ground, struggled into the wet leather, bent to pick up the roll, and when he straightened up he saw in the dusk at the edge of the jeep track the glint of shiny crutch wood and the carved ebony face of Jed Schroeder.

They stood facing each other for uncounted minutes, the one tall and straight and blond as a Viking, the other bent and weathered and black as Stygean darkness, one with the features and coloring which had ruled the earth before the third world began, the other the grim shade meant for hanging in the dead of the night.

The vanquished Viking's head dropped and the dark silhouette moved toward him in somber triumph.

"Fatback and black-eyed peas is a-cookin' on the stove, Pan. Ol' coon-dog's hollerin' at the moon 'most ever' night now. Time a body was t' shuck off the devils a-nippin' at his heels, boy."

Pan raised his eyes to the black man's face. "How did you know it was time, Jed?"

In the curious way that Jed had, he shed the boyhood dialect as a mother might shift from babytalk. "I knew, son, I knew."

An Pan recognized immediately that his daylong

157

ordeal had somehow triggered the old man's consciousness, just as his mother had once known where to look for him in the forest long ago. Jed *knew* that Pan would be coming down that trail, if not the extact hour, at least that he *would* be coming.

Although Pan probably knew the forest at night better, Jed led the way through the maze of trails, swinging his crutch confidently through the darkening forest. An owl screeched in the distance, defining his territory, and bats dove in swarms at the insects kicked up by the scudding feet of the two men. In the valley to the south a diesel generator kicked over and slowly thudded to a gentle hum and there was light in the hunters' lodge. The fetid, decaying lowland odor of wet leaves and morel mushrooms and rotting logs reminded Pan that he was no longer a denizen of the high places, was now returning to a life he had once known, would have to know again.

It was dark when they reached Jed's shack, but a half moon gave them all the light they needed. Jed was good to his word about the fatback and peas and Pan drank almost a half gallon of milk before he finally pushed his chair back and slumped in it, hands clasped on his belly. "Thank you," he said.

Jed got up, stacked the dirty dishes together in a deep blue basin, and poured steaming water over them. "You're welcome." He tipped in a few squirts of liquid detergent and swished the water around gingerly with one finger. "Your mother's been here," he announced without inflection as if he had just told an inquisitive stranger the time of day.

Pan tensed briefly, his eyes narrowing slightly and his hands clenching and unclenching several times. Then he relaxed and folded his arms on his chest, still stretched out on the old wooden chair. There were suddenly a hundred questions he wanted to ask and couldn't even put one into words.

"Several times, Pan," the old black man continued, his eyes now turned full on Pan, glowing like black beads in the semi-darkness of the kerosene lamp. "I sort of lied to her the first time. She came in July of that first summer you were gone, about three months after you left this shack. She asked if you had been there. I said yes. She wanted to know where you had gone. I said I didn't know."

"You did right, Jed."

"I don't think so. So the next time she came back, just a month later, saying she couldn't prove it but she had good reason to believe you were still about somewhere, I told her I thought I knew where you were."

Pan nodded his head, the long braids of his red-blond hair bouncing on his naked shoulders. He ran his tongue around his lips, and the heavy biceps in his arm twitched rhythmically as he brushed his mustache away from his upper lip with his fingers. Slowly he stood up, moved silently on bare feet to his deerskin shirt where it hung drying across the back of a chair in front of the wood-burning stove. He turned the shirt right-side out, slipped it over his head, and turned to face Jed.

"She'll be back again, Jed?"

The black man nodded his head in solemn agreement.

"When?"

"Don't rightly know, Pan."

"When was she here last?"

"Couple of months gone," he answered, returning Pan's steady gaze without flinching, but his speech beginning to show his anxiousness. "Keeps on a-wantin' me to go up the hill for ya' seeing as I knowed where you was. A'most did it once. Ya' prob'ly seen me."

Pan nodded, remembering the time Jed had climbed the trail as far as its end, then turned back. "I saw you,

159

but I knew you'd never do it. Relax, Jed, I'm not blaming you. You didn't really have a choice, you know."

"Maybe not, Pan, but I thought I did." He moved from the stove where he had been standing warming his hands behind his back. With a long sigh he sat at the table and leaned on his elbows, his blue workshirt stretching taut across his rounded back.

"Your mother loves you, son. Ain't right for you to treat her so."

"You'll understand I don't mean to be harsh when I say it isn't any of your business, Jed," Pan said softly, and the old man nodded his head slowly.

"Just saying what I felt I ought to say."

"Anyone else been asking about me?"

"Just the waitress at the restaurant in town. Wanted to know if you'd found my place. Told her yes. She seemed satisfied, didin't ask any more questions. That was almost two years back."

Pan sat on his bunk and leaned back against the rough planking of the wall behind it. He watched Jed with half-closed eyes as he said, "I'm going home, Jed. Decided today. Figured I'd work for you long enough to buy some clothes and a bus ticket."

Jed's head jerked up. "Hell, boy, I'll loan you the money. *Give* it to you. No need to waste time once you've made up your mind."

Pan smiled, the first time he had smiled at another human being for two years. "Ah knowed you'd say that, Jed," he said, mimicking the old man, and Jed grinned, showing a sprinkling of rotted yellow teeth across the front of his mouth. "But I can't do that, Jed," Pan said. "Besides, it'll do me good to start back into civilization the slow way. If you can use me for a couple of weeks."

"You call this shack civilization, Pan? I've seen better civilization in the South Pacific."

"That where you got the limp, Jed?"

Jed nodded. "Tell you about it some time." He grinned again. "Explain how I got the shrapnel in my backsides."

"I'll believe anything you tell me, Jed. Right now . . ."

The rooster sang out his "Happy New Year" in the early morning light, long before the sun had found its way over the mountains to the east, and long before Pan was ready to get up. Jed made coffee, fried bacon and cornmeal mush, and stole out the door on stockinged feet, leaving the blond giant asleep on the straw ticking. He stood for a moment in the doorway, looking back at Pan, wondering what terrible demons drove the boy to spend two years alone on the top of a mountain.

Couldn't have been a crime, he reasoned, for if it had been, someone other than his mother would have been there looking for him. At least not a serious business such as murder or rape or arson. Couldn't have been a love affair turned sour, for no one of that age would grieve or pine so long. That was just in books they done that. No, it had to be a witching, a diabolical devil-begotten spell cast on the lad by some satanic warlock or sorceress. Had to be. And Pan had tried to rid himself of the malediction, had tried to counteract the curse, by banishing *himself* from the world. Now he ought to know better, Jed thought to himself as he stood watching the boy, he ought to know you don't do it *that* way. You get the witch-man *himself* or the one who paid him, and until you do, the curse stays laid. Could it have been his mother? Or his father?

Jed returned later that afternoon and found Pan sitting on the porch, scratching the coondog's ears. He had washed his head and the long blond hair shone almost red in the sun. He had trimmed his mustache with a razor blade and had combed his beard neatly. Two years of sun and wind had bronzed his skin.

Crinkled white crow's feet spread laterally from his eyes onto his temples. If he's a devil, thought Jed, he's the most handsome one this valley has ever seen, and if he's not a devil but is bound by one, he's in trouble with a capital T.

"Didn't hardly earn my day's grub, did I, Jed?"

"I'll take it out of your wages, don't you worry."

While Pan pumped water, Jed splashed it over his face and hands, crying aloud in mock anguish. "Hooo-*eeee*, hooo-*eeee*, that's cold," but loving every minute of it. He playfully flicked a few drops toward Pan, and Pan sidestepped agiley.

"Sure wish I could still move like that, Pan," Jed said as he wiped his face on the sleeves of his shirt and his hands on the back of his pants.

"Bet you could, not too many years ago, Jed," Pan said.

"Yeah, that's the truth, son. But the days and years just go be too fast, and 'fore you know it, they're gone beyond retrievin'. Time's the one thing we got *no* control over. Even death and taxes is easier to manage. We can cheat death a dozen times, but every time we do, there's a little more time gone by. Didn't fool Old Man Time. No, sir. And we can keep from paying taxes by not making anything and not owning anything, or even by cheating Uncle Sam just like we did The Grim Reaper. But not time. It goes on forever."

Pan leaned against the pump and looked at Jed, knowing the old black man was trying to tell him something.

"I suspect you've cheated The Grim Reaper a few times, Jed."

"True. And been a-scared of him a mite more. 'Specially of late."

"Death isn't all that bad, Jed."

"But *dying* is!"

Pan crossed the littered yard and sat down on the porch a few feet from Jed. The sun was just dropping behind the hill back of them, and a cooling breeze swept up the valley, laden with the heavy scent of lilacs and dogwood. It was too glorious an evening to talk of death and dying.

"What's on your schedule for tomorrow, Jed? Anything I can help you with?"

"Gonna' girdle some big old beeches and aspen trees in a stand of young cedar the boss wants to get more sunlight. That way they'll stand for years without damaging the firs. Better'n cutting them and killing the young cedars when they fall. Can't use the wood anyway."

"Seems like a waste."

"Not if you like cedars better!"

For ten days they worked as a team, each on one end of a crosscut saw, rhythmically two-stepping around the big trees, never breaking their to-and-fro stroking, shuffling in perfect coordination until the first cut was made, then reversing direction and cutting their way around the thick bark six inches lower than the first cut. Then with razor-sharp adzes they gouged off the strip of bark down to the bare wood, assuring that no sap would run either way ever again.

The work was gruelling, but both the old black and the young white were conditioned for it, and neither had to pace himself to wait for the other. It seemed to Jed that this was just what the boy needed, a chance to set his mind at rest for punishing his body. And so it would have been, if Pan had been the son of John and Sylvia Reynolds. But he was not. He was the son of Hermes, heir to the forest-dwelling tribe of *Pan troglodytes* and of Penelope, heiress to a throne in the talismanic hills of ancient Arcadia.

Chapter 22

"You've got to try one more time, Sylvia," John Reynolds said urgently, pushing his glasses back on his nose in order to focus on the pipe he was holding. "Maybe I could go with you, maybe talk some sense into that Jed you think knows where Pan is."

He rolled his head slowly from side to side, holding a match steady to the aromatic tobacco packed tightly in the heavy yellow Meerschaum. From across the living room, curled in her favorite chair, Sylvia watched him apathetically.

"Maybe," she answerd. "But you couldn't browbeat him. He'd turn you out just like that." She flicked a pale finger across the arm of the chair.

John nodded slowly, puffing intermittently, his hooded lids pale and parchment-like with age like the rest of the skin of his face. His beaked nose, once subservient to the strength of his eyes and mouth, now dominated his face and seemed to hang over his mustache and chin like a falcon before his stoop. His seventy-three years lay on him like a cougar on a rock, quiet, sullen, poised, dangerous.

He looked across the room at his wife, the white *arcus senilis* drawing even blacker tints from his pupils. He had grown tired of his wife's docility, her never-ending subservience, her obsequiousness. She had reached seventy herself just the previous spring, an age at which most women knitted or played bridge all afternoon, or went with their greying, stooped husbands to Golden Agers' picnics or pinochle parties. To all outward appearances she had the persisting vigor of younger womanhood and carried herself with the aplomb of good health. Her hair was white, combed back into a small bun at the nape of her neck. Old age had not softened her face as it does with some. Deep worry-lines creased her forehead and coursed alongside her nose to the corners of her mouth. A faint mustache lay on her upper lip.

On her soul, however, she carried scars too deeply ingrained to allow her the luxury of a gracious old age. The disappearance of Pan had been just one more wound driven helter-skelter into the soft core of her unconscious, and that wound had not yet healed, perhaps never would.

The wound would certainly never heal as long as John Reynolds was alive. He clung to the only real dream he had had since he had been upstaged by the Milan scientists over thirty years before. Desperately he clung to it, nagging Sylvia persistently with the never-ending question: why did we let Pan leave? We had no choice, Sylvia had reminded him a thousand times; he left of his own free will, and we could not restrain him bodily. Besides, she said, we both thought he would be back in a few hours, full of questions and hopefully full of answers to our questions.

And always after their fitful spats she tried to placate him with her fawning posturing, taking the blame on herself for not doing this or that thing which would have kept Pan there with them.

"I'd know how to handle Jed, Sylvia," he muttered now. "I wouldn't force him to do anything."

"All right, John," she said, slumping in the chair and placing her head on the back of it in resignation. "But what if we do find Pan down there, what'll we *say* to him, after all that has happened?"

"We'll worry about that when we find him."

They drove through a dripping, thawing, late winter countryside the first day and into spring on the morning of the second day. John seemed tense, anxious, and chewed on the stem of his pipe whether it was lit or not. Sylvia crouched silently in the far corner of the front seat, morose and sullen. She answered John's infrequent attempts at conversation with sulky ill-temper.

"What's the matter, Sylvia?" he asked finally. "Don't you *want* to find Pan?"

"I want him to find himself before we find him."

"Then why did you come after him before?"

"Because you told me to."

He looked sideways at her in disgust. "After forty years and all we've been through, you still want to wait even longer? My God!"

She stirred restlessly and for just a few seconds seemed to be on the verge of a retort. Her eyes brightened and the weary look about them faded ever so slightly, then she closed her eyes and settled into her seat with a sigh.

They drove slowly through the village where Pan had gotten off the pig-truck and turned left into the hills at the barber shop. Guided by Sylvia, John found McWhirter's coulee and Jed's shack and coasted in between the two white pines which had guarded the little valley for a hundred years or more.

Jed had heard the car coming and stood on the porch, lame leg propped against the roof support, thumbs tucked into the pockets of his faded, blue bib overalls. There was an almost studied nonchalance about him which went undetected by the Reynolds only because they didn't know him well. He had recognized the car immediately and was not surprised to see Sylvia step out of it onto the hard bare ground. So he stood and waited and knew the balding white-haired man who got quickly out of the driver's side must be Pan's father.

He saw John Reynolds pause and look around him. He saw him taking in the rude shack, the littered yard, and outdoor privy, saw his eyes range up the hill behind the house and saw the malevolent shadows fill those eyes. He saw the heavy lids come down like shutters till only the lower halves of the orbits showed spitefully in the early afternoon sun. He felt terror rise in his breast until his breathing was almost shut off and his strong right leg felt an invasive weakness that threatened to fell him like a pole-axed steer.

Jed saw all this and he wished to God that Pan had followed his first instincts to stay on the mountain where he was safe. Safe from this man who might be his father but who was evil incarnate. From the depths of Jed Schroeder's soul, perhaps even from that fourth room where no one ever went and from which nothing good ever came, issued the certain knowledge that here was the warlock who had settled the curse on Pan.

He knew it, and wondered if Pan did.

"Hello, Jed," Sylvia said, and moved slowly toward the porch.

"Miz Reynolds."

"This is Dr. Reynolds, Jed."

"How do, sir."

"We've come to talk to Pan, Jed," John said and leaned back against the front of the car.

"I know."

"Do you know where he is, Jed?" Sylvia asked, her voice breaking with emotion.

Knowing suddenly he needn't answer, Jed turned his head to look at the doorway of his shack, and there framed by the rotting timbers stood Pan.

Sylvia gasped desperately for breath and the staccato rasp gouged Jed's heart with is poignancy. She stumbled forward, her thin bony legs pumping with the urgency of motherlove, and Pan stepped out of the doorway to meet her. He swept her frail body into his arms and her tears coursed down from her swollen eyes onto the smooth, faded leather shirt.

Jed lowered his eyes, then raised them to look at John Reynolds. John stood rigidly, feet widespread, arms braced behind him on the hood of the car. It was as if his brain were pulling him toward his son while his body held him back with an even stronger force. Go to him, Jed pleaded mutely, go take him in your arms. But John Reynolds could not. And Jed's mind and heart pleaded, Break the spell, man, break it, you can do it, you're the only one can do it!

But he could not.

Chapter 23

Carefully Jed eased the old truck out of the yard, between the white pines, and onto the dusty road leading into the wilderness. Jammed in the front seat with him were John and Sylvia, John in the middle so Jed could handle the shift lever without embarrassment. Pan stood in back, feet planted firmly on the splintered floor, knees slightly bent to balance himself as the truck rocked and bounced on the uneven road.

Pan's mind was awhirl with conflicting thoughts. He knew he should be pleased to see the Reynolds in a way he was. He was sorry he had caused his mother so much grief, and he felt a stirring of guilt for having never communicated with his father. And although he did not even now fully comprehend the Experiment of which he was the end product, he knew the Experiment could not be completed until he gave the Reynolds a chance to talk to him.

But what could he tell them? From *his* viewpoint, the Grand Experiment wasn't such hot stuff after all. What had been discovered by mating two different species? Well, sometimes he felt like a human (and a very normal one, he thought), and sometimes he felt like a chimpanzee (probably normal there, too.). Big deal. Is there anything here which could not have been guessed without going to such elaborate, life-long, trouble? What had this Experiment revealed?

The truck slowed and turned onto a two-wheel track which penetrated even deeper into the forest. Pan's mountain now rose above them on the left, in shadows now as the sun had already dropped behind its peak. Jed left the truck in first gear, crawling slowly along the small creek, occasionally fording it as the trail swung from one side of it to the other. Sylvia sat quietly, her arm draped over the dusty door. Her tears had dried but her eyes remained red-rimmed and she blew her nose gently from time to time. John sat immobile, his hands clasped tensely in his lap, his legs spread awkwardly on either side of the gear shift. His eyes were almost closed, but they opened periodically to watch the progress of the truck. Small talk was impossible to the tense atmosphere, and no one wanted to broach the deeper subjects which all were thinking about.

Pan had suggested in a tone which had not left much room for disagreement that John and Sylvia go with him to the camp where he had spent the past two years. He knew he would feel at home there, and might be able to talk with them more at ease than he would in Jed's shack. He did not want to *tell* them, but wanted them to see—to feel—to sense—how he had lived, how he had survived, how he had come to grips with his dual personality. Perhaps he would not even *have* to say much if they could see with their own eyes what had happened to him in the past two years.

Jed eased the truck to a stop beneath a giant white pine which marked the beginning of the tail upward.

"It's goin' to be a long, hard climb for y'all," he said, but both John and Sylvia waved off the warning.

The truck rocked as Pan leaped over the side onto the ground beside Jed. "You'll stay here, Jed? Wait for us, even if it's late?"

"All night, if that's what it takes. God knows I got nothin' *more* important t'do."

Pan stood beside the cab for a moment, studying his friend, blue eyes somber, thanking him. John and

Sylvia were climbing out on the other side. "You're afraid for me, Jed?" Pan whispered.

Jed nodded, his mouth pursed so tightly that his lips blanched.

"Why?" Pan asked, his voice soft and his eyes pleading.

Jed merely shook his head silently from side to side, swallowing the words which he knew would sound either hollow or melodramatic depending on how Pan interpreted them.

Pan sighed, took a deep breath, and moved around the front of the truck to join his parents.

He pointed up the trail. "It's about 1500 feet to my camp. Not too hard going. And we'll stop often, whenever you want to."

Sylvia smiled. "Lead the way, Pan." There was a childlike eagerness in her voice that caused John to glance at her with thinly disguised disgust, and Pan half expected him to say, "This isn't a picnic you know, Sylvia." But John held his tongue and stepped off the path to allow Pan to precede him.

They climbed slowly, and Pan told them how he had roamed this mountain until he had chanced on his campsite. When they stopped to rest, he turned them around and pointed out the jeep-trails in the valley, the mountain across the way where he hunted mushrooms and acorns, the brushstrip through the valley which marked the little brook where he picked marsh marigold and watercress. When they neared his camp he showed them the tree from which he had spotted the rockface which was not his home.

A gentle breeze flowed down the mountainside, carrying with it the scent of dogwood and cedar. Raucous jays screamed at them and startled squirrels lay flat against oak trunks or fled dizzily through the treetops.

"They're not used to strangers," Pan said.

"They're not afraid of you, Pan?" Sylvia asked.

"Not any more, not these here. But I get the same welcome you've gotten if I stray too far."

The path now lay parallel to the sidehill and they walked along it more quickly to Pan's lean-to. Even John Reynolds was now more alive, his eyes darting quickly from place to place, cataloguing every detail of Pan's lifestyle. He walked around the lean-to, touching it, bending to examine the inside, asking questions about construction.

"You've had fire, Pan?" he asked when he saw the blackened earth between the hut and the rockface.

"Mm-hmm. Brought matched at first, then ran out and kept a bank of coals going. Perhaps we should have a fire now?"

"Oh, that'd be lovely, Pan," Sylvia said and giggled like a schoolgirl. "I haven't sat around a campfire since I was a very young woman."

"I've never tired of it," Pan said. "It kept me company. Kept me warm. Cooked my food. Gave me something to do, keeping it going." He gathered some sticks and built a little teepee over a handful of dried leaves. "Got a match?"

He smiled up at John, a warm, ingenuous smile which brought a faint but nevertheless unmistakable softening of the lines around John's mouth.

"Have you been lonely, Pan?" John asked as he fumbled for a book of paper matches in his coat pocket.

Pan took the matches, deliberately tore one from the pocket and carefully held it close to the dead leaves as he stroked a match and placed it under the pile. With his fingers he moved the leaves around until they were blazing, then just as methodically moved the twigs about until they too caught the flames.

"Lonely?" he said. He pulled a branch toward him and sat in front of the fire, gradually adding larger and larger sticks to it.

"No, I don't think I've actually been *lonely*. Alone, yes. Dreadfully alone, sometimes. But when you're lonely, you've got to be lonely *for* something, somebody, some*thing* that isn't where you're at."

"Longing, perhaps, Pan?" asked Sylvia. She had sat down near the fire, almost in the doorway to the lean-to, and she stretched her long thin legs out in front of her and leaned back on her straightened arms.

Pan thought a moment. "Longing? Yes, maybe that's the right word. Longing for something, but not really knowing what I was longing for. Perhaps just for companionship with my *own,* but not knowing who—or what—my own was, and not even knowing if there was anyone like that. I guess you might say I've spent two years looking into myself, looking for *me,* searching for an identity, not knowing who I am, not even knowing *what* I am."

John Reynolds had moved closer to the fire, holding his hands over it, his face in the shadows falling on the campsite as the sun dropped lower toward the invisible horizon on the backside of the mountain. Across the valley the shadows had crept almost to the top of the ridge and darkness was only an hour away.

John sat down on a log that Pan had long ago dragged up close to the fire. He felt a dull thudding in his chest and the palms of his hands were moist as he cradled a pipe and began stuffing it with tobacco. Where do I start? he asked himself. What kind of question do I begin with? They're both waiting for me, I know. This is my moment.

"Pan," he said, and saw Pan heave a deep sigh, almost one of relief, as if he also awaited the questions and was content to let them come.

"Pan," he said again, "I was a young man like you once. I was a biologist, but not just any biologist. I was a molecular biologist, working on the cells which make up every living thing. I had a dream, yes, you might

173

even call it a vision, of the work I had to do. I worked for ten years, night and day, on my dream, until there was nothing left in life except the culmination of my work. Finally I had it. I could have cried out 'Eureka,' like Archimedes when he discovered how to test the purity of gold. But I didn't. Instead, I spent another year tying up the loose ends, getting my data into publishable form, savoring the impact my paper would have on the world.''

Pan carefully laid several pieces of oak on the fire and crossed his ankles in front of him. He did not look up.

"I waited a few months too long," John continued. "Someone else had had the same dream, had duplicated my work and had beaten me into the scientific literature. At first I was incensed, then crushed. Nothing seemed important any more. For a year I performed routine, menial taks that any graduate biologist could have done. Then gradually I woke up. I knew I had the brains, the talent, whatever you want to call it, to rank with the greatest of the world's scientists. All I needed was an idea, and idea which no one else would have, that no one else could research and beat me to the punch."

Sylvia shifted her weight, watching her husband now with wide eyes, listeneing to the still powerful voice recount in a few words of obsession which had gripped not only him but her for forty years. Again she felt the magic of his dream and forgot the horror which it had begot.

"The idea came, and I was possessed by it. It became the touchstone of my life, and all other people and all other thoughts became subservient to it. If I was successful, my name would go down in history with Galileo, Darwin and the others who have changed the world with their ideas. I would eclipse the old masters like Lorenz and Tinbergen and the new heroes and heroines like Schaller and Goodal."

It was almost dark and the fire glinted in his eyes like sparks struck from flint. Restlessly he blew the ashes from the top of his pipe, took a deep drag on his pipe and blew smoke through his nostrils.

"You are the product of that dream, that vision, Pan. You hold within you the key to our future. Only you know what it feels like to descend from two kingly lines of Primates. Only you can reach back to the time ten million years ago when our two lines diverged, when a mutation took place that separated forever the genus *Pan* from the genus *Homo*. Think of it, Pan. You are unique. There has never been anyone like you before, in the history of the universe!"

Sylvia sat forward tensely, her eyes now fixed on Pan's face, waiting. She had expected questions from John Reynolds, not this. But perhaps he had asked a question, after all. A question which only Pan could understand and therefore a question which only Pan could answer.

"I do not feel unique, Dr. Reynolds."

The heavy cloak of evening lay upon the mountain and its hush permeated outwards from the campfire into the hills and valleys, outwards further still to the plains and tundra, the hamlets and villages and great cities spread thoughout the world where *Homo sapiens* had displayed his genius. It spread like ripples in a quiet pool where a struggling insect fought to avoid a soggy death. It spread like the giant tidal waves unleashed by the slippage of millions of tons of rock beneath a mighty ocean.

An owl hooted. A fox barked. A mosquito droned. And a young man put into words the final summation of a man's life work.

"I feel sorry for you, Dr. Reynolds. You have staked so much on so little. I can't answer your question any better than a first-grader who sees his cat having kittens, or a farmer struggling to save the life of a new-born calf, or an intern helping on his first delivery. You are

175

asking me to describe for you the mystery of life as it appears to the descendant of two forms of life.

"I don't *feel* any different that if I had been your natural offspring. I do not feel a stronger kinship with the apes than any other human does. I do not feel any more kinship with humans than another ape. I can only feel a sense of horror about the way in which I was created. Is that a human feeling, or an ape-like feeling? I *do* feel akin to the forest creatures, but not because I am part chimpanzee. There are many who must feel even more closely to the other animals of the mountains than I do. I have felt a closeness to everything here in Appalachia, the trees, the flowers, and the great pines that tower over us. But that feeling does not come because I am part plant!

"I now understand better why I have acted in such animal-like ways, but this does not come because any any detailed information you told me. I understand it *because* you told me, and did not understand it *before* you told me. I realize now that I came from two worlds, therefore am caught between two worlds, and cannot function well in either. Perhaps if I were *more* like a chimp, I could go back to Gombe Stream and live with my father's side of the family. Perhaps if I were *more* like a human, I could return with you and live at Standing Oaks.

"Don't you see, I'm *neither,* and *both*!"

Total darkness had come and the only light was the campfire. Sylvia was crying softly. John Reynolds sat slumped on the log, his arms folded, his pipe out, his eyes almost closed.

The sound of the wind in the pines came softly to them and a sudden breeze lifted a few sparks from the fire and they drifted slowly upwards and then were snuffed out, one by one.

Chapter 24

There was an awesome finality to Pan's simple state-
ment, "I do not feel unique, Dr. Reynolds." After hearing that brief yet harsh summary of Pan's reaction to his
unasked yet implied questions, Reynolds listened with
only half an ear to the rest of Pan's words. There could
be no further penetration of Pan's mind. There still
would be no vindication of the humanists, nor final
denunciation of the animalists.

The stark, utter finality was plain to see. Even the unconscious use of "Dr. Reynolds" instead of "Dad" or
"Father" had punctuated the sentence with a period,
not a comma nor even a semicolon or colon. The period
meant there was nothing more to be said. Nothing to be
added by Dr. John Reynolds, after all, to man's quest
for himself in the ethological quagmire of the biological
basis for animal behavior.

His dreams of a scientific breakthrough had become a
nightmare. He had created a new being,, a new form of
life. He had nourished his ego, had sustained his
desultory life with the persistent hope of someday being
able to sit down with that being and ask him questions.
Questions which, when answered, would unlock the
doors, solve riddles, unravel enigmas. Papers would be
written, books published, lectures given all over the
world. He would have vindicated Clarence Darrow's
brilliant defense of John Thomas Scopes and would
have driven another silver nail into the coffin of
William Jennings Bryan.

Watching the sparks dying in the blackness of that summer night, John Reynolds knew his dreams were just as dead. There was nothing more to do. His body shook with sobs, and his shrunken little body seemed to almost disappear as his mind closed in around him with an alien despair.

Sylvia crawled on hands and knees to his side and took the balding white head into her arms and rocked with him in silent rapport. She stroked his face and brushed the silvery locks with gnarled fingers.

"Hush, now, John," she whispered. "Hush now. You tried, you tried, you did all that a man could do. It's not your fault. It's not your fault. It's nobody's fault if Pan can't say any more. Come away now, John. Let's go home."

From across the fire Pan leaned forward awkwardly and reached out toward the couple on the old log. In his heart was a compassion such as he had never felt before for anyone or anything. He knew as well as Reynolds that this was the pitiful denouement of a potentially grand scheme to learn more about man and his relationship to other animals. And he wondered, as he sat crosslegged before the fire and the sounds of the night-forest crooned softly to him, if somehow he had failed them, if somehow he could still salvage something for them. Perhaps something could still be done.

He led the way slowly down the mountain, breaking brush and branches to make the way easier for the old couple. They climbed into the truck without a word to Jed, and he drove them through the silent woods to his shack. John Reynolds shook hands with Jed, his eyes wet but the tears dry on his cheeks. He turned to Pan and Pan put both his arms around the old man and held him for just a moment. There was nothing to say except, "Goodbye, Dad, I'll be in touch," and he knew he never would.

As Reynolds climbed into the passenger side of the car, Sylvia stood on tiptoes and kissed Pan on the cheek. "Come home whenever you want, Pan. We'll make a life for you, a good life. Standing Oaks will be yours someday. Soon." She was the strong one now.

When they had left, Pan thought at first, things would go easier. Perhaps he should have gone with them right then, but it would have been too hard. He would stay with Jed for a few more weeks, sifting out the experiences of the past two years in light of his talk with John and Sylvia. Then he would pick up and go home to that new life.

But it was not easier at all. He was not inwardly at peace and knew he never would be if he stayed with Jed. Each day brought a stronger desire to be gone from McWhirter's coulee, to get away from Jed Schroeder, his dark black eyes and his penetrating mind. He could scarcely conceal it from himself any more.

Each morning when he got up he was afraid he would have another of his "fits," that he would again dehumanize himself in front of Jed. On the mountain he never had to worry. No one was there to witness his trances. And oddly, it seemed to Pan, he could not remember having had any. And in fact he hadn't. If he had remembered the scene in Hamlet where Laertes says to Ophelia, "Be wary then, best safety lies in fear," he would have disagreed strenuously. Pan's best safety, he felt, lay in *never* having to fear. He would also have disagreed with Roosevelt when he cautioned the American people that the only thing they had to fear was fear itself.

He lay awake at night, wondering if there was some way he could predict when the moods would come upon him. Or was he forever doomed to sudden atavism, forever fey, forever Pan? His mind travelled the same paths it had followed so many times in the first few weeks on the mountains, searching inconclusively for the key act or word which would trigger the behavior which was now so loathsome and repellent to him. No, there was none. No more than there was for the schizophrenic who unconsciously slides from one personality to another, never able to predict or control the emergence or submergence of one or the other.

He added up his earnings in his mind and knew he had far more than enough to make the trip to Standing Oaks. But still he stayed on. It was almost as if he were waiting for something to happen which would make up his mind for him. But hadn't he already made the decision to go back? Then, turning that question over in his mind, he knew that actually he hadn't. All he had done was to decide to leave his mountain top, assuming that when he did so, he would go back to Standing Oaks.

And there he was, back at the starting point. Where could he go? To whom could he turn? Was there anyone, anyplace? He had thought that in the two years he would have exorcised the fear that drove him into the mountains. Now he realized it was not so. He had only postponed the inevitable confrontation with himself.

In those long, dark, restless nights, when the only sounds were Jed's wheezing snores and the coondog's thumping as he scratched his flea-bitten mange, Pan admitted ruefully that the two years had not been entirely wasted. He had developed a real consciousness of his being, had lifted himself to another level, but in so doing had merely come to realize that there was still another level of wisdom yet unattained. A level unattained unless he left the steady platform of reason. Reason does indeed "fling open the door to wisdom," as Maeterlinck said almost a hundred years ago, but *reason* places the soul on the defense, whereas true *wisdom* presses ever forward on the offense, a craving of the soul for love.

The moon had become full in the ten days since Pan had left the mountain, and it now threw an eerie light into the house. Lying on his side on the crude bed, Pan watched the skittering shadows of bats and large insects on the floor of the little cabin. A steady hum of mosquitoes filled the room, and one would occasionally land on Pan's exposed face or arms, but this was one thing he was used to and he ignored them.

More persistent was the steady hum of his own mind, restlessly drumming a new refrain through the menage of old and familiar thoughts. Catching the thread of this unfleshed idea, but not quite able to credit it, he silently padded across the room to the door and sat outside on the porch. The cadenced sawing of crickets' legs ceased for a moment, then began again. The high-pitched yap of a red fox sounded from across the valley and the nightwinds soughed in the white pines near the gate.

At first the notion seemed incredible, but the more he thought about it the more realistic it seemed. It would solve everyone's problem, his most of all, and certainly Jed's and the Reynolds'. And it would be so easy. He could walk up the mountain to any of a half dozen places where the deadly Amanita mushrooms grew. He would have an hour or two after he ate them to half-bury himself in the soft earth and brush of his favorite wildplum thicket on the rockface above his lean-to. And then he would await the inexorable poisoning of his nerve centers. If there was pain, he could stand it. If there was not, he would sleep and never awaken. It was a pleasant thought.

In the brilliant light of the old moon, the new thought grew more and more tenable. He knew, as had Death when he spoke to the Plowman, that "he is a fool who laments a mortal's death." But had Pan been a reader, and had read further in the Plowman's chronicle, he would have found these words, "Best to die when one seeketh most to live. He hath not died well who desired death . . ."

Upon Pan fell an immense ennuei, a sudden draining of the very fire of his life, a loss of the cohesiveness which produces tenacity, an attrition of enthusiasm which stirs the body to act and the mind to think. He curled up on the porch and slept, and even the old coon-dog's wet nose on his cheeks did not awaken him.

In the morning, when Jed's crutch poked him gently in the ribs, he forgot for a moment his last thoughts before going to sleep, but then they returned in full force, burrowing into his belly like the short sword of the *sepuku*-seeking Samurai. He winced as if physically stricken, and Jed did not fail to notice it.

"Up and at'm, got to get goin', boy," he said. "Fresh side's in the pan, and coffee's a-bilin' in the pot."

"Great, Jed. Let's put a little of that side into the Pan." He stuck his finger into his solar plexus so Jed wouldn't fail to get the pun.

And Jed roared. "That's a good'n. C'mon, boy. We ain't gettin' a very good start this mornin'. Sun's halfway up the puckerbrush."

Pan poured the coffee while Jed forked the bacon on-to the old white china plate.

"You know, Pan," Jed said in his best English, "I been thinking. There really ain't no need for you to go back to your place up north, if you don't want to. If I'm not too forward, you being white and me black, and this being the South, you could stay here and work for me and finish your schoolin' down in the village till you get your feet back on the ground."

"I've thought about that, Jed. I really have. And I don't think it'd work. Not because you're black and I'm white—God knows that wouldn't stop me—but because if I'm ever going to get back on the track, it'll have to be where I came from. Even if I did say I'd never go back."

"All right, Pan, whatever you say. But the offer's there. Just like a check you ain't cashed. Always there. Won't bounce either."

"I know it, Jed. I know it."

Chapter 25

Jed sniffed the air as they climbed into the truck, then looked into the southwest where a thunderhead loomed over the mountain. "Rain in the air, Pan. That'n over there'll miss us, but we'll get it sometime today, I'll bet."

"Won't take that bet, Jed."

"Thought maybe we'd burn some brush today, but that wind's a mite strong for a controlled burn. Better we should stick to the girdlin'. That way we can always hop into the truck if the lightnin' gets too fierce."

He drove slowly between the two massive white pines which marked the gate, then picked up speed a little as they coasted down the hill to the valley below. Thunder rumbled from the rainstorm in the south and dust-devils spun in the road ahead of them. About a mile from the shack, he slowed and turned into a well-used track which ran north along the small stream. Pan knew this stream well for he had foraged for mushrooms along its banks in spring and fall for two years, and he had picked the beautiful yellow marsh marigolds there each spring. It arose from springs in a five or six acre bog only a few hundred yards from Pan's lean-to.

They followed the narrowing track almost to the base of Pan's mountain home, then angled northeast past the now deserted lodge, swung around the base of another mountain, and climbed it from the other side. Near the top the track disappeared into the brush and Jed stopped the truck and got out.

"Gonna' show you something, Pan."

Only a deer-trail gave them some relief from the snagging thickets and briar-patches. Then the big trees began, beech and oak and maple, and the underbrush almost disappeared. Further on, scattered cedars grew desultorily in the shade and Jed informed Pan that this was where they would be girdling today. But they pushed on to the crest of the mountain and started down the other side. Before they had gone far, however, Jed stopped and pointed across the valley to the mountain almost a mile away.

Pan stared open-mouthed. Near the top of the mountain was a white patch of yellow limestone, and at the base of it was his camp. He couldn't make out the lean-to, but anyone with binoculars could have. And even at that distance, any movement could easily have been detected.

"You knew all the time, didn't you, Jed?"

Jed nodded.

"Did anyone else ever come up here?"

"The boss did. Once. When he was looking over that cedar growth we just came through."

"Did he see me over there?"

"Never said nothin' if'n he did."

Without another word, Jed walked back to the other side of the hill and picked up the crosscut saw they had left there. Pan followed him slowly. So that's how Jed knew exactly where to come, he thought, when he promised my mother he'd find me. Without thinking, he peeled the bark off a basswood tree and chewed on it. Jed saw him and laughed. Pan looked absently at the bark, wondered for a moment why Jed was laughing, then tossed it into the brush with a chuckle.

The handle of the saw felt good, smoothed by the

years of rough callouses, darkened by the sweat of countless hands. The jagged, offset teeth caught for a moment on the bark like barbs on a wire fence, sank quickly and noisily through the coarse epidermis into the softer layer of phloem and then grated on the wood itself. As the sound changed, Jed and Pan shifted their feet to keep the blade out of the tree itself, and in this way worked their way around the tree. They completed the cut, then worked back around the tree at a lower level, in the opposite direction to give different muscles the major work.

Tree after tree they girdled, leaving them standing, doomed to die before leafing out again. So easy to take the life of a tree, Pan thought. Or to pull a carrot or pick a cherry or slice off a shoot of asparagus. So easy to catch a fish or shoot a quail, or down a deer with bow or rifle. So easy to kill a man, even if that man is oneself. It all depends on where you drew the line in your own personal code of death-ethics. Some people curse the deer-slayer, yet nonchalantly watch the throes of a majestic twenty-pound pike in the bottom of a canoe. Others condemn *all* hunters of beast and bird and fish. It all depends on where you draw the line.

If only, Pan thought, I could kill off just *part* of me. And knew he couldn't. For he was Pan.

Towering in the sky above, cumulus clouds reached to the heavens, black as pitch and rumbling with the voice of Zeus. The winds swept across the valley from Pan's mountain-camp to the cedar seedlings where Pan and Jed drove iron spikes into the mature growth of unneeded and unwanted giants so that the whims of man might be satisfied.

Jed looked up as a stong blast of moisture laden air struck his back. "Best we head for the truck, Pan," he said, "before we takes a tree or the lightning itself on our heads."

186

But Pan was not listening.

He stood with his face to the wind, the lean, hard, bronzed muscles of neck and chest standing out in cords, hands clenched and forearms steeled, abdominal muscles taut as if for an expected blow, knees slightly bent and feet widespread. A raindrop plopped, and then another, and still a third, and then the forest floor echoed with the rising roar of the torrential rain, a surging reverberation of wind and water.

"Pan," Jed shouted, but he might have shouted to Zeus himself.

Pan's whole body shook with a brief but violent spasm, the rigid hauteur of his face relaxed and Jed thought he had won. But without a backward look, Pan started climbing the ridge, one heavy step at a time. Rain streamed from his long blond hair and down his face and ran in rivulets from his chin. He never once looked to either side, and brushed the bushes and saplings out of his way as if they were nothing.

At the top of the ridge he paused to look out across the valley into the very center of the storm. The wind beat against his face and sent sharpened little pains into his eyes. Until now he had been silent, but slowly he began to hoot, drawing deep gasping breaths and then sending ever-louder screams across the hills. In the middle of one prolonged, eerie wail, a lightning bold and thunder clap hit simultaneously only yards from where he stood and the sickening sweet stench of charred wood and ozone filled the air.

His feet tingling painfully from the electrical charge which had coursed through them, Pan lifted first one foot and then the other, swaying slightly from side to side, almost swaggering in a rhythmical dance, his voice stilled now in the raging storm. Then again he hooted, panted, hooted again, louder and louder and faster and faster, his voice a crescendo of howls and screams which

Jed could hear a hundred yards down the hill. Pan's fists were raised against the wind, his face contorted in actual pain, his mind and soul ranging the rainforests of western Tanzania.

With one final bellow of indignation and paroxysm of wrath, Pan charged down the hillside at full speed, unmindful of the brush and smaller trees, leaping windfalls, hurdling stumps, the personification of panic. Past Jed he charged, then grabbed at a small tree to break his rush and swung around it and leaped into the lower branches, where he sat motionless while the rain pelted on his head and back.

Jed had turned to watch the display, frightened to his very core, knowing the bewitchment had returned, or had never been dispelled. He looked up at Pan, only a few yards away from him in the tree, and caught his eyes. Instead of seeing the devil himself as he had expected, he saw rather the beautiful blue eyes pleading without guile, tormented blue eyes singing Jed's soul with pity. Jed put out his hand, but it was too late, or perhaps there had never been time.

Pan leaped from the tree, plodded slowly up the slope and stood at the crest again, driven, maddened, demented. But no, none of these. Merely performing the normal acts of a male chimpanzee caught in a rainstorm, knowing his whole troop of kin were sitting in the trees around him watching his show of courage.

Down the slope he charged again, this time tearing off the limb of a tree and brandishing it like a weapon above his head, then stopped abruptly and hurled it ahead of him into the slashing rain. He tore off another limb and trailed it behind him, stopping only to rip it through the brush when it caught in the dense undergrowth. For half an hour he continued, slowly tiring, but always struggling up the slope to begin the downward charge again.

Finally, unable to continue, he climbed one more time, stood upright in the driving rain and flashing lightning, and leaned against a tree, his back to Jed. Slowly he turned his head and looked down the slope at Jed as if in farewell, as if the curtain were about to fall on the performance, and shuffled across the ridge and disappeared on the other side.

Chapter 26

The rainstorm subsided as quickly as it had come, leaving the mountains sodden and dripping. Pan slipped and slid down the slope, frequently catching at trees and bushes to slow his descent. Occasionally he stopped to brush the water out of his eyes and bomb back his sorry hair with his fingers. He had lost his moccasins, but his feet were tough and he hardly noticed. The leather shirt which he had made so long ago and had cleaned carefully at Jed's place clung soggily to his shoulders and he shrugged frequently to loosen the tight feeling.

There was a subtle difference in his posture compared to an hour before. He slumped slightly, noticeable even in the position he had to maintain in the descent. His head was thrust forward on his neck. His arms swung more loosely and he sometimes turned sideways in order to use all four limbs in clambering downward.

As he neared the jeep track on which he and Jed had climbed the mountain several hours before, he heard the roar of the truck above him. Quickly and silently he melted into the bushes beside the track and waited. The truck ground by him, Jed's anxious face peering out the open window, then disappeared in the forest. Pan waited several more minutes, then cautiously crawled out of his hiding place. Before getting up, he rolled over on his back in the mud, one foot grasped tightly in both hands, and picked at a splinter in the sole. He stood upright then, and followed the track past the lodge to the junction of the road toward Jed's place and the track to his old mountain-home.

He bore to the right, ignoring completely the more travelled road to Jed's shack, crossed the stream where he had mushroomed so often, and started up the trail to the lean-to. A gentle rain was still falling, but the wind had subsided and the woods were quiet except for the steady drip of water from the trees onto the dead brown leaves blanketing the hillsides. There were no birdsongs, no animal calls, nothing but the slurp-slurp-slurp of Pan's feet as his toes dug into the soft soil and pushed him upwards.

He reached the end of the manmade part of the trail and slipped noiselessly through the tangle of brush onto his own beaten-down pathway through the forest. Furtively he crept up the trail, stopping frequently to listen for alien sounds. Once he knelt down to examine a track in the mud, and finding it to be an old one, continued upwards.

Fifty yards from his lean-to, he stopped and stood with one hand grasping the shoulder-high limb of a dead aspen. He seemed bemused, as if thinking, wondering what he would do next. Stealthily he lowered his hand from the branch and stole forward, watching the trail ahead of him, occasionally flicking his eyes from side to side. The lean-to was unoccupied, dry inside as it had always been in the violent storms.

Pan stooped to peer inside, then stood up and tore away the ridgepole, broke it in the middle, and threw the pieces as far as he could. The tattered remnants of the canvas tarpaulin shredded and the overlain bark shingles collapsed in a heap. Pan scattered them with his feet until there was nothing left to show where he had lived for two years except a blackened, grassless spot where his cookfire had been. He sat hunched on the wet ground, a faint mist rising from his shoulders as his sweat vaporized and condensed in the cold spring air.

He was tired, wet, hungry, homeless. He was alone.

He was Pan.

He was Pan as he had never been before. It was as if his 47th chromosome had broken free of the domination of the other 46, no longer subject to the checks and balances of *Homo sapiens*. He had been set free to range the broad upland forests, unmindful of the rain and incognizant of the sun. He was no longer the same Pan who had seemed heir to Penelope's gentle humanness, who had only occasionally been subject to the whims of the alter-ego Pan of Herme's descent.

The clouds broke open and a single shaft of sunlight poured through the rent to warm the mountain-top. A subdued yellow light turned the limestone cliff above Pan to irridescent gold and a light mist drifted across the valley below. Pan struggled out of his sodden leather shirt and leather pants and lay them to dry on the rocks at the base of the cliff.

Satisfied now that there was nothing left of his camp to be seen from the mountain across the valley, he set out in search of food. It was too early for marsh marigolds, too early for ground mushrooms, far too early for berries and fruits. He walked down the hill to the small bog where he had so often found cattail shoots this time of the year and filled his stomach with the tender plants, digging in the spongy tussocks with his fingers until he uncovered them. He squatted at the edge of the bog and chewed thoughtfully on the slightly astringent delicacies.

His belly full, his body drying in the late evening sun, his muscles restored to strength after the tiring display on the other mountain, Pan sat happily in the forest he had thought he could leave and couldn't. Without consciously voicing the idea, even in the silence of his inner being, he knew he had finally, really come home.

No more for him dread thoughts of death, no more the fear of falling fits, no more the push and pull of the civilized world on his shattered personality. He was Pan, and he would live as Pan.

Grunting slightly with the effort, he rose to his feet and climbed the mountain, past the site of the old lean-to, around the corner of the rockface where the stream trickled down to the bog, and up to the wild-plum thicket where he had hidden from the nosy pointer. He sat at its edge, idly gazing out over the valley below, then across to the mountain where he had left Jed just a few hours before. Behind him the sun was setting, its last golden rays slowly climbing the distant mountains to the east, leaving the forest below in gradually deepening shadow.

A high-pitched staccato whir sounded in a huge white pine and Pan looked up into the branches in time to see a tiny red squirrel disappear into the crotch of the tree. The evening sounds of birds preparing for sleep surrounded him, lulling him with their lilting lullabies. A spotted fawn strolled down the hillside only yards away, and behind her came the doe, peering anxiously at Pan, yet apparently unafraid. Pan stared at her and smiled. She acknowledged the gesture of friendship by dipping her head to feed on the mast dropped last fall by beech and oak.

Pan crawled into the plum thicket, curled up in a tight ball, hugged his knees with powerful arms, and slept.

Chapter 27

For three years Pan lived on his mountain-top, free and devoid of fear. His body, already tough and hard, became even more rugged and iron-hard. He rolled up his leather shirt and pants and cached them in a dry crevice in the rockface below his aerie, and went naked except for a leather breech-clout which he held in place with a leather thong around his waist. Rarely did he cut his hair or trim his beard, and soon his face and head was a mass of red-blond hair, usually reasonably clean because he loved to bathe in the stream at the foot of his mountain. But in winter when he was loathe to immerse himself in the icy water, his hair and beard became matted and caked with oil and dirt.

He lived as he had done before his abortive visit to Jed's shack, except now he did not have fire, nor did he miss it. He roamed his square mile of forest, eating what he could find, when he was hungry. He used a pointed stick to dig roots, and two rocks to break open the acorns. He collected great clumps of clover and carried them to a saltlick where he dipped them in brine and chewed them whole. As before, he ate the young shoots of milkweed and the delicious young plants of the nettles. He no longer could boil and burdock stalks nor the wild violets, but he learned to eat them raw, and found their strength-giving properties no less.

So his body remained firm and sturdy. Since there was no one to give him a cold or the flu, he remained singularly unaffected by communicable disease. With a sharp-ended stone he cut out splinters from his feet and hands, and lanced boils which appeared on his legs from thorns and brambles. As Jed had taught him to do, he crushed the juicy leaves and stems of the shade-loving jewelweed and held them on insect bites and stings until the soothing poultice eased the pain.

But as his body toughened, so did his mind. Slowly, by the day and by the week, as the years rolled by, he remembered less and less of Standing Oaks, of John and Sylvia Reynolds, of Jed Schroeder and his coondog in the valley. In the years before he went out to Jed's, he had often sat in a tall tree, or on a rotting log, and thought longingly of the "outside world," but now he seldom did. If he thought at all, it was to plan his food-hunts or to think out a route of escape if the hunters in the valley seemed to be moving too close.

When it rained, he crawled under an overhanging shelf of vegetation or into the thick stands of young white pines on the back side of his mountain home. There he would sit, head bowed and arms clasped around his knees, until the rain abated. Several times the urge to perform a rain-dance came upon him, but strangely he was able to dispel the compulsion, even the one time a bolt of lightning struck only a hundred yards away.

Periodically he was subject to a desire for meat which was almost like a craze. He would awaken with an aching in his belly and he knew he had to find meat. Munching on acorns would modify the strong urge somewhat, but always he would have to spend the day searching for meat. Squirrels were the most plentiful, but almost impossible to stalk or ambush. Without a gun or knife, the bigger game like deer and bear were out of the question. So he turned to rabbits to ease his hunger. He knew their warrens, down near the valley floor, and for hours he would sit motionless near the den-mouths until one came close enough to grasp with his bare hands. He would squeeze the neck until the rabbit died, then smash its head against a tree to make sure it did not revive. The pelt stripped off easily and he would sit gleefully tearing at the succulent red meat with his strong teeth.

His meat-hunger usually lasted for several weeks before diminishing, then left as quickly as it had come, and he could return to roots and plants again. Without knowing it, he was following the patern set for Hermes and his clan in the rain-forests of far-away Africa. There they would hunt in teams for bushbucks, bushpigs, baboons, monkeys, and even African babies when other game was scarce. But as long as there were plenty of rabbits, Pan was not interested in other kinds of meat.

The summer of his fourth year came early. In the valleys where he cut cattails and burdock the heat was oppressive, but on the mountaintops there was almost always a breeze. He awakened with the sun, fed for several hours, then stretched out in the shade through the noontime heat, and fed again when the shadows began to lengthen across the ravines and glades.

One morning in late May, when the dogwoods had shed their big, white, flower-like leaves and a blue mist hung heavily in the air, Pan awoke to a strange sound. Below him, near the jeep-track where the hunters had once parked their truck, he heard the unmistakable sound of girlish voices and the clatter of pots and pans. Pan sat up, rubbing the sleep from his eyes, instantly alert. How had they come there, he wondered, without his knowing it? During the night, obviously, but why?

He sat silently for almost an hour, listening to the voices, wondering what he should do, wondering what they were going to do. Feminine voices in his hermitage were alien to his ears, almost unremembered as if from someone else's distant past. A peal of laughter echoed up the slopes, echoed in his memory like a stone dropped in an empty well.

Stirring in the depths of his long-submerged recollections was the vision of a pretty, raven-haired schoolgirl whom he had once thought of as *his* girl, even though she had never returned his affection. So he had not pursued her, had only concentrated on sending her pleasant visions of sunny afternoons in fields blooming with daffodils and fall walks through maple trees blazing in the forest. She had felt compelled to recount these delightful fantasies to him, and he was satisifed.

Could she be here? No, but someone with a laugh like hers was down there, fixing breakfast on an open fire. He could smell the bacon frying, the scent wafting upwards as the sun heated the mountain.

Soundlessly, he crept from his plum-thicket, down the beaten trail to the upper end of the jeep-track. Carefully, step by step, he cut across the hillside through the forest until he could see the campsite without being seen. There, pitched under a giant white pine, was a small blue and yellow tent, its peak anchored to one of the lower branches of the tree. Two girls sat beside a fire, eating from paper plates. Propped against the tree were two blaze-orange backpacks, and through the open flaps of the tent Pan could see two partially unzipped sleeping bags, one dark brown and the other a deep blue. The ground was already littered with the odds and ends of camping gear and clothes. The scent of the mosquito repellent mixed oddly with the cooking odors.

Pan squatted behind a bush, slowly comprehending that these girls were intending to stay for a while. There was already a subtle permanence in the taut guy-ropes of the tent, the cooking stones arranged to hold the pots

197

and frypan, and the relaxed attitudes of the girls themselves. He sensed that he should make his way back up the hill to his solitary outpost where he could keep track of the girls without any chance of discovery. But instead, he stayed and watched, held by curiosity and a strange new feeling coursing through his veins.

The girls were young, of college age, and dressed for the out-of-doors. One, a slightly chubby brunette, was dressed in a rough khaki shirt, frayed at the collar, borrowed from her father's cast-off Army clothes many years before. She wore tight-fitting bluejeans, faded and frayed from hard wear. Her hair was cut very short with just a slight curl at the neck and wispy bangs on her forehead. Her eyes were green, bright and intelligent and frequently darting around into the forest as if looking for something or someone. She scratched her perky nose with the back of her hand and sniffed. Her voice was soft and melodious, steeped in the local drawling cadence.

Her friend was slim and angular, almost bony, but moved with a gracefulness that even Pan could appreciate. Her hair was long, hanging almost to her shoulders, thick and black as an Indian maiden's, arching upwards in thick waves from her brow on both sides of a central part. Her face reflected a slightly arrogant calmness, the high cheekbones and long sculptured nose balanced perfectly in her haughty face. She would have been cast classically as the beggar-poet's daughter in "Kismet." She too wore a faded bluejeans, but unlike her friend, wore a light-colored, short-sleeved blouse.

When she spoke it was with the crisp accent of New England. "Jennifer," she said, "Why do you keep looking around? Nothing here to be afraid of, is there, bears or something?"

Jennifer giggled. "Haven't you heard of our famous

mountain man?''

"Your what?''

"Oh, Pheobe, there's been a rumor for years that someone lives here in these mountains. A hermit, like. But
without a house or fire or anything.''

"You mean,'' Phoebe asked incredulously, "he lives
off the land, without a hut or a gun or *anything*? Just
lives in the *woods*?''

"Oh, it's just talk, I reckon. Nobody's really seen
him, unless it might be Jed Schroeder over in the next
coulee, and he don't *talk* about it. Just looks up at the
sky or wanders off when someone mentions it. But he
did have a young fellow worked for him a few years
back, everyone remembers that, and my mother says he
came in here and never came out. But you know how
mountain folks talk.''

Phoebe stirred some powdered milk into her coffee
and leaned against the big pine tree. Her brows knitted
thoughtfully as she watched the swirling powder
dissolve in the cup. She cradled the cup in both hands
and blew across the surface, then sipped carefully. "A
young fellow? Our age?''

"About. No one knows. If its the same one my
mother saw in the restaurant five years ago he might be
twenty-one or twenty-two now. Big blond guy, handsome, with funny blue eyes.''

"My God. Five years. Must be nuts.''

"Phoebe, it's just a story!''

Phoebe nodded slowly, her black springy hair un-
dulating rhythmically on either side of her beautiful
face. She threw back her head to drain the coffee cup,
eyes closed tightly against the streaming sunlight.

For the next three days the girls camped at the foot of
the big white pine. They walked the forest trails
together, stopping often to study a ground-plant or a
shrub or to inspect a flower or mushroom. They had

sketch pads, and drew the leaves of the trees, then labeled them with the help of small paper-back keys. They
climbed the hills, always following the jeep-tracks or
walking trails, carefully recording in their note-books
the varied flora of the mountains.

Several times they put aside their books and papers
and fished for trout in the shaded pools of the little
streams which rushed down the brushfilled ravines. A
few small trout actually found their way into the beer-
batter of the frying pan, but the bigger ones had nothing
to fear from the girls' efforts.

In the evenings they built a crackling pinebrush fire,
then added rolling-pin sized birch and aspen pieces for a
slow-burning, coal-forming flame. Sitting cross-legged
before it with sweater or jacket over their shoulders for
protection against the cool night air, they talked about
they day's interesting finds, or about the rareness of
their wilderness experience, and sometimes about boys,
or religion, or movies they had seen. Then eventually
the conversation would falter, subside to occasional
words or brief comments, and finally cease altogether,
each girl studying the embers of the fire with heavy-
lidded eyes, reluctant to admit that the day was over so
soon.

As the fire went out and the cold crept in, they slipped
out of bluejeans and shirts, into wooly nightclothes,
crawled into their sleeping bags and zipped down the
mosquito netting. Pleasantly tired in mind and body,
they said their goodnights, and Pan would steal silently
up the mountain to his plum thicket above the rockface.

On the third night, he curled up in his usual fetal position, prepared to go to sleep as usual, wondering when
the girls would leave his territory. But this night he
couldn't sleep. He rolled over on his back, wide awake,
remembering the dark eyes and raven hair of the lissome
girl in faded bluejeans. She aroused in him sensations he

had repressed for almost five years. Like a monk, or a modern-day priest, he had slowly driven his sensuality into the subconscious, had conquered with sheer will-power the sexual fantasies which come normally to all human beings, especially the young. Without stimuli from television, magazines, and women themselves, he had found it increasingly easy to live an asexual life.

Restlessly he rolled from side to side, sat up, lay back down, got up and stood in the center of his thicket and turned his head to the stars blazing above him. Hunters like himself filled the sky, Orion most prominent and doomed by Apollo to forever patrol the empyrean with sword and club. And there was Sagittarius, the Archer, already with drawn bow, half-man, half-beast, a centaur, not unlike Pan himself. Leo was there, representing the king of the hunting beasts, who had been hunted himself and killed by Hercules and raised into the heavens by Jupiter to honor the deeds of Hercules. But Pan did not see them as figures in the sky, did not know them by their deeds, saw only that their radiance filled the night with lustrous yearnings.

Pan knew in that moment that he wanted that girl, needed her, must have her. His mind, long unused to problems greater than what next to eat, stumbled blindly through the long hours of darkness, shaping plans which would never work, grasping at strategies he knew would be discarded in the cool light of morning. Twice, in a towering, uncontrollable surge of desire he broke out of his thicket and stumbled down the hillside toward the sleeping girls. But each time he regained control of himself and stole sheepishly back to his nest above the rockface.

All the next day he paced the mountaintop, tearing at bushes and saplings and venting his lust in narcissistic outpourings of his masculinity on the ground. He ate little, snatching at the orange-red, beefsteak mushrooms

201

on the oak trees or crunching last year's half-rotten acorns with his teeth. The searing of frustration drove him half mad and burned in his eyes. He knew he could never go down to the girls in his present condition. They would be terrified beyond all words. If they had a gun, they would kill him. If they didn't, one or both would run off to Jed Schroeder's or the village and soon the woods would resound with the boots of dozens of men. He would be hunted down and killed like an animal. And for what? For trying to associate with his own kind.

Late in the afternoon Pan's rage began to abate. He was exhausted from a sleepless night and a devil-driven day. A light rain began to fall as he climbed to the summit of the mountain behind his plum-thicket lair, and up to the very highest branch in the tallest white pine there. He pulled in a few branches under him, and slept. But just before sleeping, his agile mind turned over the final stages of a plan which had been developing all afternoon. It would work. It had to work. It had to work or he was through. There would be no turning back now.

Chapter 28

Silently dusk crept over higher on the mountain until the last rays of the sun were pushed off the peaks and darkness was everywhere in the blue-black hills. The rain had stopped toward evening, and still Pan slept on his pine-tree nest. Rivulets of water ran off his brawny shoulders. He unwound his arms from around his massive legs and sprawled backward along the tree limb, then slept again.

A whispery wind soughed through the treetops, sending showers of water from leaves and branches onto the ground below. An owl hooted from its perch in the crotch of a giant oak tree, only to jump off into space again. Padding softly on rubber-soled feet, a black bear left its feast of termites and crawled into a thicket to sleep till dawn lit the world again. The forest was alive with nocturnal creatures suddenly brave enough to use the same living space used by day-feeding animals.

Phoebe and Jennifer built their fire between the stones and heated a can of Dinty Moore beef stew, giggling like schoolgirls over some little joke.

Pan stretched, scratched his groin idly, then sat up and looked out over the forest toward the faint glow in the valley where the girls were camped. Swiftly he slid down the tree and dropped lightly onto the damp pine-needles carpeting the earth. He scraped together a handful of needles and crammed them hungrily into his mouth, chewed thoughtfully for a moment or two, then quickly but quietly set off toward the south, down the mountainside to the main trail which he and Jed had followed into the hills three years before. He paused at the edge of the road, listened for alien sounds, heard none, and loped down the road toward Jed's.

He ran easily, almost effortlessly, his leather breechclout slapping rhythmically on his thighs and buttocks, his eyes piercing the blackness ahead of him and his feet following the track unerringly in the dark. The trail met the main road which climbed slowly to the white pines marking Jed's path. The coondog grunted, identified the visitor without hesitation and slunk back under the porch.

Pan stood in the bright starlight, glad the moon was new and already set. For almost a half hour he remained motionless, listening for the sound of a creaking bed or the rustle of bare feet on the floor of the little cabin. He then moved around to the little window in back where he had so often watched birds and animals feeding in the trees on the slope. Again he stood silently, listening, and now could hear the slow, even breathing of the sleeping black.

With the shadowy stealth of a stalking lioness, Pan returned to the front door, opened it an inch at a time, crossed the creaky floor to his own cot, and felt for the blanket roll he had left there a lifetime before. Knowing it had to be there, he was not surprised when his hand fastened on it. He lifted it carefully, weighing it unconsciously and sensing that it contained all he had put in it when he had gathered together his belonging and met Jed in the trail.

Jed would notice its absence in the morning, would know immediately where it had gone and who had taken it, and might be hurt because Pan had felt it necessary to come like a thief in the night for his own gear. But then he would just as quickly discern that it had to be that way, and would no longer be hurt and no longer wonder. He would sit on his front porch in the warm morning sun and bid Pan godspeed.

Noiselessly Pan closed the door, padded softly across the unpainted boards, and soundlessly bounded onto the hard clay path and set off at a miler's pace for his old campsite under the lee of the rockface. He crouched beside the trickling springhole and untied his blanket roll. There were his frypan, cooking pot, hunting knife, pocketknife, panpipes, carborundum stone, wire snares, traps, rolls of new twine, and few other things he had forgotten he owned.

He leaned back against a tree stump and with a swishing of steel on stone he sharpened the small blades of the pocketknife and the cold stainless steel of the long hunting knife. When he was done he ran his thickly calloused finger along the razor-sharp edges and smiled quietly to himself. He hefted the big knife, balancing it with thumb and fingers, sensing without verbalizing that it was an instrument to be used for cutting roots and for cutting flesh, a tool or a weapon.

With the slightest hint of hesitation, he reached up with his left hand and grasped a handful of hair. The hunting knife flashed in smooth, linear strokes through the three-year growth, and then worked its way around onto Pan's face, slower now, but with brutal frankness. The bleached blond hairs from his head mixed on the ground with the reddish blond hairs from his face and he ran his toes through the silky pile. Lots of microscope pointers, he thought idly to himself, then stood up straight with sudden realization that he had not thought of a microscope (or any other modern instrument) for years. It sobered him, and he sat down on the ground and ran his fingers through the soft hair.

These hairs, he thought, were once a part of me, but now are cut off, banished from me and my life forever. There is no way they can be engrafted onto me again or any other living being. They will die, wither, decay, break up into thousands of tiny segments, then finally into millions and billions of molecules of protein which will find their way into the grass or the trees, or float down the mountain in a rainstorm and be absorbed into a fish or a crawdad or a worm. And then they may become part of me again, if I eat that fish or a bird that ate the worm. It is too late for me to remain part of the human experiment, too late to rejoint he human race? Or have I already been cut off? Subdivided. Annihilated. Decayed. Cast off, estranged, insularized? Am I like those beautiful blond tresses, of no use now until they are dismembered? Am I of no use now until I am just as dead and just as decayed? Would I be better off, physically dead, than I am now, spiritually dead? He remembered the night when he had seriously contemplated suicide. Maybe that was still the best solution.

He closed his eyes and drew down the black curtain between his eyeballs and his brain. He had not tried to communicate with anyone for so long that at first he had a little trouble with the total concentration necessary. Drawing his feet up under him, he bowed his head almost to the ground until the blood ran red before the dark screen and scintillating lights flashed intermittently like stars blinking through the smog of a great city. The gray fog lifted and long wavering lights flowed like the aurora borealis and he saw shimmering on the screen first the raven-black hair and then the slate-gray eyes of the girl called Pheobe.

Then a strange thing happened, something which had never before occurred in any of his auto-hypnotic trances. She smiled, not so much with her mouth, but with her eyes, and not looking directly at him, because he was not looking at her with *his* eyes, but into the far distance, as if she saw a sail on the sea or a dust-trail on the desert. As if she was searching the horizon for something she wanted to find and now fancied she saw. The vacancy of his real mind could not cope with this innovation and the face disappeared from his view like a mirror image when the lights are dimmed.

More slowly now, and with greater care, he trimmed his hair to about the same length it had been when he first came to these mountains. He splashed cold water on his face and shaved off his beard, leaving long sideburns down to his jawline. He debated about the mustache, then finally cut it off also. Twice he had to hone the knife and several times he made small nicks in his tender skin, but finally he was done.

Next he removed the dirty, oily, breechclout, sat in the trickle of water from the spring, and scrubbed himself all over using clumps of leaves as a washing cloth. He stood up and brushed the water off, then felt his way along the lower edge of the rockface until he found the cache into which he had stuffed his rolled-up shirt and pants. They were dry, dusty, smelled of mold, but they were intact. He carried them to the spring, rinsed them off, and lay them on the bushes to dry in the night breeze.

He had no shoes nor even the moccasins he had fashioned so long ago, but he could do nothing about that now. He remembered that he had once seen the moccasins on the mountain where he had kicked them off, but they had been exposed to rain and sun and would be useless even if he could find them in the dark.

With a start he realized that the stars were beginning to fade with the false dawn and he had not slept for two nights. He was suddenly aware of an extreme fatigue and with great difficulty he gathered his belongings onto the blankets and rolled them up. With the blanket roll under one arm and his clothes under the other, he laboriously clambered up the steep slope to his plum-thicket and crawled through the tunnel of twigs and leaves to his lair. He unrolled the blankets, put on under him, and one over him, and fell into a deep sleep.

A black-capped chickadee hopping along his leg awoke him in mid-morning. He opened one eye, then the other, and watched the little bird as it cocked its head and twittered merrily. It flitted away, up into the trees, and pecked at almost invisible insect eggs on the tiniest twigs. Oh, to be a bird, thought Pan, and be able to just flutter around in the trees all day, minding only the sure instincts bequeathed him by an unbroken line of identical ancestors. Not torn by two conflicting strains of antecedents, not driven by forces he needed to examine and work out in order to survive.

He walked slowly along the ridge, rubbed his hand against the smoothness of his face, and savored the odd sensation of contentment. He pulled a few new shoots of a poison sumac, peeled the rind, and chewed on the sweet meat like a cane of sugar candy. His faded brown leathers were dry and he pulled on the pants, noticing that they were slightly loose around the waist but tight on his thighs. The shirt felt snug also and he shrugged his shoulders restively at the unaccustomed restriction of movement. With a tinge of sadness he rolled up the dirty breechclout and tucked in into the hole in the rocks which had protected his clothes for three years.

With an aching poignancy in his heart he climbed the tallest tree on the mountain—a massive white pine which dwarfed every other tree in the area—and stood in the loftiest crotch which would support his weight. Three times he shifted his position to face in the four directions of the compass, savoring the desolate loneliness of his aerie one more time. His final stance placed him facing the east where he could see the winding jeep-track on which the girls were camped. He could not see their tent, but he could make out the tree under which it was pitched.

He was ready.

And he knew he was still Pan. But he also understood better than ever before that this was his last chance to break with the legacy of Hermes and place his inheritance from Penelope into the forefront. If he did not make it now, he never would, and must then face the choice of instant deliverance from this life, or resignation to a truncated life as the off-spring of Hermes ten thousand miles from home.

Chapter 29

A soft, warm summer breeze riffled the silvery-green leaves of the young aspens lining the track as Pan walked slowly along it. The cloying sweetness of ripening clover filled the air and a couple of times Pan reached down to clutch a clump and pop it into his mouth. He chewed methodically, sucking the juices and spitting out the residue like used-up gum. Several times he stroked his chin and found again the bushy beard gone. The corners of the eyes which Jenny's mother had called "soft, not hard and bright like most people with blue eyes," crinkled with wry amusement.

The girls were not in their camp when he arrived, so he sat down with his back to the pine tree and waited. For two hours he sat there, dozing periodically in the early afternoon heat. Though he heard them coming a long way off, he sat with his eyes closed until they stood before him, quietly watching him.

It would have been understandable if they had screamed and bolted. They saw a blond young giant, bronzed like burnished copper, faded buckskins obviously years old, bare feet thickened with almost pure white callous, hair bleached silver and cut oddly. But when he opened his eyes, they did indeed see that they were soft and gentle, penetrating their innermost souls.

Jenniver spoke first. "So the rumors were true," she whispered and looked quickly to Phoebe to see if she comprehended. It was obvious that she did, for she stood with feet braced slightly apart, hands clasped in front of her holding a notebook and pencil, lips parted, eyes cloudy and lids drooping.

"I know you," Phoebe said, her voice resonant with emotion. "I saw you last night. In the flames of the fire."

Pan nodded without moving, gripping her eyes with his. The mesmerization was complete, and he knew she was unaware of it. But she was now fey like him, enchanted and charmed, her destiny his, their lives forever intertwined, and without the other neither would be quite whole again.

"Are you hungry?" Jennifer asked.

"Yes," he answered.

With quiet calmness she laid and lit a fire while Pan and Phoebe spoke to each other with their eyes. Jennifer sliced a canned ham and fried several pieces in the pan. She handed them around on slices of buttered bread and they ate.

"Who are you?" Jennifer asked finally.

"I'm Pan."

"And I'm Jennifer. You met my mother years ago in the restaurant in town. And this is Phoebe. She's from Vermont. She thinks she wants to be a botanist, always studying planets and trees and stuff."

Pan nodded.

Jennifer giggled. "Some people who live alone just can't stop talking when they're with others again, but you can't seem to get going."

"I never was much of a talker, I guess, and living alone doesn't give me much to talk about. Suppose I could ask you what all's been happening in the outside world, but right now I couldn't even ask the right questions." He looked at Phoebe and she returned his stare.

"Do you mind if we ask *you* some questions?" Jennifer said.

"Not if you don't get mad if I don't answer some of them."

"Fair enough. Oh, you ask him, Phoebe, he doesn't pay any attention to me." There was laughter in her eyes but her voice was serious.

Phoebe got up and filled their cups with dark black coffee, then stood back of Jennifer with the coffee-pot still in her hands. It was now late afternoon, so her face was caught by the rays of the setting sun, turning her hair to a shimmering sea of lustrous purples and blues and multiple shades of black.

"I would just like to know," she said, "who you are."

"I'm . . ."

"Pan," Phoebe interrupted. "I know. But who is Pan?"

Pan shrugged his shoulders, stroked at his chin and glanced up at Phoebe with a muttered "Used to have a beard," and then sat forward on his haunches to poke at the fire with a stick of kindling. If I tell her, he thought, she'll run like a scared rabbit, and if I don't she'll keep after me till I do.

Without looking up, he spoke, his voice not much more than a whisper, but the girls could hear him clearly. Jennifer sat crosslegged, leaning her elbows forward on her knees, her chin cradled in one hand, her cup in the other. Phoebe remained standing behind her, but she had put down the pot and held her cup in both hands like a Chinese priestess of the Anyang culture presenting her p'an to the priest.

Pan poked idly at the embers and sparks shot upward into the lacy needles of the white pine overhead. He looked up and watched them die out. "I *am* Pan," he said finally. "The Pan who lived in these mountains, and whose haunts are these high hills. I am like Pan of Greek myth, for I am part man and part beast, and never do I know which will dominate my actions. My father is Hermes and my mother Penelope and I think they are both dead but they live on in me. Sometimes I am one and sometimes the other, but always I am Pan."

Jennifer shivered and clutched her jacket closer around her, but Phoebe moved closer to the fire and sank down on both knees, still holding the coffee cup in front of her. "I remember Pan," she said. "He was the god of the flocks and herds, and he was a piper. He could send visions and dreams and he had a lover called Syrinx. He was young, and vigorous, and sometimes lustful, even though he had promised his mother he would never have a woman."

Pan's eyes opened widely, staring across the fire at Phoebe. In the deepening dusk his face was almost black but there was enough light behind him to form a halo around his silvery hair. The firelight reflected from his eyes with a carmine lambency and both girls tensed.

He shattered the spell with a coarse laugh and the girls relaxed. "Tell us more about yourself, Pan," Jennifer said, "about how you live and that."

Pan smiled, bounced a bit on his haunches, then sat back against the tree again. "Not very well, by your standards, Jennifer. But very well, by the world's in general. Plenty of food, if you know where to find it. Good water, too. No liquor or tobacco."

"I couldn't live for two days without going to the store," Jennifer said. "Just what *do* you eat?"

Pan waved at the forest around them, now dark. Then he told them how he had survived, how he had learned from Jed Schroeder and by experience, how he hunted the rabbits and how he collected honey and nuts and mushrooms. He told them of his first lean-to, his attempt at living on the "outside" with Jed, and then about his last three years without shelter or fire or tools.

He talked for an hour, sometimes slowly, searching for the right words to convey his thoughts, sometimes in torrents of speech which held the girls enthralled. Once Jennifer interrupted to take back what she had said about him not being able to get started talking, and once Phoebe stopped him long enough to ask him if he wanted some more coffee or food.

"So there you have it," he said finally. "My whole life in a nutshell."

"No," Phoebe said. "Not your whole life. How you lived, yes. But not why."

Pan stood up, his huge body exaggerated by the darkness behind him, the fire casting flickering lights on his faced leathers. "Some day, Phoebe, maybe some day. Not tonight." He turned, and disappeared into the forest and the girls could not hear him going.

For a few moments they sat in silence, watching the crackling flames. "I don't think," Jennifer said, "that we need be afraid of him."

"No," Phoebe answered, "not at all. I think he has more to fear from us than we from him."

Jennifer nodded. "Poor kid." She got up and started getting ready for bed, but Phoebe remained by the fire. "You coming?" Jennifer asked, but Phoebe shook her head.

"I think I'll sit by the fire awhile. I don't seem to be very tired tonight."

"Don't let him get to you, Phoebe."

"He already has."

Jennifer stood by the tent watching her friend for a moment, then with a gentle sigh which Phoebe could not hear, she entered the tent, zipped down the mosquito bar, and crawled into her sleeping bag.

From time to time Phoebe fed the fire a few small branches to keep it alive, thinking as she did so that she should have come out like this before. But in her family no one had ever camped, and she didn't belong to Girl Scouts or any other group which would have taken her into the woods. Now her father was dead and her mother was caught up in a constant round of social activities which did not include her only daughter. Phoebe had gone home from school on a few semester breaks and summer vacations but soon found she was just a stranger in her own home. Her mother was never there, always playing bridge at the Country Club or involved in some do-gooder project with the church or Women's Club.

She found she loved the study of botany, and could spend hours or whole days roaming the woodlands around the college, just poking along with a friend, identifying flowers and vines and trees. It became a challenge to find a new plant, then laboriously work down the keys until she knew the name of the specimen. She loved particularly to have Jennifer along because she had grown up in a small village and already knew many of the species of flora without having to study them. So when Jennifer had suggested the camping trip just outside her own hometown, she quickly agreed. Airily her mother waved goodbye, and was probably glad to be free again.

Now as she squatted before the little fire, Phoebe knew she had found someone else to share her life with. She laughed softly, almost aloud, as she pictured the scene with her mother.

"There's this guy, see, Mother, who lives in the mountains down by Jennifer. No, not with his parents. No, I haven't met his parents. But he's really great, Mother. No nonsense to him at all. And he really knows the woods. As a matter of . . ."

No, she could never tell her mother about Pan. *Could* never tell? NO. *Must* never tell. If there was one thing she was sure of, it was that her mother would have absolutely no comprehension of a man like Pan.

But there was another thing she was sure of. She loved him and he loved her. There had been that instant sharing of thoughts when their eyes had first met. There was the same of *deja vu* which had to mean something. Pan had merely nodded when she said she had seen him in the fire the night before. Could he have known? Was he really Pan, and could send visions? It was a little frightening to think of. But *he* was not frightening. So gentle, and well-mannered, and obviously so intelligent. A little strange, maybe, but that would be because he had lived alone for so long. She was ready for him, and he for her.

She scratched at the fire with a stick and it burst into flame. She saw again the blue eyes, the badly cut silvery hair, the broad shoulders and tapering hips, the heavily muscled thighs, and yes, the dirty bare feet. But most of all she saw the enchanting, eldritch, brooding eyes with the haunting visions just out of reach.

The next morning, an hour after dawn, the girls were awakened by the sound of piping outside their tent. Jennifer dressed and zipped up the tent flaps and crawled out of the tent on her hands and knees. Phoebe rolled over on her back and listened. At first the tune seemed recognizable but then wandered off into trills like birdsong, ululating reedily in the quietness of the forest, returned in swooping melodies to the lower ranges, booming like bullfrogs in the swamp. There was a mystical, runic quality to the music, echoing the deep forest itself yet not of the forest, unworldly, beghosted.

Jennie busied herself with the fire but Phoebe lay in the tent, listening to the serenade which she knew was for her. Then for two or three seconds the piping stopped, only to start up again with a deep booming on the lowest note on the scale. The same note was repeated again, and again, each pause slightly shorter than the

216

one before, twenty-five or thirty times, until there was no longer space between booms and the sound became a steady staccato whir which died out like a jet engine disappearing into the sky. Phoebe recognized the performance as a perfect rendition of the drumming of a mature, male, ruffed grouse.

Jennifer laughed and called to Phoebe, "Sounds like Pan is establishing his territory and calling for a mate."

So he is, Phoebe thought, but I knew that last night. She slipped into a clean pair of bluejeans and a cool, light white blouse, and joined Jennifer at the fire.

"Where is he?" she asked.

Jennifer pointed up the hill. "Somewhere up there. I can't see him."

They ate their bacon and eggs in silence, each wondering when Pan would appear. Jennifer was curious and Phoebe almost anxious.

"Maybe he's not coming back today," Phoebe said.

Jennifer looked at her friend with just a trace of sadness in her eyes. "He'll come," she said.

He did come, about midmorning, with hands full of the foods he had been living on for so many years. He placed them carefully in front of the girls on a patch of sweetclover. Methodically he brushed little flecks of dirt off the roots which had been washed in a stream on the way to the camp. He identified the young shoots of milkweed, burdock, nettles, skunk cabbage, and sumac. He showed them dandelion, clover, fiddle heads of fern, wild violets. He cut open the unearthed roots of cattail, bulbrush, groundnut, Indian cucumbers, Jerusalem artichoke, and man-of-the-earth. He tumbled onto the ground a cloth full of chestnuts, post oak nuts, white oak nuts, beechnuts, and a scattering of wild strawberries, choke cherries and red buds.

From the more edible roots and shoots he cut small slices and the girls gingerly tried some of them. He laughed with them when their attempts fell short of their desires.

"You're not very hungry, Jennifer," he said, "or you'd think all of these were gifts from the gods."

"Which they are," Phoebe added.

"Too much bacon and eggs this morning," Jennifer said. "We'll not eat all day and you'll see how much we eat tonight."

"But don't you ever cook this stuff, Pan?" Phoebe asked.

"Used to. Haven't had a fire for three years." There was a momentary silence as the girls remembered, then Jennifer said, "Well, will you cook some of it up for tonight?"

"Sure. It does taste better."

For almost a week Pan visited the camp daily, appearing in the early morning with his pipes to awaken them. His repertoire seemed endless and he never played the same tune twice. "I make them all up as I go along," he explained, "so there's no way I could repeat. Oh, I do remember some segments of melody, or a particularly thrilling sequence of tunes, and I like to do the partridge drumming and that's got to be the same. But the rest of it is all spontaneous and unrehearsed."

"You could make a fortune with that pipe," Jennifer observed.

His whole philosophy of life and his entire attitude toward the world was reflected in his answer, "For what?"

During the day they roamed the giant valleys, probing into Pan's secret places, seeing, as it were, the underside of the forest, understanding it in terms which had not yet come into their ken. Pan showed them the life cycle of the forest, the primary growth of bushes and short-lived deciduous trees, when the gradual maturing of the forest into pine and fir, which stood forever unless burned or cut away. He described the intricacies of the interaction between flora and fauna until the girls' heads swam with facts. He was a walking encyclopedia of nature lore, nature personified, and they marveled that any one man could have observed so much.

"Wasn't much else to do," he said with a smile.

At dusk he sat with them around the fire, and they listened while he talked about his mountain home and the unending beauty which surrounded them. Never once did he volunteer any information about his own identity. It was as if he were to forever remain apart from them and their world, a world which he had once known and had now uncompromisingly renounced.

When he talked, he included both girls in his discussions, but Jennifer knew from the way he looked at her that she might as well have been a hundred miles away, and his eyes might as well have been closed. But when he looked at Phoebe, his whole soul poured forth. There was a yearning there, a longing which could not be hid, a desire leashed temporarily.

One night, after Pan had silently disappeared into the forest, Jennifer asked Phoebe, "What's going to happen?"

It had been an unasked question for days, and Phoebe had been waiting for it. "I'm going to stay if he asks me."

"For how long?"

Phoebe shrugged. "How long? Until we leave."

"You think he'll ever leave?"

"Maybe. Maybe not."

"This is really what you want to do?"

"I'll never know until I try it."

Jennifer leaned against the pine tree where Pan usually sat and looked up through the branches to the starlit sky. "Do you think this is where you really belong?" she asked.

Phoebe sat thoughtfully, staring into the embers. "There was a quote," she said so softly that Jennifer had to lean forward to hear the words, "in Twain's story of *The Gilded Age* that has stuck with me, probably because I sort of identified with poor Ruth Bolton when she was looking for her own milieu and finally found it. It went like this: 'if you should rear a duck in the heart of the Sahara, no doubt it would swim if you brought it to the Nile.' That's me. The duck. And this is the Nile. And I think I know how to swim."

Chapter 30

A driving rain lashed the forest, sending all its denizens into shelter. The deer stood unmoving in the thick timber, rumps to the wind, heads bowed, a steady stream of water trickling off their noses. The birds crouched in dry niches under thick branches and the squirrels and rabbits lay snug in hollow trees and underground burrows. Even the insects and arachnids hid from the storm, fearful that the huge and heavy drops would crush or drown them.

The girls lay on their sleeping bags, Jennifer on her side watching Phoebe, Phoebe propped against ther rucksack, arms hugging her knees, rocking slowly back and forth. From time to time the tent seemed ready to tear from its moorings, but it was well pitched and held. A few drops of water seeped through the window flap, ran down the inside of the tent and formed a small puddle near the back.

"He's out there in that storm," Phoebe said.

"And enjoying every minute of it," Jennifer added.

"Do you think so? Is he really such a creature of the forest? Is he really the god Pan?"

"Do you think so?"

"He must be," Phoebe answered. "How else could he identify so closely with Nature?" She turned to look at Jennifer. "What else do you remember about Pan?"

"Not much. He was the god of the woods and fields. His name signifies *all*. That's where we get Pan-American, Pan-Hellenic, pantheon, and so forth. He played the pipes while the wood-nymphs—the Dryads and Oreads—danced for him . . ."

"I should like to dance for him. In a secluded glade, the sun shining through the trees, with garlands of flowers around my neck and a wild rose in my hair." She lay back against the rucksack, her legs straight out in front of her, a smile of rapture on her face.

"Whoa there, girl. This Pan is a *real* man. He's no god. He's just a mixed-up boy and he's lived alone so long he wants a woman."

The smile faded from Phoebe's face and the grey eyes blazed. "Don't *say* that! He's never yet even touched me."

"Not with his hands he hasn't. But I've seen his eyes when he's watching you."

"Well, you're crazy if you think he's the first one to look at me like that."

"No, not the first. I just hope to God he's not the last."

The fire faded from Phoebe's eyes. "I don't."

Jennifer sighed, then crawled to the front of the tent and zipped up the flap a little way. "Storm's over, but it's almost dark. Suppose we can get that fire to going? Might as well try."

Phoebe followed her out of the tent and they stood in the rain-washed air, breathing deeply. The black overcast of the passing storm whirled out of sight to the east, dragging behind it the last remnants of grey scudding clouds. In the west the sun was almost down, hidden behind the hills, but the sky was mauve and purple and crimson.

"Red at night," Jennifer quoted, "sailor's delight. A nice day coming, Phoebe, tomorrow."

"You still want to go tomorrow?"

"I've got to. Really should have left a week ago."

Phoebe nodded and began to peel the plastic cover off their firewood. "Looks dry. Ought to burn real well." She stooped over to pick up the wood and tears fell from her cheeks onto the oak branches and spread like ink on a blotter. She stood up with a small piece of kindling in each hand and turned to face Jennifer.

The two girls looked at each other, Jennifer's eyes now filling with tears also, the salty drops coursing down her cheeks and onto her lips. She licked them away, her mind telling her she must remain aloof from what was happening to her best friend, her heart saying she should wish her well.

With a little cry of anguish Phoebe threw the wood onto the ground and rushed into Jennifer's arms. "Oh, Jenny, Jenny, what'll I do if he doesn't ask me to stay?"

Jennifer wound her arms around the stricken girl and swayed with her like she were a small child. Words came to her lips and were frozen there because she knew the best thing that could ever happen to Phoebe would be for Pan not to ask Phoebe to stay with him.

The haunting sounds of the syrinx floated down to them from the mountain above, tormented, bewitched rhapsodic. It was like nothing Pan had ever played before and it held them gripped tightly in its spell. It was now a fugue, then a sonata, then finally a symphonic poem which faded into the enchanting strains of a pastorale. Phoebe broke away from Jennifer and turned away, face uplifted, long black hair flowing down her back. Jennifer picked up the sticks Phoebe had thrown down, gathered a few more and a lit a fire. Still the music descended to them, now slowly getting louder till it seemed that it came from just outside their camp, and there was Pan, slowly moving toward them in the dusk, pipes to his lips, eyes on Phoebe alone.

The fire was burning brightly now and Pan stood at the edge of the circle of light. He had shed his leather garments and replaced them with the breechclout. His body glistened with water, each muscle standing out in *bas relief* in the glow of the fire, his massive chest heaving with each breath, his flat belly tensed with the effort of playing.

Phoebe stood mesmerized, feet planted firmly in the wet earth, her body facing slightly away from Pan, but her head turned toward him and her eyes filled with longing. Jennifer had squatted by the fire, her gaze shifting slowly from Pan to Phoebe and back again. Pan never knew she was there.

The music faded into a thin reedy piping, then broke wildly in a decrescendo of tumbling notes to the very bottom of the scale, where it wallowed, and softened, and died.

Pan cradled the pipes in his right arm and raised his left arm in the classic, studied invitation of the ballet master, palm open and turned slightly upwards. An invitation to the dance, or to live. Without a word, without even a glance at the girl by the fire, Phoebe took Pan's hand and he led her out of the camp into the forest. Led her from the prosaic heartland of Appalachis to the arcane heights of Arcadia.

There was laughter and there was love, the unleashing of long-repressed love. He was Pan, he was the god-king of Arcadia, he was *all,* and he was the personification of all Nature. And she was Syrinx, she was Panpipe, and she was a Dryad nymph who danced for him in the forest glades and on the mountain heights. In the sun and in the rain, in the hush of evening and in the cool crisp dawn she danced for him while the pipes played rollicking tunes and mournful, haunting melodies. And they made love with tenderness and with passion and with all the strength of a new love born fresh for them alone. There was a new sound in Arcadia, the sound of girlish laughter carried aloft on the summer breeze.

But there was also fear. The cold fear that followed them in the darkness of night and rummaged around in the maelstrom of buried lineages. He felt it more than she did, for he knew the precariousness of his ancestry, but she too nurtured in silence a dread of strange and misbegotten offspring. For she was not yet convinced that Pan was not a god come to earth.

Jennifer had left them the tent and they pitched it under the lee of the rockface where Pan had built his lean-to. Carefully they carried a pan of coals from the fire in the old campsite in the valley, translocating thereby the heart of their first meeting-place.

They roamed the hardwood groves and the tag aldered streams, the brush and sumac-choked hillsides, the thickets of plum and the rockstrewn barren places. Hand in hand they sat on the rockface above the lean-to and watched the sunlight climb the mountains in the evening and descend in the morning. They snuggled warm and happy in the tiny tent while wind and hail tore at their hillside home. They marvelled at the violence and they were awed by the grandiloquence of the tiny cheep of a newly hatched sparrow in its nest above their heads.

And there were the hum-drum days of lassitude when the summer heat came and the mosquitoes hummed and the crickets chirped and a heavy hand of ennui lay upon them.

It was then that Phoebe asked Pan, "When will you tell me who you really are?" And he answered, "In time, Phoebe, in time, when it's the right time, the right time and place."

There were times of loneliness, too, for Phoebe, when Pan would disappear for hours at a time, sometimes even over night, and she would not know where he was or if he was ever coming back. She would have been even more troubled if she had known that he was lying curled up in a tree-nest, sleeping in hidden coverts while the ghosts of Hermes dissipated themselves in slumber. Whether it was merciful or not, he had learned to recognize the premonitory symptoms of his trance-state and could slip away before they became evident to Phoebe.

But even though there was a constant shadow of foreboding over them, there was always love. They slept in each other's arms and they spoke in each other's embrace. She loved to listen to him talk about the forest and its creatures. He did not know the names of many of the plants which he had studiously observed for so many years, so she supplied them, but he knew their flowers and their leaves, and where they grew and flourished best. He understood the habits of most of the animals: rodents and birds and snakes and great game animals like bear and forest boar. He showed her how a blue heron fishes and how an oriole builds its nest, how a frog can trip its tongue and how an owl can digest its prey whole.

He in turn never tired of hearing her recite poetry and quote from the great writers both of antiquity and modern day. She knew Twain and Shakespeare, Mencken and Dobzhansky, Tillick and Plato, Mitchener and Dickens. When she did not remember the exact words, she paraphrased and he never knew the difference. But most of all he loved to lie back against a tree and watch her face and hands as she "read" to him a passage from the classics. When she forgot a phrase, and screwed up her face in concentration, he laughed, and she threw a clod of dirt or a stick at him or stuck out her tongue in mock anger.

The cool winds of fall came and the geese flowed

overhead in endless streams. Robins arrived in flocks from the north and redwinged blackbirds by the thousands flickered against the setting sun. Phoebe kept a fire going most of the day and its heat reflected off the rockface into the open tent just as Pan had planned it would.

One night they sat in the doorway of the tent, warming themselves by the fire, listening to the nightsounds in the forest. "I've got something to tell you, Pan," Phoebe said, her eyes black in the hollows beneath her brows.

"I don't think you have to," Pan answered.

"No, maybe I don't." A smile flickered in her eyes and was gone. "You've always known more about me than I know about myself." She paused again. "The child?"

He nodded.

"What will he be like, Pan?"

He shrugged and was silent.

"Like me?" she said. "Or like you? Or like . . .?"

He turned his somber blue eyes full on her and she shuddered involuntarily. "Or like what?"

"I don't know. Do you?"

A cloud passed over his eyes and she was no longer there. Too quickly it had come upon him and he had not felt the warning signals in time. But his animal instincts of survival tore at his guts and he stood up and stormed out of the campsite and up the edges of the rockface and she could hear him clambering higher and higher, pants of despair and grunts of fear falling like dead leaves around her. Finally she could hear him no more and the night wind blew cold on her neck and she was afraid.

Chapter 31

The sharp tap of knee or elbow in her womb had awakened her, and she lay listening to the strangely silent world outside their tent. The muffled thud of a deer's hooves just below their tent sounded so odd that she crawled out of the sleeping bag and peeked out the tent. The ground was blanketed with a new snow, inches deep, and it clung to bushes and trees in thick, wet clumps.

"Pan," she cried softly, "wake up and look. It's snowed. I didn't know it ever snowed down here."

He sat up and looked out at the glistening whiteness. His hair was touseled, and his beard had grown out again, giving him the appearance of a wooly sheepdog. She laughed and rumpled his hair, then dragged at it playfully. He grasped her arm and pulled her back into the sleeping bag, where they lay together in love.

She had never spoken to him about his rampage up the mountain, and he never volunteered any information. But there had grown a certain restraint which had not been there before. It was unnatural, and anything unnatural in their idyllic life seemed out of place. So many times she had been on the verge of talking to him, but each time he had sensed her discomfort and had walked away or had changed the subject. He would shake his head with the clear implication that the time had not come.

This morning, after they had made love, they lay warmly snuggled together, with the world outside hushed, the voices of the wilderness mute.

"Pan," Phoebe said, easing away from him so she could see his eyes, "Isn't it time to talk? The baby's moving. I can feel it kicking me, and in just a few months it's going to be born. There are things you haven't told me, things I've got to know." She brushed his hair with her hand. "Darling, please!"

He sat up slowly and put on his leather shirt and pants, then zipped up the tent flap and gathered some wood. She could hear him pounding the snow off the branches, but soon the fire was crackling and hissing as the snow melted and vaporized. Pan crawled into the tent, tied back the flaps so the heat could enter, and sat beside her on the sleeping bag.

"Yes, I guess it's time, Phoebe."

She waited, wondering if she really did want to know.

Without preamble, without euphemisms, without attempt at restructuring the facts, he began.

"Over thirty years ago, a research scientist by the name of Dr. John Reynolds of Standing Oaks, up north, had a brilliant idea. He had devoted his professional career to the study of biology on the cellular level. Most of his research had followed a pattern designed to uncover the cause of cancer. He had his laboratory at the University, but he also had a fully equipped lab at home where he worked on projects which might or might not have anything to do with the discovery of the cause of cancer. It was with this background that he chanced upon an article in a magazine read primarily by laymen who are interested in—but not particularly well versed in—basic research. The article posed the question: If we really want to know what goes on in the minds of the lower animals, why don't we use our scientific skills to create a crossbreed between man and the highest of the lower animals, the chimpanzee.''

Phoebe gasped, her face drained of blood, and she lay back on her pillow, her hands clutched together on her breast. ''Pan . . .,'' she whispered hoarsely, ''Pan, don't. I don't think I can take this.''

Pan continued as if he hadn't heard her, and perhaps he hadn't. He told her of the kidnapping of Penelope, the room in which she had been raised without contact with the outside world, the training in Ameslan, and her slow growth into a dwarfish analogue of what she might have been. He hinted at the death of Jan Wheeler but did not know the details. He described the capture of Hermes and his joyful meeting with Penelope. In a low, monotonous drone he pictured for Phoebe the scene in the laboratory just as John Reynolds had told him, and not knowing the scientific language, he told in his own words of the micro-surgery and the implantation of the fertilized egg in the Fallopian tube of the still unconscious Penelope.

Outside, the snow was beginning to melt in the mid-morning sun and clumps of snow fell from the trees into the fire with a sizzle. The fire needed replenishing and Pan went out and threw several logs onto it and returned to the tent without a glance at Phoebe. Phoebe lay prostrate, eyes staring at the soggy tent roof, mouth agape, breathing stentorous. Her ears still heard, but her mind was blank.

Still Pan plodded relentlessly on. He told of his bloody birth and his mother's inevitable death. He related in fine detail his early years, the knowledge within him that he was different from his playmates. Painfully, pitifully, pleadingly, he reconstructed the scene in the living room at Standing Oaks when John and Sylvia Reynolds had told him just what he was now telling Phoebe.

Phoebe had recovered some of her senses, and now

sat halfway up, leaning on one outstretched arm. She reached out to touch Pan, and his hand closed over hers gently and held it. Tears of compassion streamed down Phoebe's face, and she listened as Pan told of his flight through the cold March morning, the ride on the hog-truck to Jennifer's village, then the meeting with Jed Schroeder.

"You don't have to go on, Pan," she whispered.

"Yes, I do. I'm not done yet. I had my first spell just before I met Jed, up on a mountain just to the east of here. I could feel it coming, I guess, but I didn't recognize it for what it was, and afterwards I didn't really know what it was, except I knew enough about chimp behavior to realize that I'd just recreated one of their displays. I wasn't really frightened then, because I figured it was just an isolated incident. How wrong I was."

He heaved a deep sigh, seemed to retreat deeper within himself, and let go of Phoebe's hand. For a while it seemed he could not go on.

"I should have been all right at Jed's. He's so kind, and in a way not often seen any more, compassionate. He never accused me, never probed, never asked for my pedigree. Just accepted me, put me to work. Even after one of my spells erupted right in front of him, all he said was, 'You need a doctor, Pan,' and I knew I didn't. What could a doctor do?" He sighed again, and hugged his knees.

"I came up here thinking I could get rid of all my troubles. And I did. It was just what I needed, but then I got the scare of my life when a hunger and his dog almost found me. I knew I couldn't hide out forever so I went back to Jed. He didn't even ask me where I'd been. And of course, he didn't have to. He'd known all along. He'd come up after me, and somehow I'd com-municated with him so he'd even known what day it

231

would be. Usually I have to exert a real conscious effort to do that, but with Jed I didn't. I suppose it's his heritage.

"I've wondered a couple of times if Jed might have phoned or wired my folks that I was coming off the mountain. But I don't think so. They did come down though, probably coincidentally, and we came back up here to this camp."

Phoebe's eyes widened with astonishment. "You mean you actually brought them up *here*?"

"Yes, that was when I still had my lean-to and fire and was living reasonably like a human being." He grinned at her just a trifle sheepishly and she felt a surge of love for him. "We talked for awhile. I don't think I told them what they wanted to hear." He stopped, his head hanging down, his eyes closed.

Phoebe didn't press him for the details of that conversation.

"Well," Pan continued, his voice soft and rumbling, "it didn't work out to come down to Jed either. A rainstorm hit while we were up on the mountain girdling trees, while we were killing those big beautiful trees with a saw and adze."

"You know," Phoebe said, "about the legend of the Dyrad nymphs who live in trees and die when their trees die?"

"No, I didn't know that. But I did know the trees would die, and when a lightning bolt struck near us I went completely berserk. And by the time I had regained even part of my senses, I had torn down my leanto and hidden my clothes and was living like an animal.

"I just existed. Animal-like. Without any thought for tomorrow. The seasons came and went. For years, Phoebe, I lived just like an animal. Until you came. Then something in me broke open, let loose a flood of

232

thoughts and memories that I hadn't experienced for years.

"And at first it was o.k. I was able to tell when my spells were coming and I could go away. Until you told me about the baby. That time it came on so suddenly I couldn't hide it."

He closed his eyes as a wave of exhaustion swept over him. He bowed his head and his heavy shoulders shook with sobs, but no tears came. In a few moments the shuddering ceased and he looked out at the melting snow.

"Your love for me is a lot like that snow, Phoebe. You came and your love for me was able to cover a lot of the things in me which should be hidden. Your love blanketed me, sheltered me, purified me. But look outside, Phoebe. The snow is melting, and when it goes, you'll see the drab brown earth and the dead leaves on the ground and the barren hillsides and all the other things which should remain hidden."

"Pan, you think my love for you is a temporary thing? That it's going to fade away like melting snow? That just because you've told me about your ancestry I'm going to fold my tent and steal back to mother?"

His huge arms reached out for her and encircled her bulging body and pulled her off the sleeping bag onto his lap where he cradled her.

"Phoebe, I wish I'd known you'd react like this. I'd of told you months ago. But I was afraid, no, terrified, that you'd leave me. *Knew* you'd leave me. And I couldn't bear to think of it."

"Pan, I need you. And I'll need you even more when the baby . . ."

She stopped, her eyes reflecting her abject terror. She pulled away from Pan and could see that he was thinking the same thoughts.

"No, Phoebe, I don't know just what Reynolds did to my chromosomes. Or rather, he did tell me, but I didn't understand it then and can't remember it now. Something about trouble with a 46th or 47th chromosome. Does that mean anything to you?"

"No. I don't remember much about my genetics."

She leaned back into his arms and snuggled her head in his belly and he could feel her sobbing gently, the tears trickling onto his bare skin.

"Phoebe," he whispered, "it's going to be all right. You just wait."

But she continued to cry, uncontrollably, moaning softly and rocking back and forth with her bare feet in the dirt. Pan stroked her hair, patted her shoulder like a father with a child, and murmured consoling words which he didn't mean and knew she would not hear.

Gradually her grief subsided and she lay in his arms devoid of feeling, sucked dry of emotion, and this was good. Pan turned her toward the doorway of the tent and pointed. "Look, Phoebe, the snow's almost gone. And it doesn't look so drab and barren after all. More like it should look. Maybe our love will be the same, not so much a blanket hiding the deeper things, but a kind of cement holding us together forever."

He held her at arms length and stared into her eyes. "For you know now at least *who* I am. I am Pan."

Chapter 32

It was the time of vernal equinox, the period of the celestial calendar when the days and nights are equal in length. Spring had come to Appalachia, bringing warm rains and sunny days and the bursting of long dormant buds and flowers. The hibernators roamed the hillsides again, fattening their lean flanks. Bucks no longer travelled with their does, and the does ate twice as much to nourish their unborn fawns. From the hollow trees the bees began to send forth their scouts in search of nectar, and when they returned they danced for their workers and told them where to start collecting food for their newest generation.

Each day Phoebe foraged closer to home, and when there was not enough food nearby Pan brought back handfuls of juicy roots and young shoots after he had eaten his fill. They had learned to live with their fears of the future, and waited now only for the birth of the baby. Early they had decided to stay on the mountain for the birth and never discussed it again.

Her contractions began on a cool summery night just after the equinox. A light wind soughed in the pines above the rockface, and the honking cacophony of a northbound skein of geese carried down to Phoebe when she awoke. At first she was not quite sure she was actually beginning labor, and fell asleep. Fifteen minutes later she was awakened by an even stronger contraction, and then she knew. The odd mix of elation and dread, which every mother knows, filled her body and her mind, and at the same time she felt a peace descend upon her spirit.

Slowly the time intervals shortened to twelve minutes, then ten, then eight and she could actually feel the mass in her belly rise up slowly and hold there for a minute or two, then relax. She did not awaken Pan, wanting to savor this moment by herself for awhile.

Between contractions she lay half-asleep, thinking of the millions and millions of mothers who had preceded her in this adventure. But none of them were like her, none of them had been made love to by Pan, none of them had ever carried his child in her belly for nine months. She did not even let the thoughts of "What if . . . " enter her mind. She had long ago repressed the first aching fears of that 47th chromosome and what it might mean to her and Pan. She had reasoned that since he was human and she was human, there *was* no need to fear. Pan was *not* half-god, half-man, *not* half-human, half-animal. He was Pan, her man, her husband.

Sunlight streamed across the valley and warmed the tent as Pan had planned it would. It broke against the rockface and reflected into the tent in shimmering beams of light and heat. Pan awoke, rolled over on his side and looked at Phoebe. She said simply, "He's coming, Pan. Today."

His eyes crinkled at the corners in silent approbation and if he felt the morbid dread he once had, he drove it deeply into his subconscious where she couldn't see it. Slipping quickly into his leathers, he started a fire and boiled wild violets and the young leaves of marsh marigolds he had gathered the night before. He made a tea of wintergreen leaves and cherry bark and handed her a cupful of the delicious stuff. She sipped slowly, propped up against the rockface in the full light of the sun.

During the day he tended her as no nurse or doctor

would ever have done. He fed her a nourishing broth concocted from dandelions which he gathered in a lightning trip into the valley, and carried water to her from the spring at the edge of the rockface. She laughed at him and told him to go for a walk or something, but he grunted and stayed.

Late in the afternoon her contractions were spaced at four to five minute intervals, powerful and painful. Her face mirrored the effort she was making to relax and let the womb do the work, but occasionally a little cry of pain or a gentle moan escaped her lips, and he ran to her and held her gently in his strong arms. He fashioned for her hair a garland of wild red roses and tucked lavendar violets under the stems.

He talked to her soothingly of the forest creatures he had known in the years he had lived in this Arcadian retreat. He told her of the yearling buck he had seen striding majestically through the oak grove despite a shattered hind limb. He described the flights of hawks which passed over each spring in their annual migration north. With the meticulous detail of a naturalist he painted for her a picture of the pattering string of a dozen fuzzy partridges following their mother through the tag alders. With each of her contractions he held her tightly and waited till they subsided, then continued on in his narrative as if he had not been interrupted.

If there was ever a stronger love between two people on this earth, it has not been described. She wished she could share the full impact of this new creation with him, and he wished he could share her pain.

"Y'know, doctuh, I'm not even sure I should be talkin' to y'all, aftuh whut happened las' time y'was heah."

In the tense atmosphere which pervaded the scene,

Jed had lapsed completely into the patois of his youth. He stood stiffly on the porch of his house, looking down on the old couple with an anxiousness that could be read in his eyes and in the way he held his hands in front of him as if he were warding off a pack of angry dogs.

"What do you mean by that remark, Jed?" John Reynolds shot back with an alacrity which belied his wrinkled face and stooped back.

Sylvia stepped forward, almost to the steps of the porch, and tilted her head backwards to look directly into Jed's tired old eyes. "Yes, Jed, what do you mean?" she said imploringly. "Has something happened to Pan?"

Jed responded to the old woman's pleas and dropped his hands to his side, then, shuffled forward to the edge of the porch and lowered himself slowly and with obvious pain to a sitting position.

"Nothin's happened lately that I knows of, Miz Sylvia. Fact is, I don't know anythin' of Pan of late. Hain't seen him for years. Took off in a fit jus' days after y'all left four years ago, and none of us has seen him since, 'less it's those two young gals camped up there last summer. And one a'them didn't never come back. Seems as if she stayed with Pan."

"God!" John Reynolds said.

"Jed," Sylvia cried, "you can't mean the girl stayed up there with Pan? For a year now?"

Jed bowed his head, his mind awhirl. He knew without a shred of doubt that this man was the cause of all Pan's trouble, and he wasn't at all sure that the woman wasn't in cahoots with him. Lived with him, anyway, and shared his bed, and shared his secrets, and should have been able to do something to break the spell if she *wanted* to, kill him even, if she *wanted* to. He shuddered as a new thought came to him: maybe she's

238

bound to him, too, just like Pan, and *can't* do anything. Maybe, just maybe, he, Jed, should take it on himself to free Pan. He wished with all his heart that he had kept alive all the bits of knowledge and the techniques he had once known, fifty, sixty, years ago, back when his folks were alive and it was common to have to take care of these problems yourself.

He raised his head and stared into the eyes of John Reynolds. Those eyes had lost their glitter, were no longer suffused with perpetual bitterness, no longer the hooded orbs of the spitting cobra. Could I be wrong, Jed thought, about this man? Is this little old man with the bald head and wispy white hair around his ears a demon, a warlock? What power could he still have over Pan, as young and as strong as Pan is?

"Jed?" Sylvia asked again.

"Yes'm, I do believe it. I don't get up in the hills like I useta' but Pan ain't come out, and the girl ain't either. Must be they's livin' up there somewheres."

"At Pan's old camp?" John asked.

"I reckon."

"I'm going up there," John said and turned spryly on his heels and shuffled rapidly to the old Ford, his run-over shoes sending up clouds of red dust in the late afternoon sun.

"John, you can't. You'll never make it. Your heart!"

Reynolds turned and looked back at his wife and then at Jed. "You two stay here. If I'm not back by morning, come looking. But not before. You hear?"

With laughing eyes and sure, tender hands, Pan stripped off Phoebe's jeans, which she had been wearing in hip-hugger style for months, and led her into the tent. And without a word of complaint he cleaned up the mess when the waters broke and helped her roll over onto the other sleeping bag.

Thunder rolled across the mountaintop and Pan looked up to see giant cumulus clouds backlighted by the setting sun. Behind them towered the black front of the approaching storm. Lightning flashed between the clouds and a light breeze stirred the tops of the trees above their tent.

Phoebe laughed. "My mother was born in the worst storm ever to hit our part of Vermont. She said babies are always born in the rain. Something to do with the low pressure."

Pan was not laughing. "Going to make it tough if that front gets here before the baby."

"We didn't time this very well, did we?" asked Phoebe, but the laughter was fading from her eyes as well. For the first time, there was just a hint of fear behind the lovely grey eyes, and she closed them so Pan wouldn't see.

Pan stirred up the fire and threw new logs on it. The wind whipped embers into the air and he watched them warily until they died out. Phoebe's contractions were coming every minute or two and she grunted involuntarily.

"You can help now, I think," Pan advised. "Wait for the full pain, then strain down and help. When the pain is over, stop straining and try to relax."

"You sound like an experienced mid-wife," she chided, and he grinned.

John Reynolds had no trouble finding the track along the small creek, and he followed it relentlessly in the swiftly falling dusk. He was driven by a demon just as surely as he had been when he created Pan long years before, but this time it was different. This time he was trying to prevent a creation, not initiate one. He had no way of knowing he was already nine months too late so he raced the old car through the shallow fords and around the twisting curves of the jeeptrack.

Maybe, he thought, just maybe, I can talk some sense into that son of mine who is not really my son but a creation of my mind and not my body. Perhaps he and that girl are really in love and together she and I can take him away from this godforsaken place. Perhaps it's too late. God, maybe it's not too late to save him.

In Jed's perceptive way, he had recognized instinctively that John Reynolds was changed. Jed had read him as a demon, a sorcerer, a warlock, when Reynolds had first come to McWhirter's coulee. And he had not been far wrong. But now, four years after that highly unsatisfactory meeting between Pan and John and Sylvia, he had real doubts. Jed had not known what happened up on the mountain, but all three of them were changed when they came down, John Reynolds most of all. Pan had merely been quieter, more subdued. Sylvia had cried almost continuously, scarcely acknowledging Jed's presence, but she was a weak woman from the start and almost anything could have precipitated her behavior. But John Reynolds was more than subdued. He was broken. Ignoring Pan, he leaned heavily on Sylvia as if she were the stronger of the two, and when they left, it was she who drove and he who sat staring straight ahead of him with eyes almost closed and mouth hanging open.

Reynolds had spent the past four years in nearly unbroken solitude in his study. There was a certain vigor with which he attacked the voluminous piles of notes and records which he and Sylvia had accumulated during he forty years since he had sat in his study with the Grand Experiment forming in his brilliant, fertile brain. If was as if he had finally said to himself, Well, this is it, I guess; if I can't solve the riddle of whether or not

Homo differs from *Pan* in degree or in kind from my in-
terrogation of the offspring of those lines, perhaps I can
do it by studying my notes of Hermes, Penelope, and
finally of Pan's life with us at Standing Oaks. Perhaps,
he thought, the clues are here all the time, in my mind
but unrecognized. But so far it had been to no avail. If
the clues were there, he didn't recognize them. If the
answer was in those notes, and therefore somewhere in
his brain, he had not received the insight to decipher it.
Perhaps, after all, he still hadn't asked the right questions.

As Reynolds parked the car by the big white pine
where the girls' camp had been, he felt a freshening
breeze and saw high over the mountain the build-up of
thunderheads which Pan and Phoebe had already
detected. He pulled open the glove-compartment and
took out a flashlight, then opened the trunk and took
his old hooded rain-slicker out of it. It was too hot to
wear, so he folded it over him arm and started upwards.

He drew in a long breath of air and blew it out slowly.
A faint wheeze emanated from the depths of his chest
and he knew he would have to climb slowly and carefu-
ly or he would never make it. A hundred feet up, then
rest, another hundred and rest again. Take the pulse and
try to keep it under a hundred. Slowly, slowly. Rest
before you're tired, he kept repeating to himself. Take it
easy. Don't worry about the heart, nor the darkness
falling, nor the scattered raindrops splattering on your
bald spot. Save the raincoat till later or you'll overheat.
Better yet, throw the coat away and ignore the rain.
You'll dry and this old suit needs cleaning. Steadily the
hillside dropped away below him. He took off his tie
and coat and tossed them on a bush.

He switched on the light and played it on the smooth
path ahead of him. Up, up, he climbed, checking
himself frequently, cursing his age and shortness of

breath and aching thighs. Cursing himself for not coming sooner. Cursing, but cursing softly and without rancor. Accepting his mission for what it was: an atonement.

Chapter 33

Long before the baby crowned, the storm was full upon them. Pan zipped down the front flaps and tied the window flaps snugly. The fire outside was no match for the torrent of water which descended upon it and it sizzled and exploded and hissed and went out, the black charred logs steaming in vain attempt to burn.

Inside the tent it was totally dark, except when the lightning flashes illuminated the canvas with a green, eerie light. Pan knelt beside his bride, cognizant of the awful weight of responsibility resting on him, but never once wishing it could be some other way. She was his woods-nymph and he was Pan. In the interludes of quietness between contractions he held her and wiped her perspiring brow.

"Play for me, Pan," she said.

He sat beside her, where she could rest her hand on his thigh, and he played. A single note, high and ready, hauntingly sweet, hung tremulously in the air, contrapuntal to the desparate thrashing of the trees nad bushes just a few feet away. The tone wavered, dropped an octave, then climbed slowly over the black notes of hte scale. Phoebe's fingers dug into his thigh and his pipes played wildly in surging empathy with her pain. Her hand relaxed and the pipes played softly and slowly, almost aimlessly in concordant harmony with her peace.

A lightning bolt hit the great white pine on the rockface above their tent and with no interval of time the thunder shook their tent and almost drowned the cry which escaped Phoebe's lips, "Pan, Pan, help me!"

She writhed and groaned and struggled with the efforts of birth. In the blackness which surrounded them, Pan laid aside his pipes and reached blindly for the newborn thing which lay inert on the slimy sleeping bag. A shudder traveled the length of Phoebe's body and she sagged limply on the ground with a great heaving sigh of mixed pain and relief.

Pan's hands searched out the infant and ran his hands over it in wonderment and awe. He felt its head and its thickly matted hair, its wizened little face and toothless gums, its body thickly coated with slippery muck, its legs covered with a thin layer of soft hair, the small genitals of a male infant. Gently he turned it over on its stomach and plunked at the viscid muccous in its mouth, waiting for the infant to cough or breathe. The cord pulsated violently in his hand as he steadied the abdomen in the mucilagenous ooze on the sleeping bag.

Slowly the cord ceased to beat, and the infant wriggled imperceptibly, then its chest convulsed and a great gasp of air filled its lungs and a high thin cry escaped the tiny lips. Phoebe struggled again and the heavy, boggy placenta cascaded out onto Pan's hands, hot and reeking with the odor of blood.

Lightning struck once more at the mountains, its rumbling thunder tumbling down the hills into the valley below. In the instant of green light which flooded the tent, Pan caught a glimpse of Phoebe's tired face turned halfway on the pillow, her raven hair haloed with the crushed garland of flowers. His anxious, straining eyes flicked across the back of the tiny babe he held in his hand just as the light was gone and darkness engulfed them again. His uneasy mind, already haunted by fear and apprehension, created one more shameful illusion and he fancied he saw tiny black hairs covering the baby's back. A roar of pain erupted from his lungs and tore the night with its anguish.

His lips pulled back in a kind of grin and he pounded his forehead with a bloody fist. Reason, judgement, and all rationality poured from his great brain in a flood, deserting him for the last time. All awareness was gone, and he stood up with the infant in his hand, the placenta hanging from its belly, tugging at its moorings. He banged his head on the ridgepole and the tent reverberated but stood.

With clumsy fingers he tore open the tentflaps and stood in the pouring rain and whistling wind. His huge body trembled with fear and his eyes were blind with blood and his neck cords stood out in stark relief.

On the trail below John Reynolds found the end of the bull-dozed trail and pushed through the screen of bushes. He played the light on the narrow path before him and then stopped as lightning flashed through the dense foliage and thunder ripped at him with tentacles of sound. His ears rang with the echoes and he fancied he heard pipes playing wildly in the night. He shook his head to clear the rain from his eyes and the plaintive sound from his ears and bore on through the brush.

In the clearing ahead he heard the angry roar as Pan stood up and stuck his head on the tentpole. John shone the light ahead of him and there in the wavering beam stood Pan, the baby hanging limply from his huge hands.

And suddenly John Reynolds was back in Gombe Stream, the hunched and hairy creature in front of him staring at the infant in his hands with hate and horror. The chimpanzee slid his hands down the baboon baby's body until they reached the feet and then grasped the feet strongly and swung the infant in lazy arcs back and forth, back and forth, the placenta twisting grotesquely and bouncing up and down on its elastic cord.

Slowly the creature moved foward toward the rockface and even more slowly raised its arm behind it, the baby dangling like a wet fish from the hairy hand. Lightning struck again and lit up the agonized face of John Reynolds holding his hands outward in mute despair.

Reynolds' tongue was stuck to the gummy roof of his mouth and all he could manage was a raspy scream of pain. It was enough. Pan slowly lowered the baby to his side and then Reynolds found his voice.

"Pan!" he screamed, rainwater and saliva spewing from his mouth in a shower of foam. "Pan! Stop! For God's sake, stop!"

For long moments Pan stood there, his face turned upward to the heavens, the infant cradled in one arm. Now a change came over him, and he laid the baby gently on the soggy ground, took off his shirt, and wrapped the baby in it. He stood up again with the child, glanced swiftly back at the tent, ignored the pitiful cries from the girl lying inside, ignored the anguished cries of John Reynolds, and strode rapidly to the edge of the rockface and started the upward climb to the ledge above.

Reynolds tried to follow but his strength did not match his courage and he soon gave it up. With thudding heart and gasping lungs he crawled back down the hill and stood outside the tent for several moments. Torrents of water cascaded from his face and he wiped ineffectually at his eyes to clear the tears and rainwater. It was the first time he had cried in over forty years.

He parted the tentflaps and knelt beside the weeping, exhausted Phoebe. She looked up at him anxiously as he propped the flashlight on Pan's rolled-up sleeping bag.

"Who are you?" she asked, struggling to sit up.

"Lie down, child, I won't hurt you. I'm Pan's father, John Reynolds. I've come to take you home."

She shrank away form him, curling up in a tight ball on the bloody, soggy, sleeping bag.

"Where's Pan? And the baby?" Her widened eyes shown like a fawn's in the dim light of the tent. Reynolds could hardly hear her whisper above the wild roar of the storm outside.

"He's climbed the mountain, child. What's your name?"

"Phoebe."

"He's gone with the baby, Phoebe. I tried to follow him but he's too fast and he knows where he is and where he's going. I don't know either."

"What had he *done* to the baby?" she asked, and her mouth stayed open and her pupils dilated as she waited for the answer.

"Nothing, Phoebe, nothing. He wrapped it up in his leather shirt. He hadn't hurt it. I don't think he could."

"Not if he thought it was his." She rolled over on her back and tried to sit up again.

"Lie down, Phoebe. Let me help you get washed up. Is there water? Warm water?"

She pointed to the five-gallon jerry-can in the corner of the tent.

"He had heated that."

And John set about with the meticulous care of which he was capable to wash Phoebe down with warm water. He removed the sleeping bag from under her, turned it over, and put it back under her. She lay passively while he worked, and wondered at the depth of his feeling for her. He in turn remembered another delivery over forty years before when he had felt the surge of genius within him and had coaxed out the little blonde girl named Penelope. And he remembered with an involuntary shudder the bloody delivery of a small baby boy whom he had called Pan. And now the wheel had come full circle and here was the culmination of all he had worked for. All the years fell away as he rubbed the girl dry and found dry clothes for her and helped her crawl into Pan's warm sleeping bag.

She moaned softly with the aching in her belly and the greater aching in her heart. He'll come back, she thought, he'll come back. And then she fell asleep.

Rain lashed Pan's face and the sharp rocks cut his hands but he did not notice. Scrabbling over the rocks, using his one free hand to pull himself upward, he reached the ledge and stood looking over the dark valley below. The wind caught furiously at his hair and he brushed it back, leaving a dark red streak of blood on the silvery locks.

Ponderously he turned and climbed laboriously through the heavy brush, past the plum thicket where he had lived for so long, through the stand of small pines to the giant white pine which had just been struck by lightning. The smell of charred wood and thick ozone hung heavily in the air despite the deluge.

He placed the baby in the first crotch, swung up into the tree, reached down and picked up the swaddled babe. He tucked the baby between his knees, and pulled himself up hand over hand into the very topmost branches. There he stood, as he had countless times before, surveying his domain in Arcadia, black and brooding below him. Home of the son of Penelope for two years and home of the son of Hermes for three more. His racked and sundered mind did not register the fact that for another year he had been the son of neither, but Pan, the son of man; not lover of the nymph Syrinx, but husband to the lovely grey-eyed, black-haired girl Phoebe, who now lay exhausted two hundred yards below him.

His trembling hands were guided by instincts ten million years old as he built a nest of branches under the topmost sheltering limbs of the great tree and laid the tiny baby in it. He stripped off his leather pants and wrapped the infant in them. He straightened up again and stood defiantly in the wind and rain. Dimly, with hooded eyes, he saw the retreatding edge of the storm outlined by a half moon in the west. It might have been an omen, and it might have saved him, but as he turned to stare at the faint light, his foot slipped and he fell.

Instinctively he grasped at the branch and his fingertips clutched it for a moment, but then slipped off, stripping the bark with his nails, and he fell again, tumbling, turning, crashing against the trunk, ricocheting from limb to limb in a devilish dance of death. He thudded against the needle-carpeted ground with a sickening, muted, thump, and lay still.

The keening of the wind sounded a final flourish of pipes, and Pan was dead.

Chapter 34

The old truck climbed slowly along the sodden jeeptrack in the valley, but Jed kept the wheels clear of the ruts on the thick carpeting of sweetclover. The roar of the engine drowned out the sounds of early morning in the mountains, and neither Jed nor Sylvia could hear the silvery chirping of chickadees nor the angry chatter of red squirrels in the pines.

"Do you really know where they are, Jed?" Sylvia shouted above the clatter.

Jed nodded without looking at her. "I know where they *was*. If'n they's still at Pan's old camp."

Jed slowed the truck and then stopped. "Here's where they was camped, the girls, ma'am. Likely you remember this old pine. You can still see the place where Jennifer and Phoebe had their campfire, but the marks of the tent's all growed over. This was their camp, all right, though."

"I'll never make it to the top this time, Jed."

"No need, ma'am. You jest set right there, or on the runnin' board. It won't take me long to find'm if they's there."

"John's up there, too, Jed."

He nodded and swallowed. "I knows. I'll find'm."

Sylvia sat on the running board, unmindful of the thick layer of red mud, as Jed headed slowly up the old bull-dozed trail, his crutch digging deeply into the wet earth. He had not needed urging to come. He had

251

wanted to come with Reynolds the night before but knew it would have been foolish to argue with the old man. He had a feeling that few people had been able to stand up to him.

After a few hundred yards he stopped to rest and turned around to look down the mountain. He knew something was wrong up on the hill above him. Terribly wrong. He had felt it all night, had felt an emptiness, an aching void in his subconscious. Even now in the full light of day he couldn't dispel the feeling that whast was wrong up there was wrong with Pan. In his reasoning mind he knew that couldn't be, for Pan was big and strong and wilderness-wise. But in his heart he knew that when a man has been trapped by the devil (as he knew Pan had been) there is only one force stronger, and Pan hadn't called on God for years, maybe never.

As he came closer and closer to the end of the track, his foreboding increased. He stopped to rest once more before pushing through the brush at the end of the trail, and it was then he heard the cry and a man's soothing voice over it. Faint and far away, but a human cry, up by the rockface he had never visited but which he had seen from the mountain across the way.

He pushed roughly through the bushes with his crutch and followed the well-worn path. There were no footprints on it and it was obvious no one had used it since the storm.

The blue and yellow tent was faded from the sun, but it had weathered the lashing wind and rain one more time. Jed hurried forward, stumbling in his haste, and threw open the tent flaps.

John Reynolds' bleary eyes looked up at him and Phoebe stopped her whimpering.

"Thank God, Jed, you've come. Pan's gone, with the baby, and I've tried to find him and can't."

"Don't you know where he might have went?" Jed

asked Phoebe as he knelt beside her. Chracteristically he made no comment about the baby, although his eyes clouded slightly and his black face softened with pity.

She shook her head savagely. "Find him, Jed, please find him. He's out there, somewhere."

"He started up the rockface, Jed," Reynolds said as Jed crawled out of the tent. "Up the trail by the spring. Go there first."

He studied the ground but the rain had washed away all traces of footprints except those John Reynolds had made that morning. As if led by the great God Zeus himself, he started up, groping on the narrow dirt track which paralleled the rock-edge.

For half an hour he climbed, swinging his crippled leg up a few inches, bracing himself with his crutch, then taking a long step upward with his good leg. When he reached the ledge on top, he stopped to rest, and looked down into the valley where his truck stood. He could not see it, but he knew where it was, and he understood now why Pan had chosen to live in this particular place. The whole valley lay spread out before him, shining in the mid-morning sun, the light green stands of poplar, the dark green fir and pine, the alder-bordered streams cutting through them all.

Unerringly he threaded his way through the wild plum thicket, picked his way through the small pines, lead by some latent genius to the giant white pine where Pan lay still on the thick carpet of pine needles.

Jed stood in the shade of the old pine, knowing there was no hurry now, no need to rush forward to shake the lifeless form. Pan was dead. A rush of wind swept through the branches of the old tree and a cloud covered the sun and Jed shivered. He bowed his head and his lips moved, "You're free now, boy. God's torn the devil out'n your soul and you're free. God strike me down for thinkin' it, but I do believe you're better off this way,

Pan.''

He sat silently at the foot of the tree, breathing heavily, and wiped the sweat from his forehead. As he did so, he began to ponder how Pan had died. There were bruises and scratched all over his body. He could see that very clearly. Where had he fallen? Off the rockface? Not likely. Where was the baby? Had he hidden it somewhere before he had fallen, and was it still alive?

Jed grunted to his feet and turned to look up the tree. There was nothing to indicate that Pan had climbed it or had fallen from it. He stepped back a few paces and with his head thrown back he moved slowly in a circle around the base of the tree. Through the thick, lacy-needled branches he caught sight of the edge of a tattered leather sleeve fluttering in the wind almost at the very top of the tree.

Never once asking himself if he could make it, or what might happen if he slipped, he started to climb. While Pan had climbed the tree in a few minutes, Jed clambered upward for almost a half hour, pulling himself from one thick branch to another. Frequently he had to stop and rest, but the sight of that leather jacket and the thought of what it probably contained drove him on.

When he was about half way up he heard for the first time the tiny whimpering cry high above him. He stopped to listen, thinking he might have heard the wind or a birdsong or even Phoebe below him in the tent. Then he heard the almost constant mewling, achingly human, and it urged him on, infusing his aging body with the strength of a young man. He cursed his flailing leg and then ignored it, throwing it around with his hips as he pulled himself upward with his powerful arms and good leg.

With a final shove upward he reached the branch on

which Pan had stood to make the nest. The baby cried continuously, but its voice was muted and Jed now saw why. Pan had mummified the baby, leaving a tunnel of leather as an airway so only the top of the baby's head showed. With scarcely a glance at the curly black hair and the pink scalp showing through, Jed lovingly tucked the entire package under his right arm and began the laborious descent.

Grasp a branch, swing the dead leg forward into space, sit down slowly on the closest branch using the good leg as a lever. Rest. Grasp another branch slightly below, stand up, swing the left leg, sit down. Rest. Over and over. Till finally his right thigh ached with the burning pain of fatigue and sweat broke out on his body and ran in rivulets down his spine.

He sat on the lowest branch, a full seven feet from the ground, pondering the impossible distance to the soft carpet below him. A soft carpet which had been hard enough to kill Pan. Tears of frustration filled his eyes. I've got to jump, he thought, and not hurt the child and not break a leg.

He crooked his right arm, holding the tiny bundle like a halfback with a football, slid forward on the limb until he teetered uncertainly, then pushed off with his left hand against the trunk of the tree. Absorbing most of the fall with his good leg, he twisted sideways and fell heavily on his back. A grin of triumph spread across his face as he realized he had made it.

He laid the baby at the foot of the tree, leaned his back against the trunk, and rested. He had been on the mountain for almost two and a half hours, and the others would be frantic, knowing something was wrong. But he had one more thing to do before he went down to them.

He retraced his steps to the ledge atop the rockface and picked up several large fragments of limestone. He carried them to the foot of the tree and dropped them there. For two hours the old man carried rocks until he knew he had enough, and then he lovingly placed them over Pan until he was completely covered.

"Should say a prayer, or something, Pan, I should," he mumbled softly. "Send your soul off right, like. But you know we loved yuh, Pan-boy. Like a son *I* loved yuh, Pan, and like a husbin' *she* loved yuh. An tuhgethuh we'll mourn, Pan, and God'll take care. 'S'long, boy."

He picked up the baby with his strong right arm, tucked his crutch in his left armpit, and hobbled down the trail through the pines.

> "The lonely mountains o'er
> and the resounding shore,
>> A voice of weeping heard and loud lament;
> From haunted spring and dale,
> Edged with poplar pale,
>> The parting Pan is with sighing sent;
> With flower-enwoven tresses torn,
> The nymphs in twilight shade of tangled thickets
>> mourn."

Milton